Descendants of Atlantis

ATLANTIS
BOOK THREE

COURTNEY DAVIS

5 PRINCE PUBLISHING
5PRINCEBOOKS.COM

Published by 5 PRINCE PUBLISHING & BOOKS, LLC

PO Box 865, Arvada, CO 80001

www.5PrinceBooks.com

ISBN digital: 978-1-63112-356-6

ISBN print: 978-1-63112-357-3

Cover Credit: Marianne Nowicki

To my family who are supportive of the time and energy I put into my writing life. I couldn't do it if they didn't listen to me talk about my characters and focus on writing amid the chaos of our daily lives.

Acknowledgments

Thank you to the amazing team at 5 Prince Publishing for giving me the chance to share this trilogy with the world.

And the amazing editor Cate Byers who pushes me to be a better writer with every exchange.

I hope to work with you all many more times in the future!

Descendants of Atlantis

Prologue

ELANTRA RAN from the city of Atlantis, the sun still brightening the sky and keeping the vampire inhabitants in their homes.

She was to be the last to leave before the sinking because she'd had to make sure that King Barnabas, the king of vampires, didn't suspect anything off today. She had to be certain that he wouldn't go looking for anyone else to satisfy his lusts or hear any of his men complain that they couldn't find a citizen of Atlantis to sink their dirty fangs into. For how many years had the citizens of Atlantis been nothing more than blood slaves to the vampires? Elantra had no idea, but she did know that today, because of her, it would stop.

She'd done her job well, spending the entire day in bed with the man who spouted false words of love as he took everything from her as if it was his right. Even her children had been taken, convinced to become like their father and carry on in his vampiric way of life. Convinced they had a duty to humans that excuses their abuse. The vampires protected the humans of earth by containing fearsome monsters and beasts in a prison created by the goddess herself, the first mother, Maeve.

But Maeve had also created the eternal monsters with

bloodlust as guardians of the prison. It seemed to Elantra that the vampires were just another monster to prowl the earth and harm humans. Elantra didn't understand, didn't see the reasoning, but who was she to try and understand the desires of a goddess? All Elantra could do was try to survive, try to protect herself and those around her who suffered.

And she had to let go of what was lost. Her sons who had chosen that monstrous life. Her heart had broken for them a long time ago, and as she ran farther from the city today, she only hoped they would regret their choices.

Elantra passed no one as she went, thankful that the human citizens had listened to her. The human citizens of Atlantis had been held under the spell of the Stone for so long, a stone that took their will and gave it to the vampire who possessed it. They were understandably shocked and scared when the spell had broken, and they realized what had been happening to them. Elantra had managed to keep them calm with promises of safety, but they had to bide their time through the night and then make their way out of the city as soon as they could that day, but not before the sun came up. They had to play it right or they'd be found out. They had to leave while the sun kept the vampires inside and be gone well before sun set again because as the sun sank into the ocean that night, so would Atlantis, and anyone still within its boundaries would be contained at the bottom of the sea at the mercy of vampires.

A fate worse than death, Elantra thought.

"Sister," Sparah's voice stopped Elantra at the edge of the city, her heart thundered in her chest and fear iced through her veins. She was so close to freedom.

Elantra spun around. She was breathing heavily. Her dark hair loose and wild around her shoulders. Her makeup smeared from sex, and blood was dried onto her throat. There had been no time to clean up. She'd stayed with Barnabus as long as she'd dared and left in a hurry with a mumbled excuse, taking nothing with her besides anger and hate. There was no memento from this part of her life she wanted with her, no keepsake she wished to tuck away and gaze at fondly. She only hoped to wipe the memory of these years from her brain and move on.

Sparah stood there looking clean and perfect, always so perfect, but it hadn't been enough to attract the vampire king, likely because of her dirty dog blood. They shared a mother but their fathers were quite different. Sparah's was a werewolf, the first Maeve had created and Elantra's had been a simple citizen of Atlantis. Though Elantra was the elder sister, it was Sparah who had inherited the strongest magic from their witch mother. Elantra had gotten the ability to be controlled by a Stone that called to her father's blood in her veins.

Life hadn't been fair to Elantra from the beginning and as she stood and stared at her sister, she wondered if it was going to continue to favor Sparah over herself.

Sparah was dressed for spelling, a long black robe trimmed in gold to enhance her magic. She had her black hair swept up in a high ponytail and tied with a leather strip. It left her mangled ear visible which she usually tried to hide from the world but today it only added to the picture of powerful witch she was presenting.

Elantra's lip twitched up in a near smile at the sight, a bit of imperfection on the outside that hinted at the beast she knew her sister held on the inside. It wasn't right, Elantra had always thought, that a dark and twisted soul should come in a package that glittered and caught the eye. It was the same with the vampires, all broad shoulders and muscles, looked like a dream but they were nothing more than a nightmare. Sparah would be a good match for the vampires really, and she'd always wanted to bed the king even though Elantra had been there first. Elantra narrowed her eyes at her sister, wondering if Sparah's jealousy would work in her favor tonight. Would Sparah see Elantra's leaving as a way to get close to Barnabus? "Will you sound the alarm, Sparah? Will you hope to finally get in his bed by holding off on casting the spell so we can all be dragged back to the city and thrown into a prison cell among monsters until it is too late?" Elantra lifted her chin in challenge. If she had to, she was prepared to fight her sister on this. "Or will you let me go, so you will be the only witch left for him to bed?"

Elantra tried to keep her fear under control. She was responsible for all the citizens who had escaped. Sparah obviously didn't care about the lowly humans whose bad luck had given them a genetic link to a spelled Stone and their blood a special draw to vampires. Sparah had never suffered through the effects of compulsion, had never given her heart through coercion only to find it smashed and smeared and her body used, all while the person who you once thought you loved, smiled and said how much they love you.

It was a torture that no human should endure and Elantra planned to keep it from happening ever again. She had broken the spell of the stone by coating it in Barnabus's blood, and then hidden it so that no vampire could ever use it against the citizens of Atlantis in the future.

Sparah shook her head sadly. "You would leave your sons behind?"

"My sons chose to live the life of a monster and one day, when one of them becomes king, they will make all the same mistakes their father has made. They will never know love; they will never know anything beyond bloodlust and the desire to control," Elantra spat the words with disdain and hurt. "They stopped being my sons when they chose vampiric living over real life." Elantra shook her head. "The spells I cast, the blood and sweat I put into creating them despite the dead body of a father they have. And they betrayed me. I never should have borne them," she spat.

"Do you not see the sacrifice they are all making? Do you not see what good is in them?" Sparah pleaded. "This is the only way to keep the world safe. Your sons are a part of that, it is an honor. You created them because you were desperate for someone to love you truly, sister. But you are blind to the fact that you created two men who want their lives to carry more meaning for the world. They don't just want to be *your* world. Are you really so selfish?" Sparah accused.

"Do *you* not see what he puts me through, Sparah?" Elantra cried, wiping at the healing marks on her neck. "Is this really what you wish for, sister? What you're so jealous of?" She held up a hand covered in her own blood. "Be my guest, go crawl into his bed and let him take from your body whatever and whenever he wants." Tears streamed down Elantra's face as she faced her sister with all her hurt and fear no longer bottled up.

"I wish to help good men keep monsters away from humans, Elantra. I wish to serve alongside a great king who wants only to protect those who are the weakest."

Elantra met Sparah's gaze, feeling the weight of the situation pressing on her. "And I wish to protect those he wishes to prey upon. I ask you again, sister. Will you be alerting them, or will you set the spell when the sun sinks and give us a fighting chance?"

Sparah's face showed the war she was fighting with herself and Elantra wasn't sure which side would win. The sun was about to set, and time was running out. They'd grown up together, they shared a mother, but they had always had their differences. "Sparah, please," Elantra whispered. "You might be willing to choose this, but we aren't. Doesn't everyone deserve a choice in their lives?"

Something dark flashed in Sparah's eyes. "Go," Sparah finally said. "I can see what good the vampires are doing here, but I can also see what you are doing, Elantra. This is the journey you have to go on."

"You've always been good at predicting the future, Sparah," Elantra said with tears in her eyes now for a different reason. "I hope you see us meeting again one day, sister."

"I do," she said sadly. "You must go straight to Mother now. You must guard her against my father. There is a magic that will be cut off, a magic that I have to take with me. She will need you, Elantra. Don't fail her."

Elantra pulled her sister in for a hug. "He doesn't deserve you," Elantra whispered, then pulled back and rushed away from the city.

As soon as Elantra crossed the line etched into the ground marking the perimeter where the spell would cut the land, she felt magic take shape behind her and sweep over Atlantis. So many had sacrificed for this moment, she knew that, but her people wouldn't any longer, not ever again against their will. She would build a safe home for them all and protect it forever from the vampires.

Her sister's words floated through Elantra's mind, and she switched directions, heading north instead. First, she would see that her mother was okay, she'd never trusted her werewolf stepfather.

One

SORCHA MADE a cup of tea and stared out at the dark barns and sheds scattered around the south Georgia compound. Elantra had them rebuilding this whole place, replanting the gardens and they'd brought in animals to tend as well. They would be as close to self-sufficient as they could get within another month or two. Sorcha wondered at the necessity, with a town right outside the walls. It had made sense at the Florida compound because it wasn't so simple to head to the store, but here, they were practically in the middle of civilization.

Elantra wanted them separate from it though so that's the goal they were all working toward. Sorcha's clan of Descendants had left their own damaged compound in Florida for this safety offered by Elantra. She was a powerful witch and after their home had been invaded by vampires and monsters, destroying the barrier that kept it hidden from anyone who wasn't a Descendant and killing some of their people, they'd had no better option.

Sorcha shivered at the thought. It must have been a truly horrifying event because her mind had chosen to completely block it out, along with the entirety of the year preceding.

She couldn't remember a moment of the attack on her

compound or the events leading up to it, but she'd walked into the compound after apparently having fled to safety outside its walls. Her sister, Julie, and the others had been in the middle of packing up to leave at the urging of the witch Elantra when she returned.

Sorcha had been so confused and disoriented at that time, she hadn't questioned anything else her sister or Elantra had said as they quickly moved everything north.

Now she questioned, because she couldn't stop dreaming about things she shouldn't. Passionate embraces by a vampire and horrifying attacks by a pack of werewolves. Something didn't add up.

Sorcha sipped her tea and, as she often did when she was alone and still, she wondered about Elantra's true intentions. She wondered about the witches who followed Elantra so closely and wondered what had changed in the last year to make the Descendants follow her orders like a mindless army.

Elantra was a very powerful witch, so it would make sense that she would attract other witches hoping to learn from her. But Descendants had no magic, unless you counted their ability to be attractive to vampires. Not a super power in Sorcha's mind. So other than hoping for safety under her magical umbrella, there was nothing to motivate the Descendants.

They'd survived so long without the direct daily guidance of a witch though, just the occasional beefing up of the security around their compounds. Why would they all decide now that it was best to live alongside them?

There had to be something in that missing year that explained it all. But how was she going to fix that? Every bit of research she'd been able to do said wait for something to trigger the memories. Selective amnesia or trauma-induced amnesia would likely just as suddenly go away as it had come on. But if it was some kind of brain damage, she may never get it back. That seemed less likely as a cause since she hadn't woken up bruised and battered. She'd just had a massive headache and lots of confusion.

No easy answers, that was for sure.

"You're up early." Elantra slipped into the room, silent as a shadow. She tended to do that. She creeped around the compound like she wasn't quite solid, and it really made Sorcha squirm whenever she was caught off guard. Elantra was a middle-aged woman; at least in looks. Sorcha had a feeling she was much older, though she hadn't been able to pinpoint how old. Either no one knew or no one was allowed to say and asking Elantra directly was out of the question. She had long black hair and brilliant green eyes that spoke of youth, or spells. Her skin was the color of the desert sands, and her lips were pure black when she didn't cover them with a bright red lipstick to go out among humans.

"I couldn't sleep so I thought I would get some training in before anyone else went down into the gym and got in my way." It was true, she trained daily because not only had she been told from birth to be ready to go up against vampires, but her last memory before waking up in that field, was of being attacked by a pack of werewolves. She had managed to fight them off apparently, she wasn't sure how and she wasn't going to take the chances of not making it out alive again if it ever came to it. Vicious uncontrolled beasts, but, something fuzzy in her mind prickled and sometimes she dreamed of a werewolf who had attacked another that night.

She couldn't be sure—not about anything in that year—and it really grated on her nerves.

"Hm, yes, it's good to keep in top form. We never know how long our peace will last," Elantra agreed, but eyed Sorcha suspiciously.

Sorcha sipped her tea so she wouldn't have to respond. She wasn't sure what to think about the plan or worries Elantra seemed to have. While Elantra assured everyone that they'd found peace and they were preparing for a lifetime of living on the land here, she also had them training hard daily for war. Both couldn't be true, and Sorcha was hesitant to point it out to the witch.

"Can you sense them out there, maybe that's what has you unable to sleep?" Elantra asked casually.

Sorcha knew it wasn't a casual question. Elantra was constantly asking her if she sensed the presence of vampires beyond the walls, as if Sorcha had some kind of special feeling for the bloodsuckers. She'd never posed the question the same way to anyone else. She asked guards if they'd seen or heard anything suspicious. But she always asked Sorcha if she *sensed* anything.

As far as Sorcha knew, she didn't have any kind of special sense for vampires and she had told Elantra that more than once.

"No, nothing," she said without inflection. She wouldn't tell Elantra about the dream that she'd woken from. It was one she had often. Passionate embraces and forbidden desires with a vampire whose face eluded her and left her wondering if it was more than a dream but perhaps... a memory? Whatever it was, it felt way too personal to share with this woman she didn't really trust. Even if her roommate, Devon, probably already had. Devon was a witch and utterly devoted to Elantra and Sorcha had confided in her about some of the dreams before she realized it might be better to keep that secret to herself.

"You'll tell me if that changes," Elantra said firmly. She had moved as they spoke, so she was standing behind Sorcha and laid a hand on her shoulder. Sorcha was starting to feel like Elantra's words might be a threat.

"Have there been more signs of vampire activity in the town?" *Activity...* Elantra wasn't specific about what had tipped her off to their presence out there but again, no one questioned her statement that vampires were there just waiting to take them all for blood slaves.

Elantra stepped away, casually moving to the window looking out into the night. "There's always signs of evil. We just don't all see them the same way," Elantra said sadly, then gave herself a little shake as if she were trying to get rid of whatever thoughts had invaded her mind. "I'm sending a few people to town today. I don't want to, but we need the supplies."

"I'll go, I can act as bodyguard and scout," Sorcha said quickly, earning a sharp look from Elantra.

"You want to leave the compound? I think it's best if all Descendants stay behind the walls. I will send witches. They can take care of anything they might come across in the daylight."

"Werewolves walk in the day," Sorcha reminded her. "And weren't there some tracks spotted just outside the walls yesterday? I think an extra trained hand would be useful. I've come through werewolves alive before, I could do it again."

Elantra's face twisted in anger for a moment, as if the careful mask of sanity slipped but was quickly put back in place.

"I don't mind taking weapons," Sorcha said quickly. "I know werewolves well enough to confidently pick them out in human form too. Can all your witches?" Sorcha asked and forced herself to take another casual sip of tea as if it didn't matter that much if Elantra denied the request. Sorcha suddenly, desperately, wanted out from behind these walls. She needed some breathing room. She needed some perspective because she had a feeling Elantra was controlling everything they saw and heard here.

Elantra frowned at Sorcha for a long moment. "I suppose a quick trip to town would be fine for you as bodyguard. There and back, make sure everyone makes it back, Sorcha. That is your job." Elantra jabbed a finger in Sorcha's direction and the words she spoke were heavy, as if laced with compulsion that prickled the back of Sorcha's neck wanting entrance.

"Of course, everyone will be fine," she assured Elantra and barely resisted the urge to rub at the back of her neck.

Elantra nodded sharply. "Take Devon and two others. Arm yourself thoroughly but nothing that will alert humans. Do your duty and return."

"Yes, of course," Sorcha agreed calmly, but inside she was giddy with anticipation. A feeling of destiny was washing through her.

"Keep an eye and ear out among the humans. Any mysterious deaths, any missing livestock, that sort of thing. I want to know about it."

"Got it," Sorcha said, quickly finishing her tea and taking the cup to the sink. She would be ready to leave as soon as possible. The idea of a day out of the compound was filling her with an energy she hadn't had in a while. Maybe she would skip the workout.

Elantra watched her with narrowed eyes but didn't say anything more as Sorcha rushed from the room. She decided not to change her routine, she didn't want to seem overly eager to leave the place. Couldn't risk Elantra changing her mind... and *letting* her out? Why was that a thing?

Sorcha's sister Julie had run a tight ship back in Florida, had made sure she knew what everyone was doing and why. As leader of the Florida Descendants, Julie had controlled a lot, but she hadn't kept them prisoner inside of the compound. They could have gone out for a walk any time day or night, though most of them weren't stupid enough to venture far in the dark unnecessarily, they knew what went bump in the night.

The way Elantra ran this place though, it was stifling, and Sorcha didn't trust it. She hoped she could find some answers in town. They wouldn't be among the humans however and she wasn't sure her desire for answers would outweigh her self-preservation.

The last thing she wanted was to end up as Elantra's prisoner or worse—in the clutches of a werewolf or vampire.

Two

"ELANTRA WANTS you to help move the cows, they finished roofing the permanent barn for the milking cows and so we need to take them out of the back pasture and put them in."

Sorcha glared at her sister from around the shower curtain. She'd had a quick workout and now was in a rush to get herself ready to leave the compound.

She didn't have time for moving cows across the goddamn property.

"I'm already booked today. I'm heading to town with Devon and some others to get supplies. I'll even pick you up a new pair of boots," Sorcha added, hoping it would appease her sister and send her on her way.

Julie looked confused. "No, Elantra specifically said *you* need to help move them."

"What the hell," Sorcha grumbled, sure that this was the end of her dreams of getting outside the compound gates. Elantra had probably changed her mind and this was the way she was letting Sorcha know.

She stepped out of the shower and grabbed a towel, aggressively drying off as Julie stared blankly.

"Tell her *Highness* that I'll be out there in ten minutes," Sorcha hissed, because what choice did she have? Whatever Elantra said, they all did. Sorcha had never seen anyone tell Elantra no and Sorcha wasn't eager to be the first to find out how she'd react.

Julie walked off without another word.

Even before Julie had taken over the managing of the Florida Descendants from their father, she'd been bossy and eager, always telling anyone who would listen what to do. Watching her be the messenger for Elantra's orders just didn't make sense.

"Invasion of the pod people," Sorcha muttered and made her way to her bedroom.

"What?" Devon asked, meeting her in the doorway.

"Nothing, just need to get my cow poop walking boots on I guess," she said.

"You drew the short stick too, huh," Devon laughed and motioned to her own tall yellow boots. "I guess our trip to town is postponed?"

"You don't think it's canceled? She isn't sending someone else?" Sorcha had a hard time holding in the desperate hope in her voice.

Devon shook her head. "No, she said we should go once the work is done." Devon shrugged, work then play I guess.

Sorcha's outlook brightened and she hurried to dress, the faster the cows were in their new home, the sooner she could get away from this oppressive compound.

Moving the cows turned into also corralling some goats into the now empty field and putting up a new fence around the pigpen.

After all that, another shower was a must and by the time they were ready to head to town it was well after lunch and Sorcha was sure Elantra was going to tell them it was too late, too close to sundown.

But she didn't even see the witch as she quickly gathered her small group and hurried them out to the van.

"Do you think we'll be back before sundown?" Tara asked as she got in the back of the van. She was a young witch and Sorcha didn't have a lot of patience for her.

"Have to, Elantra would have our asses if we didn't," Mary said, taking the seat next to Tara.

"Sure will," Sorcha said and started the van before the three witches were even buckled.

Sorcha smiled as she drove toward the gate that surrounded the compound. In theory, it was ideal for an off the grid compound encased in magic to keep it from being identifiable. In reality, it was nothing in comparison to the compound they'd left in the Florida wilds. It didn't feel like home and Sorcha was happy to be leaving its oppressive walls for even a few hours.

Devon was in the passenger seat happily chatting about what she knew of the town, which didn't seem like much. Neither Tara nor Mary had anything to contribute but they listened excitedly. It seemed they were all anxious to get away from the compound. Perhaps being completely devoted to Elantra was as suffocating as Sorcha imagined it would be.

Sorcha waved at the guard as they passed through the gate and he surprisingly just waved them through, no questions or curious looks.

"He must have been expecting us," Sorcha said.

"Oh yeah, Elantra probably told him," Devon said as if it were obvious.

They probably wouldn't have even gotten this far if it hadn't been pre-approved. Sorcha had a rebellious streak that made her want to try at the next opportunity, just to see if Elantra would forcibly keep her inside.

Her ears popped when they were through the gate, indicating they'd passed through the spell surrounding and camouflaging the compound. She sighed heavily because for the next couple hours, she was free.

Devon turned to Sorcha and gave a wide grin. "Feeling antsy?" Devon asked, tucking a black curl behind her ear.

"I guess so. We've been preparing for months and I'm starting to wonder how long we'll prepare for nothing to happen."

"What do you mean nothing? Vamps and weres have been sniffing around the compound the last three nights," Mary said from the back. "I'm freaked as shit that they are going to figure out a way in."

Tara smacked Mary's arm.

"How do you know?" Sorcha asked, her hands tightening on the wheel. "I mean, I heard about the wolf prints, but how do you know vamps have been out there too? Could be wolves in human form leaving regular footprints. It's not as if they're hooved demons," she added with a laugh.

Devon glared back at Mary and Sorcha's gut clenched. Something was being hidden from her.

"Just a feeling I have," Mary mumbled.

The feeling of unease grew in Sorcha the farther they drove from the compound gate. She concentrated on the road ahead but couldn't miss the glances Devon kept sending her way and it made her uneasy.

"Who has the list?" Sorcha asked, to try and keep Devon from noticing the way sweat was starting to bead up on her neck.

"I have the grocery list," Tara said brightly.

"I have a list for the hardware store and the farm supply store," Mary said.

"We also need to grab a few things from the gun and pawn," Devon said.

"Lots to do, shall we divide and conquer so we aren't out past curfew?" Sorcha suggested. "I want to hit up a clothing shop, I ripped my favorite leggings this morning, and I told Julie I would pick her up a new pair of boots."

"I don't want to do all that," Mary said. "Drop me off, I don't mind getting my stuff alone."

"I don't want to do groceries alone," Tara whined.

Devon rolled her eyes at Sorcha, they'd had plenty of conversations about the helplessness of Tara. She was the youngest of the coven, and not well suited for the workload that Elantra was putting on all of them.

"I'll go with you, Tara, we'll hit the gun and pawn first, then groceries. Sorcha can do the mall."

"That'll work," Sorcha said, keeping her voice even and as uncaring as possible. "Well, I mean, as long as you guys don't need a bodyguard. I am supposed to be making sure you all make it back alive." She said it with enough derision that it would challenge any of them to say they needed her to keep them safe.

"I don't need you," Mary said with a huff, and she was probably right. Mary was one of the toughest witches in the coven. Muscled and tall, she worked out twice as hard as Sorcha. Devon was no slouch either and only Tara would be considered weak among the group, but with Devon she was safe, Sorcha had no doubt. And likely to only run across humans anyway—not that humans weren't dangerous to a pretty young girl—but Devon could certainly handle human problems.

"We'll be fine," Devon said. "No reason to stick together and take three times as long. I'm supposed to work with Elantra on some spelling tonight and if I miss it, she'll call Stephanie in instead."

"That shouldn't be a problem, let's get in and get out," Sorcha said. "No reason to let Stephanie get a bigger head by learning more from Elantra."

"I second that," Tara said. She was Stephanie's roommate and complained about her constantly. Apparently, Stephanie was a real kiss ass and didn't hide the fact that she was in love with Elantra. And for one of the witches to be infatuated to the point that it annoyed the others, that was a hell of a lot of devotion the girl had.

Sorcha pulled into the hardware store parking lot and Mary hopped out with a wave, then Sorcha drove a couple blocks and dropped Tara and Devon. Devon stood in the open door and looked at Sorcha as if she wanted to say something, then just shook her head and smiled. "I'll text you when we finish up here so don't plan to hang out at the mall and hit on all the hotties who are hanging out after school."

Sorcha laughed, "I don't think young and inexperienced is my type."

"Oh, I know what your type is," Devon said and flashed her teeth briefly before she shut the door. Sorcha regretted sharing the erotic vampire dreams with her roommate.

Sorcha waved at Devon and watched her walk away.

Alone in the car, she gripped the steering wheel and stared ahead, unsure what to do. The urge to drive south and not look back until she hit Miami was strong and she wasn't sure what was really behind that feeling. Was it the desire to get out from under Elantra's thumb, or was there something down there that she'd forgotten she wanted? Would the familiar city trigger her memories?

She turned north toward the mall because she couldn't justify leaving her sister behind. And even if she could, there was something deep inside telling her there was something here for her. A heaviness and burning in her soul that told her to stay in this town and root out the cause of it. It didn't feel like a desire to escape control, it felt like a destiny wanting to be found.

* * *

"What the hell are you suggesting?" Ian snapped and bared his fangs.

"I am suggesting that you send your wife and her new little friend out for a goddamn stroll!" Samson snapped back and bared his own fangs. Ian might be the king of Atlantis, but if he stood anywhere close to between Samson and Sorcha he was going to be beheaded in a very royal fashion.

Katherine put a hand on Ian's chest and the big vampire visibly relaxed. They'd only been together a few months, but it was obvious they were deeply in love.

And it grated on Samson's nerves in such close quarters.

Katherine was a Descendant, but she hadn't grown up with them, hadn't known anything about them, or that she was supposed to hate vampires. By the time she'd figured it all out, she was already in love with Ian despite his bloodsucking tendencies.

"I would love to get out and stretch my legs," Lilly said, breaking the uncomfortable silence. Lilly was a werewolf who, along with her protective mate, Tray, had shown up with Katherine and Ian a week ago. Ian and Katherine had emerged from Atlantis and been concerned when they found that the Miami clan of vampires and the Florida Descendants were nowhere to be found.

Apparently, Katherine had befriended the wolf pack on their trip to Miami after she'd been let out of the Descendant's Florida dungeon. She had been coerced into trying to help them find the Blood Moonstone so the werewolves could control their full moon shifting. They'd ended up finding it themselves, along with the surprise of a female werewolf no one thought existed.

Samson wasn't a fan of werewolves since they'd historically been enemies of vampires. The Aristotle Society, a group of men hellbent on ridding the world of vampires along with the help of the witches, had enslaved the werewolves as weapons against the vampires. A very useful weapon, they could take out a vampire like nothing else in existence. Of course a vampire was just as deadly to them. Balance, the universe always created balance.

Samson was willing to put aside those old notions though in the face of a common enemy.

The witch, Elantra, and her revenge plot scrawled in blood on the walls of the Florida compound.

For Samson though, it was first about saving Sorcha from

whatever trouble she had found herself in. Whatever insanity Elantra was planning was second only to that.

Katherine looked up at her mate. "I think it's a good idea, Ian. Obviously, they aren't being let out of there during the night, this is maybe our only chance to find her and see what's going on," Katherine reasoned. "See if she's there willingly."

Ian gave Katherine a look of pure love before turning a glare at Samson. "I don't think putting the women at risk is smart."

"I am more than capable of taking care of myself, and Katherine," Lilly pointed out.

Lilly was a match for any human or Descendant, but maybe not the witches. They were unpredictable in their power abilities and under the tutelage of Elantra, who knew what they were capable of?

"My mate isn't going anywhere without me," Tray said, putting a hand on Lilly's shoulder.

"Two wolves, you know Katherine will be safe," Samson said, meeting Ian's fierce gaze.

"Fine," Ian agreed, and a wave of relief washed over Samson.

He would have answers by nightfall.

Samson watched the threesome leave and fisted his hands. The desire to walk out into the sun and find Sorcha was nearly overwhelming. He rubbed the spot over his heart where he'd been shot with a wooden splinter bullet. If she hadn't sucked the pieces out, he would have died. And that act might be what would save her now. It was his blood coursing through her body that he could sense so well. When she was behind the protective walls of the compound, he could just barely sense it, but as soon as she had apparently passed the barrier it had been a sudden strengthening. Which further proved that the magic hiding the current Descendants' compound was far more powerful than anything they'd had in the past. He could feel her strong and clear now and it killed him to not be able to touch her and ascertain if she was truly alright. If she was even in that place willingly. It didn't make sense that the Descendants would have all just abandoned their Florida home in a day, there was something going on here and it had everything to do with that psychotic witch Elantra.

Samson ignored the whispering of the others behind him, his coven mates and Ian all helpless against the sun that shone outside. Beltar was the ruler of their little coven above the waterline that included Samson and three other vampires living in and protecting Miami and the passageway to Atlantis, which was just off the coast. Beltar was a good leader and although Samson didn't do well with any amount of authority, he'd been able to find a place in Beltar's coven when living in Atlantis under Ian's thumb had been too much.

He hadn't thought much of his life on land either though, until about a year ago when one little Descendant had given him a reason to exist.

Samson had nursed Sorcha back to health after a vicious werewolf attack and she'd inexplicably fought every instinct she'd been born with, every rule that had been drilled into her head for years, by trusting him. It had been the only good thing in his long life and it had overwhelmed him.

Then Samson had fucked everything up. He'd lost her all too soon and it had nearly killed him. The only thing that had kept him from simply walking into the sun since then was wanting to continue to protect her even from a distance because she was amazing and beautiful and kind. She was a light in the cruel world.

She deserved better than what he could offer her.

Everything he touched, he destroyed.

She needed him now though, he was sure of it. He had followed Sorcha's scent here after she'd disappeared. That was two months ago, and they still had barely any information about what was going on behind the compound walls. It was locked down tighter than the Florida compound had ever been and it drove Samson mad.

At least they'd been able to locate the walls of the compound thanks to the fact that Sorcha's blood called to him. She had to feel the draw too and it irked him to no end that she was able to resist it. That until today she had stayed tucked behind the compound walls where he couldn't see or smell or touch her. The only thing he was able to do was stalk around the perimeter of their invisible compound every night and growl and grumble and wish she'd show herself so he could drag her away and keep her forever.

He vacillated between thoughts of taking her and making her forgive him and a realization that it was impossible so the best he could hope for was to assure that she was safe and happy. He could watch her from afar until she died a human death and he plunged himself into the sunlight to end his own suffering. Just one endless life of suffering, that's all he'd had aside from the short bright spot that had been Sorcha.

Vampires as a species had been created by the goddess Maeve to keep humans safe from the monsters that were now held captive in Atlantis. Maeve and her lover, Peleseus gave their lives to become the prison that held the monsters and to hold the spell which had kept Atlantis whole, contained, and sunk to the bottom of the sea. The honor of protection was passed down among families and it was a warrior's honor to take it up. All the vampires took the honor willingly and seriously.

Samson hadn't had the same upbringing as the others. He had been created in hate and anger, he had been used and abused and he was twisted in ways that none of the others could understand. Ways that had made him do the unthinkable, had made him lose the love of Sorcha, his soulmate.

He wanted more than anything to deserve her love no matter how hopeless the desire might be.

"Do you really think it's her?" Beltar asked.

"You all saw the note scrawled on the wall of the Descendant's compound that they left. *Fray's Revenge.*" Ian said. "We know it isn't Fray, she was killed right after the sinking, but her daughters..."

"You mean *your mother*," Samson challenged. "Because we all know Sparah hasn't set foot outside of Atlantis since it sunk." She couldn't. Sparah set the spell binding her grandmother's body to the sinking city and supposedly used her own blood as part of the magic. If Sparah left, the whole place would either fill with water, or it would rise again, no one was sure and no one wanted to find out because risking the monsters escaping was too horrifying to imagine.

Ian's face darkened. "*My mother*. Elantra, is no mother. She chose them over me, then and now. I think the years have only addled her mind and made her more dangerous."

"And what about Sparah? Do you think we should let her know that her sister has decided to make moves against us?" Samson asked.

"Perhaps once we know what Elantra's plan is," Ian said bitterly. "If Sparah doesn't already know."

Sparah was a powerful witch and she could see into the future, or possible futures anyway. She wasn't very forthcoming with those predictions usually because they weren't sure things and messing with the natural selection of chance and choice she said, could damage the brittle fabric that held the universe in balance.

That's what she'd told Samson anyway when he'd asked her if he would ever find peace.

He was pretty sure she just didn't want to tell him that no, he would never find peace until death.

Multiple grumbles went up around the room, every vampire knew the nature of Sparah and that there was nothing to be done at the moment. They all settled, most dozed, since it was daytime, but Samson just glared at the stairway and concentrated on the feeling of his bond with Sorcha. As long as he still felt it strongly there was a chance that the others would find her before she was once again locked behind those magical walls.

Three

TWO BAGS IN HAND, Sorcha left the mall and headed across the parking lot. The sense of something she couldn't name was getting stronger the longer she was outside of the compound, a humming in her chest and a tingle in her blood. She had hurried through her shopping in the mall for proof that she'd done as she said and planned to spend whatever time she had left following her instincts and hoping to uncover some kind of truth.

A short woman with long black hair called her name and waved from across the lot distracting her thoughts and making her steps stutter and stop.

"Sorcha!"

Her first thought was that Elantra had sent someone to check on her but she didn't recognize this woman who was now rushing forward. Sorcha scanned the rest of the lot, not recognizing anyone and no one seemed to be paying either of them any attention.

Was this a trap or was this what she'd been hoping to find?

Not trusting, Sorcha put a hand on a small knife she had strapped at her side.

"Sorcha, it's so good to see you," the woman said while

breathing heavily and grasping her side as though she had a stitch from the short jog.

She wasn't a werewolf if she was this out of shape, not a vamp because she was out in the sun. Could definitely be a witch, could be one of Elantra's spies.

"Do I know you?" Sorcha asked with a less than cheerful tone.

The woman frowned at her. "Seriously? We met in Miami and spent a little time in a dungeon together," she said with a laugh. "How could you forget that wonderful experience?"

A spike of pain shifted through Sorcha's mind at the woman's words. As if whatever memories her explanation might have brought up were being forcibly shut down.

This wasn't good.

"Shit, are you okay?" the woman asked and reached out to touch Sorcha's arm.

"I don't think you have the right person," Sorcha said with an eye twitch and took a step away from the woman. She rubbed at her temple and tried to calm her brain.

The woman continued to frown, a look of deep concern on her face. "Okay, you need to come with me. Something is definitely wrong."

Sorcha didn't disagree with that assumption, but she wasn't stupid either. "Like hell, I don't even know you. Did Elantra send you to check on me? I'm just doing a little shopping for necessities." Sorcha held up the bags.

"I don't know Elantra personally, but I've heard the name. A real witch, right? My name is Katherine. We've met. We have spent time together," she explained again slowly. "And I need you to trust me and come with us so we can figure out what's happened to you and the other Descendants."

Katherine flicked her gaze over Sorcha's shoulder and Sorcha turned just in time to see a man and woman flank her and grab an arm on each side. Instinctively she knew, both werewolves. She didn't think there were any female werewolves.

Panic spiked through her as she looked at the male.

"Friends," the female growled, low and dangerous. "We are friends. Don't fight us, we just need to take you somewhere to talk privately. That's my mate, he won't harm you."

Sorcha knew she could put up a fight, she wasn't helpless, and if it was just the human in front of her she might, but against two werewolves she knew she could just as easily be on the losing end. They said they were friends, but that didn't stop the panic and memories of attack swamping her. Her heart was beating wildly, and her breath was coming in pants. She felt a sheen of sweat break out all over her body.

She turned her narrowed eyes to the male and snarled. "Get your hands off of me."

"Calm yourself, you are safe," the male said but he did pull his hand off of her arm.

Sorcha studied his face as his voice hit buried parts of her brain. He looked familiar.

"You," she whispered. Had this man been there when she'd been attacked? Had he attacked her? Panic swelled again. She continued to stare at his face, trying to understand, trying to remember. A new piece of the memory surfaced with a painful snap. Him naked and bloody standing with a limp body of a werewolf at his feet, not dead but nearly. Something told her she could trust him.

Had he saved her? was this the wolf she vaguely remembered killing another and stopping the assault on her? She hadn't been sure that was a real memory, didn't believe a werewolf would turn against its own kind to help her.

"You were there," Sorcha whispered.

"Yes, I was there, and I helped stop them. My name is Tray. Now don't fight, just come along, we aren't parked far, and we are trying to help. Something bad is definitely going on with Elantra and the Descendants. We need to figure it out."

"That attack was traumatic and I—have some kind of amnesia around it all," she explained as she grimaced in pain.

Terrifying memories filled her mind, threatening to overwhelm her. A mix of old and recovered memories of that night swirled painfully in her mind. A new face threatened to peek through the shroud of forgotten but when she tried to clear it the pain spiked and she cried out. She clutched at her head, the pain too much for her to tolerate right now.

Tray moved closer and grasped her chin, forcing her to look into his eyes. When he spoke, his words were gentle and soft. "Sorcha, I was there, and I saw what they were trying to do to you. I was there and I stopped them long enough for you to go on the attack. I promise, I mean you no more harm now than I did then. It is important that you trust me and come with us. I don't know what's happened to you to make you forget, but I can assure you that *we* aren't the enemy. Whatever is hurting you now, we want to help."

She nodded, sure that he wasn't lying even if the memories were polluted in an unnatural haze that hurt her head. This was the most she'd uncovered since waking up and she wanted to pursue it. Was he the trigger for lifting this amnesia?

She looked at the woman, Katherine, and tried to place her face. The effort made her head hurt but when she looked at the female werewolf, she felt nothing.

"Have we met, too?" she asked the woman.

"No, my name is Lilly, I'm Tray's mate." She held out a hand and Sorcha took it cautiously.

"Sorcha," she said weakly. "I don't know what's going on, but it doesn't hurt to look at you," she said with a laugh that bordered on psychosis.

"Let us help you with whatever this is," Lilly said. "We can't talk here though."

Sorcha nodded, not sure it was the right thing to do, but she followed them willingly. She didn't relax however, and she kept darting her gaze around expecting to see one of Elantra's witches at any moment or more werewolves rushing out to attack.

She was always ready to fight off danger, it's what she'd been raised to expect. In this moment, that drive had switched from predominantly danger of weres and vamps, to danger of witches. She didn't want to be stopped from whatever discoveries this journey might lead her to. She knew that the witches would never let her go along with these enemies even to possibly have her memories back.

She hesitated to think of them as enemies, because that would make her stupid as fuck for following them willingly. Strangers was better. Were they strangers? The way her head hurt when she tried to place the small human woman and the painful rising of memories of the male werewolf indicated they were a part of that lost time. But it didn't prove they meant her no harm. Her guard was up, her knife was near her fingertips and her eyes darted between them all when she wasn't searching the surroundings for Elantra's spies.

Sorcha studied the small woman, Katherine, for a moment as they walked. She said they knew each other, had spent time together. But there was nothing in Sorcha's memory of the woman, only a black, painful hole.

The woman in question turned and smiled at her as if sensing her uneasy gaze. "I'm a Descendant too, well half, anyway," Katherine said as they walked.

That surprised Sorcha and eased a little of her worry. "Don't tell me your other half is werewolf," Sorcha laughed.

"I never knew either parent, I was adopted by two regular humans as an infant, but as far as I can figure, my mother was a regular woman and my dad was a Descendant who didn't know he'd impregnated her. Probably a one-night stand sort of thing," Katherine shrugged. "Honestly, I'm glad I didn't grow up with the clan. No offense, but all your baggage seems like a lot."

Sorcha just grunted. She loved her clan, well maybe not so

much recently. But they were her family, and she wouldn't want anything else. She couldn't imagine growing up not knowing what horrible beasts were out there, not being prepared for dangerous encounters. Just living life as if you were the top predator.

She shivered at the thought. Knowing what could eat you in the dark had kept them alive for centuries.

What would it have been like to discover that later on? To suddenly be thrust into a world full of fangs and claws. Questioning every bump in the night and shadow. Her eyes swept over Katherine. She was small and lean, obviously not trained to fight, she'd be helpless against the vampires who would want to use her. Leaving a baby outside the clan was forbidden for that exact reason. Sorcha wondered who her careless father had been.

Probably someone from the now deceased Georgia compound, they were obviously not following all the rules otherwise they'd still be alive.

Katherine had eventually figured out what she was, apparently, or she wouldn't be here with a couple of werewolves. She seemed happy, too. There was an air of relaxation and ease about her that Sorcha wasn't sure she'd ever had in her entire life. She'd lived in a constant state of preparation, fear, and watchfulness.

She wanted what Katherine had and just the thought made her feel like she was betraying her ancestors who had fought so hard to free themselves and protect their clan.

Four

THEY LED Sorcha to a windowless van parked in an alley next to the mall. Sorcha paused and put her hands on her hips. "Do you think I'm suicidal?" she asked as Katherine opened the back door.

"I promise we don't mean you any harm, we really just want to talk to you. Help you, maybe. You mentioned Elantra back there. We think she's up to something bad, and since you don't remember me or Tray, I'm guessing she messed with your head to get that done."

Sorcha couldn't deny that. The only thing that would spike pain through her like she got trying to remember this woman's face was a memory charm, or curse depending on how you looked at it. The only problem with that was, they only worked well if the recipient was willing.

So the real question was, what was she trying to make herself forget?

"Fine," she said and climbed into the van.

Lilly smiled brightly as she followed Sorcha in.

"I don't think I've ever met a female werewolf before," Sorcha said.

"I can still rip out your throat," Lilly said, still smiling.

Sorcha laughed. "Well, honesty is always the best policy."

Katherine hopped in next and lastly Tray, who closed the door behind them. Sorcha relaxed a bit since no one was in the driver's seat ready to take her to a secondary location to murder and Tray didn't flip the lock. Even a false sense of escape was better than feeling trapped.

"Okay, start talking," she demanded and looked at her watch. She didn't know how much time she had before the others would be calling for a ride and she wanted as many answers as possible before then.

"We were actually hoping you would be able to tell us what's going on," Katherine said. "All we know is that The Descendants' compound down south is empty. Tray traced your scent here and we followed him to help. According to the message scrawled on the abandoned compound wall, Elantra wants revenge for her mother, Fray? What can you fill in?"

Sorcha took a deep breath. "The last thing I remember was being in the woods and fighting for my life against a pack of werewolves. Vaguely I remember you," she said glancing at Tray. "Then I woke up in an empty field outside the compound." She shook her head.

"Like I said, I came upon you being attacked and I tried to stop them, you started fighting back as soon as I got a few of them distracted."

"By yourself?" she asked, surprised. There were at least six wolves that night, she'd been surrounded, and they had made their intentions very clear. She shivered and rubbed at her arms remembering the searing pain of claws and teeth. So much blood and not all of it her own by the end.

He just grunted. "They are all dead."

Beside him, Lilly clutched his arm and gave him an adoring look, as if she thought he was the reason the universe spun.

"Good. Monsters don't deserve to be on this earth." Sorcha's face heated a little, knowing she was talking about their kind. But he'd saved her, what did that mean? Just because one monster could show human decency didn't change the fact that they were mostly all monsters. It just meant maybe indiscriminate hate and killing might not be the way to go.

"No, they don't," Tray agreed darkly, and Lilly rubbed her face on his arm in a very animalistic gesture of love and affection. "That was a year ago."

"You lost a year?" Katherine asked.

Sorcha nodded, "It literally felt like moments before waking in the field, but I know that's not possible because it was miles north and I—" she hesitated but gulped and lifted her chin in defiance of the painful memory. "I was unharmed when I woke up."

"What happened after you woke up?" Katherine pressed.

"I stumbled back to the compound. It was midday and everyone was rushing around, packing. My sister was pissed because I hadn't been there to help." Sorcha frowned as the oddness of that day came back. "I tried to ask her questions, I tried to make sense of what I had been through, but Elantra was there barking out orders and her witches were moving everyone around like it was some kind of emergency. I had no choice but to follow along. I was scared," she admitted. "It felt like my attack had just happened and I couldn't make sense of anything. I just wanted to feel safe again and that is what Elantra was offering. She wanted to take us to the Georgia compound where she could fix the wards and keep us all together and safe, witches and Descendants."

"And is that what she's doing?" Katherine asked. "Is she keeping everyone safe in there behind the walls and heavy wards?"

Sorcha nodded. "We are fixing the place up. The whole clan that had lived there was taken out by a pack of werewolves, probably the same ones who attacked me that night."

Tray nodded agreement. "Weston's pack was vicious but he's dead. He also had his pack take out all the witches west of the

Mississippi and was coming into our territory to take over and, I think, go after his stepsister Elantra to avenge his father's death. She killed Gilead after the sinking of Atlantis because Gilead had lost control and killed her mother, Fray."

"Fray's revenge," Katherine nodded.

"She blames the werewolves for her mother's death and she blames the vampires for taking her children and being generally assholes to the Descendants," Tray said.

"Did they kill her children?" Katherine asked with a gasp.

Tray looked at her curiously for a long moment. "Elantra is Ian's mother."

Katherine gasped beside Sorcha. "That bitch is Ian's mother! And how the hell did I live with Sparah for two months and she never mentioned she was Ian's aunt! What the hell?" Katherine crossed her arms over her chest and glared across at Tray.

"Fucked if I know," Tray scoffed.

"That family has problems," Lilly said.

"You live with the vampires?" Sorcha gasped, turning wide eyes onto Katherine.

Katherine's face blushed. "Happily. Ian is the love of my life, the love of my... eternity."

"But he's a *vampire*, doesn't he..." Sorcha darted her eyes to the woman's neck where there was a hint of redness, a bite mark? Sorcha's body heated at the thought, the memories of dreams that had to be so much more than fantasy reared up in her mind. Did this woman have all of the pleasure that Sorcha craved in her sleep? And she was surviving it?

"Wait, does he have the Descendants' Stone? Are you enthralled?" Sorcha asked, worried for the woman. She leaned close and peered into her eyes, looking for what, she didn't know.

"No," Katherine assured her, pulling back out of her grasp. "The Descendants' Stone doesn't work on people who have drank vampire blood."

"Oh." The implication was obvious and Sorcha looked at the

woman with morbid curiosity. She was admittedly taking and giving blood with a vampire, having sex with a vampire, being in love with him and living with him in Atlantis.

It was everything that every Descendant would tell you is impossible to be done willingly. And yet here was proof against that impossibility. Katherine was queen of Atlantis, a Descendant. It flipped Sorcha's world around to think about it.

"Has Elantra said anything about her plans?" Tray asked, bringing them back around to the point of their conversation.

"She doesn't tell me much, I don't think she trusts me," Sorcha admitted. "She watches me with a wary eye she doesn't seem to give the others. I don't know why."

"I think I have a theory," Katherine said. "Ian doesn't have the Descendants' Stone because his brother found it and tried to use it against the Descendants there in Florida. When we helped take him out, we returned the Stone to Julie. So where's the Descendants' Stone now?"

"That evil thing is supposed to be buried in Atlantis where no vamp can ever use it against us again. How did it make it back up here?"

"Ian's brother, Jovi, managed to find it. Your sister though, she is supposed to be keeping it safe now. I guess you don't remember any of that because it was in the last year," Katherine frowned.

"Are you saying you think my sister is using the Stone?"

Katherine shook her head. "No one can use the Stone except a vampire and no Descendant would ever even consider such a thing. It takes your will; it makes you a happy zombie. It—"

Sorcha froze as realization hit. "Oh my god, exactly like how they have all been acting. But my sister too, which means Elantra—"

"Elantra could be using it. She is a powerful witch. Vampire powers originate from a witch's spell creating a creature that was strong enough to capture and contain the monsters in Atlantis.

She could have what it takes to make the Stone work for her. She could be using it to control all of them, but it doesn't work on you because you had Samson's blood recently."

"Samson's blood," Sorcha whispered, and her mind nearly exploded with pain. She rammed her hands to her eyes to try and stop the lightning that was spiking through her head.

"Jesus, is she alright?" Lilly whispered.

Sorcha felt a cool hand on her back. "Sorcha, relax, breathe. Whatever it is, we will fix it. Just breathe," Katherine said.

Sorcha breathed as Katherine instructed. She drew in deep and let it out slowly, then another. After a few more she stopped shaking, her mind settled to a dull thud and she was able to open her eyes.

She couldn't live like this, pain at every memory that tried to push through but what if the fix brought forward forgotten pain worse than this? She had to think it would, why else would she have agreed to such a terrible spell?

Across from her, the wolves both looked on edge as they watched her.

"What happened to you?" Tray demanded. "It isn't simple trauma-forgetting, is it?"

"I think I took a spell to get rid of a year of my life." This wasn't a trauma response, no selective amnesia. This was a deliberate act to forget.

"Why the hell would you do that?" Lilly gasped.

"I think that's a very good question. Another good question is why the hell do I have vamp blood in my system?"

"It's nothing to be ashamed of, actually it's a real benefit in this situation," Katherine defended. "You saved Samson's life recently. When we were all in the Descendants' dungeon together, thanks to these guys, who your sister had hired." Katherine jabbed a thumb in Tray's direction.

"How—why—" Sorcha stuttered. It was a lot, it was so much

and she felt pinpricks in her brain even as she tried to not make an effort to remember what Katherine was talking about, for many reasons.

"I willingly took vamp blood," she whispered, that seeming like the biggest part of the story at the moment.

"Yes," Katherine said.

"And I *saved* a vampire?"

"Right, you two already had some history I guess," Katherine shrugged, and Tray nodded.

"These guys imprisoned us?"

"Well, Tray and his pack, not Lilly. She was being held prisoner by the Aristotle Society at the time. And it was all under Julie's direction so really they were just hired goons trying to keep the vampires away from the Descendants."

That made sense, at least the vampire part. "Why would we have been imprisoned with the vamps? Well, I guess you would be with your, uh, mate?"

Katherine nodded with a grin pasted on her face. "Julie was pretty pissed about you choosing the vampires over the Descendants so she stuck you in there to think on what you'd done. I don't think she intended to leave you there for long, but then Jovi and his monster broke in with the Stone and things got a little crazy."

Sorcha groaned and she grasped her head again. "It doesn't make sense. Why would I do that?"

"I think we should let Samson explain," Tray said. "I want to get out of here before anyone comes looking for her."

Katherine pressed a bottle of water into Sorcha's hands. "Will you come with us? Will you hear what Samson has to say and maybe we can figure out how to help the others? You know something's wrong with what Elantra is doing; you feel it in your gut, right? That's why you are talking to us at all and not just trying to kill us or run."

"My sister, and my clan, they're being held prisoner." The realization that her niggling thoughts were right was heavy. "I have to do what I can to help them. But they will know something is wrong as soon as I don't pick up the others from the shops." She took a sip from the bottle. "They will come after me and they could hurt all of you." Sorcha wasn't a hundred percent convinced these people were on the side of good, but she wasn't ready to sentence them to death at the hands of the witches yet.

Just then her phone dinged. She pulled it out and stared down at a text from Devon.

Come get us.

She looked up at Katherine and frowned. She didn't know what to do. Could she really trust these people to be who they said they were?

"Turn away Tray," Katherine said and started to push her pants down.

"Woah, what the hell are you doing?" Sorcha said, sliding back on the small seat.

"I'm one of you, Sorcha, I need you to trust me."

There in the dim light Sorcha could see the small mark on Katherine's upper thigh that indicated their shared ancestry. It was the mark of Atlantis—a circle with a triangle inside and a lightning bolt through it. It had appeared somewhere on the body of every Descendant born since forever as far as Sorcha knew. Sorcha touched the back of her neck where her own mark was. Katherine really was a Descendant of Atlantis like she claimed. Despite the fact that she was shacking up with the king of the vampires, she was family, and Sorcha wanted to trust her.

Katherine pulled her pants back up and pulled out her phone. "I am going to let the guys know we are bringing you back so there's no surprises."

"The guys?" Sorcha asked, fear creeping into her voice as she imagined a bunch of werewolves waiting for them somewhere.

"Vampires," Katherine clarified.

Sorcha was certain that didn't make her feel any better.

Five

⟨≈⟩

"SHE'S COMING HERE," Samson said as he stared down at the message. He wanted to shout with joy and he wanted to kick everyone out so he could be alone with her.

He didn't do either though. He just leaned against a cold wall and stared at the stairwell where soon she would descend. How would she react to seeing him again? His arms ached to embrace her, to bring her body against his and feel her heart beating against his. He ached to press his lips to her flesh and feel her tremble with desire. He would give anything to have those perfect moments of passion back.

But he knew he didn't deserve them; he wasn't Prince Charming. He hadn't slain her dragon; he had shown her he was every bit the monster she thought he was.

Ian watched the stairwell with a similar anxiety showing on his face. At least he would have Katherine flying into his arms once she reappeared in the basement.

The other vampires were further back in the shadows. Hopefully they wouldn't frighten Sorcha when she arrived. Beltar, Laric, his second in command, and the twins, Trent and Prat.

Samson wished he could send them away, but it was still light out and the basement didn't leave much room for getting out of each other's way.

He didn't think Sorcha was in danger with any of them, even in such a small space, Trent and Prat went out nightly to satiate their desires with the locals. Beltar and Laric had gone out recently enough to not pose a danger, Ian made sure of it. He wouldn't allow anyone around Katherine that was unfed. Samson knew they would make Sorcha uncomfortable though and he wished he could prevent that.

Samson had indulged as well out of necessity, though he hated it and himself when it was done.

He despised what he was and what he had to do. Hated how they squirmed and gasped, how they moaned with desire as he drew their blood. They practically begged for death in his grasp and he'd only recently learned how not to give in to that desire.

It was everything he'd been trained to do, forced to do for so long as his tormentor's weapon of choice.

Samson shook off the dark thoughts that drove him near the desire to step out into the sun and destroy the monster he was.

Sorcha had no idea how she'd saved him that night. How healing her had healed a small part of him. He'd found hope in her.

It had been the desire to deserve her warm looks and smiles that had drove him to his old habits. He didn't want to become the monster in front of her, but he had become a monster anyway, it hadn't mattered.

The look of betrayal on her face had destroyed him. And he knew that she was right. He was nothing better than the others. He hated himself, hated vampires, hated humans and the pain they could wield against each other. He hated werewolves for what they could do. The only thing he didn't hate was her.

Sorcha.

And that is what had kept him going for the last year.

Thoughts of her were the sun in his eternal night.

A strong prickle of awareness washed over him, then a wave of heat. They were here. She was upstairs. He heard the sound of a door opening, footsteps moving across the floor.

He held his breath as the door at the top of the stairs opened and let in a painful bit of sunlight. But he didn't move further back, he squinted as shadows moved down the stairs. His entire body was tight, stiff, and strained. He was holding himself back, just barely. He wanted to rush forward, throw aside anyone else in the way. Sorcha, she was all that mattered, all he wanted, all he needed for eternity.

Four shadows on the stairs and he wanted to scream at them to hurry the fuck up and move.

He had to bite back a groan as the door at the top of the stairs shut out the light and the darkness once again surrounded him. He could see her clearly now as she descended. Her red hair was loose around her shoulders begging for his fingers to run through it. He knew it would smell like the honey shampoo she favored. Her green eyes swept the room with a practiced precision that spoke of her years of training. She was calculating danger, she was noting who was where, and her hand was gripping a small knife.

She was here. She had chosen to come. But she wasn't sure she was safe, and it killed him to see fear hidden behind her calculating expression. He wanted to reassure her, but he didn't move. She wasn't even looking at him and it made his soul ache. He could take her anger, but her dismissal was gut-wrenching.

Katherine was already embraced in Ian's welcoming arms, having been the first one down the stairs. Sorcha finally met his gaze as she flicked her eyes back through the room a second time. He saw a slight widening of her eyes and then she grunted and pressed a finger to her temple as she quickly looked away.

"Sorcha?" he asked, confused by her action. Hadn't she expected him to be here, had they not told her he had led the charge to save her?

She turned back to him and pressed her lips as if it pained her

41

to look at him. "You know me too? Are you the vampire Samson they mentioned?"

Samson was shocked, what the hell was she talking about? "What do you mean, am I Samson?" he demanded.

"She seems to be suffering some memory loss," Katherine explained, returning to Sorcha's side.

"What kind of memory loss?" Samson asked, a little softer but no less frantic. Something was wrong with her; she was harmed and he needed to fix it.

Sorcha gave a bitter laugh. "Unfortunately, I think it's intentional and self-induced. Which begs the question..." She met his gaze firmly even though it was obviously causing her significant discomfort. "What the hell did you do to me to make me want to erase you from my life?"

Shame filled Samson at her words and he stepped back as if he'd been struck. This was his fault; he'd driven her to this awful choice, and now he didn't exist in her mind at all.

* * *

Sorcha was fighting back a pressing pain as she looked at the huge vampire. There were five others in the small basement, but she couldn't even think about them enough to be afraid. She was so consumed with the sight of him.

Samson.

Her dream vampire.

She knew it the moment she'd descended the stairs. In her dreams he was a faceless shadow but now that shadow had a face, a beautiful face. His hair was black as night and cut short. His eyes a brilliant purple. Her gaze trailed to his lips, perfectly kissable. Did she know what those lips felt like in reality and not just what her dreams had come up with? Had they really trailed down from her ear to the sensitive space where her neck and shoulder met?

Had she moaned in pleasure and begged for more from him?

"Sorcha?" Katherine asked. "Are you alright?"

Sorcha snapped her gaze from Samson's lips and pulled her hand from her neck. She locked her eyes on Katherine and shook her head. "No, I'm not."

"Sorcha?" Samson said, taking a step closer.

"No," Sorcha snapped and held up a hand, but she didn't look at him. "I was attacked by wolves." She jabbed a finger at Tray. "He saved me. Then I woke up nearly a year later outside of the compound in Florida, destroyed by vampires and Elantra taking control, moving us all up here." She took a shuddering breath. "When I don't dream about that awful night, I dream about you," she whispered and looked back into his deep purple eyes. "I ask again, what did you do?" She sucked in a hiss as another sharp pain exploded behind her eyes and moved to the base of her skull. "Why did I erase you?"

"What is wrong?" Samson demanded. "Why are you in pain?"

"Whenever I try to remember, the spell fights back," she groaned and rubbed at her head.

"Stop remembering," Samson demanded.

"Okay, asshole, I'll just do that, maybe if you go walk out into the sun for a minute, I can stop my brain from trying to place your fucking face among the deliberately blocked memories."

Katherine snorted a laugh that she covered badly with a cough.

Two of the vampires in the back snickered loudly.

"Okay, this isn't helping," Ian said, taking control of the situation. "Sorcha, obviously you are here for answers, and we are too. What can you tell us about what's happening in the compound? Are the Descendants in danger? Is Elantra planning some kind of attack on the pack or Atlantis?"

Sorcha took a breath and turned from Samson to look at Ian. He had a protective arm around Katherine and she was touching his chest possessively. Something about the obvious familiarity and comfort between the two made a new sort of ache fill her chest.

Longing?

She shook it away and concentrated on his questions. "I don't really know much about Elantra's plans. She isn't sharing with me. It seems like she's merely trying to make the compound self-sufficient so everyone can stay safe."

"But you don't believe that?" Ian pushed.

"No, something is off."

"She's a fucking nutcase," one of the other vampires murmured.

"Oh! How about you not telling me she is your *mother!*" Katherine snapped, hitting Ian's chest. "And Sparah is your aunt? Why the hell didn't you tell me that?"

Ian grunted. "It wasn't pertinent information."

Katherine glared up at the vampire as if she didn't have an iota of fear. "Everything about your past is pertinent to me, Ian. I love you."

Ian looked down at her with a hungry expression and kissed her long enough to make Sorcha uncomfortable and Samson cleared his throat multiple times to get their attention. It didn't work and the couple continued their kiss.

Sorcha could feel Samson's eyes boring into her, but she refused to look at the vampire. She didn't want to think about that sort of embrace with him, didn't want to wonder if her dreams of him were a memory.

A spike of pain shot through her head because she couldn't quite make her mind not try to remember when her body wanted to react to his nearness and the promise of passion. She hissed and rubbed at the back of her neck. This situation was not going to work.

"Ian," Samson snapped. "Could you concentrate on something other than your woman for five fucking minutes?"

When Ian pulled back, Katherine was wobbling and clinging to him with a look of pure ecstasy on her face.

"No, five is long enough to not be paying her attention," Ian said with a grin and Katherine laughed.

Sorcha took a deep breath. "They know you're here. Somehow she knows that vampires and werewolves are in town so she's being more watchful but she hasn't asked us to attack or anything like that. Just more of an excuse to not let us out."

"She's going to be upset when you disappear," Samson said simply.

"Very," Sorcha agreed. Her phone had rung off the hook on the drive over. Devon, Tara, and Mary were obviously already pissed and had likely alerted Elantra by now. If she was careful, she could still play it off like she'd been busy at the mall the whole time, maybe left her phone in a changing room or some shit. "I need to go back, my sister is at the compound, my whole clan is. I don't know if they are safe. I don't think they are," she corrected. She pulled out her cell and stared down at the multiple text messages and missed calls.

"You can't go back in. Elantra will never let you back out if she even *thinks* you're not with her a hundred percent," Samson argued.

Sorcha wasn't sure that was true. Elantra didn't fully trust her now, Sorcha was certain, yet she'd let her out.

Why had she? Why now?

The missed messages had stopped about ten minutes ago, they'd been near constant for twenty minutes and now they were silent. Why would they stop trying to find her?

Twenty minutes was enough time for them to get someone else at the compound to come pick them up. Which would mean more Descendants were in town. Her phone lit up with Elantra's number.

"Shit!" Sorcha hissed and dropped her cell, stomping on it until it was splintered into a thousand tiny pieces.

"Why did she do that?" Lilly whispered to Tray.

"Tracking spell," Beltar said darkly.

Sorcha met the gaze of the fierce dark-haired vamp. "What if it was a setup? She kept asking if I could sense vampires, she kept asking and watching me. She hardly lets anyone out of the compound, never a Descendant. Only her most trusted witches come to town for supplies when necessary. But today she let me." Panic swelled inside her as she realized what she may have done.

"We need to get out of here," Ian said and there was a chorus of agreement.

"But the sun isn't down yet," Katherine pointed out. "There's at least another hour of daylight."

The basement was silent for a full minute as they all weighed the chances of a witch attack in the next hour.

Sorcha wanted to say it was impossible, it was no big deal. Elantra wouldn't be able to launch an attack against them on such short notice.

But she knew that wasn't true because not only did Elantra have everyone in some semblance of battle ready at all times, she could have been planning this exact scenario. "It's a trap," Sorcha whispered. She looked at Samson despite the pain that it caused. "You all have to get out of here."

Just then a loud bang sounded upstairs. It was too late; the witches had arrived. Sorcha had led them here; these people were going to die and it was all her fault.

Lilly and Tray shifted to wolf in a blink. They were massive and Sorcha couldn't stop herself from stepping back. Lilly was a pure black wolf with large yellow eyes and Tray was a beautiful red, they both bared their teeth in a snarl at the stairs and Tray stepped forward slightly, guarding his mate. The four vampires that had stayed back in shadow for the entirety of the conversation moved forward now, ready to fight and Katherine was pushed behind her mate and the rest of the group so fast, she looked shocked by the movement. Seconds later Sorcha found herself in a similar situation.

"Hey, I am not helpless," she snapped at the blond vampire who was now standing guard in front of them both.

"Still one of the weakest links, so you go to the back, babe," he said.

Footsteps sounded above, it was impossible to tell how many, but it was more than a couple, and icy fear crawled up through Sorcha's stomach.

What if her sister was among them? She couldn't stand by and let them fight her sister. It would be hard enough watching any of the Descendants fight, but she would have to stop them from harming Julie.

"Sorcha, I am disappointed," a voice echoed through the basement, sent on a spell. "You walked right into the den of the enemy. What would your father say to see you like this?"

Katherine reached out and gripped Sorcha's arm and even though she wasn't sure they'd ever been friends; she appreciated the comforting gesture. At least she wouldn't die alone.

"What did you do?" Sorcha shouted, hoping whatever spell Elantra was using worked both ways.

"What did *I* do? I am only trying to make the world safe for the weakest, the humans, and the Descendants. I lost my life, my children, my sister, my mother. I lost everything because of them, and I refuse to let that go unpunished any longer."

"You abandoned us," Ian snarled to the disembodied voice. "You ran from your family and your duty to serve the greater good of Atlantis."

There was a heavy silence that followed his words and no one in the basement breathed, waiting to see what Elantra would do, knowing her son was among them.

"You all made your choice," Elantra hissed and there was another explosion.

This time the ceiling fell. Debris came down and Sorcha found herself on the ground with Samson using his body to shield her. All around her she could see nothing but fallen ceiling and pieces from the floor above. It was dark and suffocating, she coughed at the dust that rose around her and she felt panic rise quickly. Was this how she was going to die? Crushed beneath a vampire?

"I'm sorry," Samson whispered in her ear. "I will protect you to my last breath."

"You're going to die as soon as she decides to move the fallen pieces of this house," Sorcha gasped out. It was hard to breathe, she was smashed between the ground and Samson's hard body. Every time she breathed in she got a new lungful of dust.

"My last act will be protecting you, I can die happy with that," he said.

She didn't know how to respond. He was happily going to die as he protected her, that wasn't something she'd expect from an immortal vampire. And it would be for nothing, Elantra would rip her apart for this so she'd die anyway.

The sound of things being tossed aside above them was frightening, how long did they have? How much of the house had fallen on top of them?

"Tell me what I forgot. I think it's fair that I don't die not knowing why you're an asshole."

"I'm a monster, but I'm not an asshole," he grunted, and she wondered how long he could keep up with holding his weight and the crush of the house off of her even this much.

Her body hurt where it pressed into the concrete floor, but she wasn't going to complain while he took the brunt of the pressure off of her. It would almost be romantic if it wasn't so terrifyingly close to a horrifying death.

A round of howls from above seemed to surround them, hope of rescue stopped any further conversation.

"Sounds like Tray's pack just arrived," Samson said.

Sorcha shivered. More werewolves?

Screams above met the howls and snarls. Sorcha shuddered at the sound.

"It's okay, I would never let them harm you," Samson whispered.

"Sure, unless you're on fire in the sun or crushed under the weight of an entire fucking house," she said, deciding anger was a more comfortable emotion than fear right now.

Suddenly there was nothing but the sound of victorious yips from the pack.

"Sent those witch bitches on their way. We're not digging you all out until the sun's down," a voice called. "Unless you want us to."

A chorus of *No* surrounded Sorcha.

"Is everyone okay, any wounded?" the voice asked.

"Sorcha is okay," Samson called.

"Katherine is fine," Ian said.

"Lilly is bleeding, get us the fuck out of here," Tray called a bit frantically, apparently having shifted back to human form.

Sorcha listened to the pack carefully removing the debris over the werewolves. With imminent danger set aside she had to try hard not to think about the hot, toned body stretched out over her, keeping her alive. She would have squirmed if she could have moved even an inch as her body thought it liked this position very much now.

She gasped as a new pressure grew against her thigh. He was enjoying it too, apparently, now that the most pressing danger was over.

Samson cleared his throat as if embarrassed, he moved slightly, but it only resulted in a slide of something against whatever was above them and his lower body pressed more firmly into her. "The sun will be down in about thirty minutes," Samson said as if in apology.

"Just keep your fangs to yourself until then," she said, as if that was the part of him she was obsessing over entering her in this moment.

"You know I would never—"

"I don't know anything," she snapped, cutting him off, pissed that she had no idea what this man was to her, what they had done, and not done. She felt robbed and betrayed by her own self for taking away whatever had gone on between them.

How the hell had she ever thought it was a good idea to erase her memories?

Six

AS SOON AS the sun had been down enough to risk it, Samson had shoved off the rubble as if it were nothing and pulled her up to safety. The house was completely collapsed in, and they had to climb up out of the basement atop everything that had fallen.

There were a lot of werewolves standing around, talking with local police, and assuring them that no one was inside when the place exploded. So when they began crawling out, the police started shoving forward and pulling weapons. Luckily the vampires were able to use their little mind trick and get the police to leave thinking the place had looked the same for months, no big deal.

Handy trick, but a scary one. The idea of being convinced of anything so easily made Sorcha shiver.

Samson put an arm around her. "Cold?"

She shrugged him off. "No, just thinking about how you all are creepy as fuck."

Samson grunted as if in agreement and Sorcha almost felt bad for the statement. He'd just saved her life, he'd just had her pinned beneath him—helpless—and he hadn't made any move to bite her.

It didn't fit with what she knew about vampires, and that made her mad.

"You guys in here," Ian called from outside a van already full of werewolves.

She stared at it unmoving, she had absolutely no desire to get in a van with a bunch of strange werewolves, even if they had likely just saved her life. Werewolves she didn't recognize, werewolves who she had no proof weren't like the others. She couldn't make her body move in their direction, their predatory eyes staring out at her expectantly. She wanted to turn and run, no weird forgotten instinct was telling her they weren't enemies like with Tray. She took a step back.

"Sorcha," Samson demanded quietly and put his hands on her face, forcing her to meet his gaze.

"I think I'll walk," she whispered, knowing there was fear in her eyes and not caring in that moment if he saw it.

"They are not going to hurt you," he said. His purple eyes bore into her with familiarity. He knew her fears, knew what she would think about this situation and why she'd hesitate. His thumb stroked her skin soothingly. "I would never let them hurt you, but they won't even try. They aren't like that I swear it or I would never ask you to get in the van. But we need to get out of here before Elantra decides to come back with reinforcements, Sorcha. It isn't safe to stay here."

She had absolutely no reason to trust him other than the fact that he hadn't harmed her yet today. And the weird feeling that at least at one point, she'd willingly given her body to him and that had to mean he hadn't been hurting her, she wasn't into that sort of thing. With a heavy breath she nodded and pulled out of his grasp, clenching her eyes shut and looking away. "Looking at you hurts, Samson." What she didn't say was that it also sent spikes of desire through her that were utterly confusing. That she wanted to wrap herself around him and drown in the comfort he was offering. That she hated him for whatever he'd done to make her want to forget all while trusting him with her life.

She took a hesitant step toward the vehicle.

"Do you want me to ride in the other?" he asked with a note of sadness that made her heart squeeze.

She was tempted to say yes. She couldn't look at him without pain shooting through her mind, but his presence did offer a touch of comfort in this situation that seemed so far beyond out of control. She was only going to be okay in there if he was with her.

"No, I would like you to be in there with me," she said. "I just can't look at you."

Samson grunted and grabbed her hand, pulling her toward the waiting van and a very annoyed-looking Ian.

She avoided looking in the back seat as she slid in behind the driver and grabbed at the seat belt, pulling it on with a little more irritation than necessary. "I hope my sister is okay. Were there any Descendants with Elantra up here?" she asked Tray who was in the driver's seat. Lilly was in the passenger seat too and that offered a bit of reassurance as well. She tried not to think about or acknowledge the three male werewolves behind her. Samson got into the seat next to her and pulled her hand into his lap, laying his other over the top, offering her comfort.

"Nope, just a bunch of witches," one of the werewolves in the back said as the van took off following the others.

She was glad to hear that, she wasn't sure how she would react if she'd known her sister was involved in trying to harm her. Or if she knew these werewolves had been forced to fight her sister in order to save them.

"Stay safe, sister," she whispered out the window as they left the little town heading south. Samson squeezed her hand having caught the words. She didn't look at him, but she liked knowing he was there. She felt safe and warm from his touch. She had no doubt that he would keep anything from harming her if he could.

So why the hell had she decided to forget him?

After a while she steeled her nerves and berated herself into bravery. She turned to the men in the back without fear in her eyes. They were shirtless she realized, probably a regular thing for werewolves, since they had to undress or ruin their clothes every time they changed anyway.

"I'm Sorcha," she said as introduction.

They were all handsome, muscled. One had a young fresh face, though that didn't indicate age in a werewolf, he could be a hundred for all she knew. Another looked older, maybe fifty but still handsome with his grey streaked hair and bright, intelligent eyes. They looked similar enough to be siblings, or father and son. They had light brown hair and green eyes.

"Pete. This is my brother, Jacob," the younger one said, indicating the older lookalike who gave her a soft smile. "We are part of Tray and Lilly's pack."

"I'm Brighton," the third said. A dark-skinned man with deep, almost black eyes and black hair. He had a wide smile that made it impossible not to smile back. "Part of the pack as well. Nice to meet you, Sorcha." He had a vicious scar on his neck that ran down his chest, looked like claw marks and Sorcha shivered as her eyes ran down them. She couldn't resist touching her own body where similar marks lay hidden beneath her clothing.

This man had been attacked by a werewolf. Her eyes snapped back to his and there was a soft knowing there that eased her.

"Thank you for helping back there," she said to all of them.

"Never turn down a good fight," Pete said with a big grin and the others nodded and howled agreement.

Sorcha had to turn away. She knew they'd saved her life probably, but that didn't mean she liked being stuck in a small space with them. It didn't mean that the sound of their victory howls didn't drag forward memories that made her eyes tear up with fear and had her squeezing Samson's hand as hard as possible as she stared out the window.

"Keep it down," Samson snapped at them and squeezed her hand back. "Try to rest, we have a long drive," he told her softly.

"Where are we headed?" Panic started up for a new reason. She was leaving behind everything. She had nothing but the dirty clothes on her back and she was headed away from her family, abandoning them to whatever hell Elantra had them wrapped up in. Was she making a mistake? Putting herself at the mercy of these monsters while leaving her sister to the mercy of another?

"Packhouse. There's a light-tight place for the vamps to stay and we can figure out our next move from there," Tray said.

Sorcha let a fearful sound slip from her throat.

Lilly turned in her seat and gave her a smile. "You're not being kidnapped," Lilly said as if she had read into Sorcha's fear. "We are going to keep you safe but we aren't trying to make you do anything. If you really want, Tray could turn around and take you straight back there. We don't force people to do what we want." She spoke as if she'd experienced exactly that. Lilly looked at Tray like he was the savior she'd been waiting an eternity for. She reached out and stroked his arm as he nodded agreement.

That reassurance eased Sorcha. "I don't think there's a welcome mat out for me back there," she said. "What's the next move?" she asked Samson.

"We followed Elantra and the Descendants because we didn't trust what they were up to, not just because I wanted to make sure you were alright. I think we've confirmed that trouble is on the horizon," Samson said. "We need to figure out how to deal with her before she can do any serious harm to anyone."

Sorcha couldn't argue with that. "Yeah, vampires and werewolves are one thing, but humans won't stand a chance if they are between Elantra and what she wants."

"We won't let humans become a casualty of her revenge," Tray growled.

His intensity surprised Sorcha. "I didn't realize werewolves were so protective of humans," she said.

"It is our reason for existing," Lilly said softly. "We protect the humans from the vampires."

"And the vampires protect the humans from the monsters," Samson snarled in defense of his kind.

"Who protects the Descendants?" Sorcha asked with a sigh.

The van was silent.

"Witches," Brighton said from the back.

Sorcha twisted around in her seat. "What?"

"Witches protect the Descendants. Elantra pulled them from the city of Atlantis before it sunk. She set up the barriers around their compounds and she trained other magically inclined humans to follow her and harness the magic. All in an effort to keep the Descendants away from the vampires," Brighton pointed out. "She's a Descendant after all. She hated the king and what he did to them all. She is looking for revenge against that," he said with a surety that left no room for doubt.

"How do you know?" she asked, suddenly wondering if he was as old as Atlantis itself.

He shrugged. "I used to date a Descendant a million years ago," he said with a wink to say he was exaggerating that bit. "She talked of their history, pillow talk you know."

"And now Elantra sees us as a tool for her revenge plot. I wonder what's changed? If she was okay to just protect before, now she wants to destroy."

"Time does funny things to a person," Samson pointed out. "Imagine how much time Elantra has had to twist her thoughts and darken her soul until all she desires is death and destruction of the ones she blames for everything that went wrong in her life."

"You sound like you're talking from personal experience," Sorcha whispered.

He squeezed her hand but didn't say anything more. She wanted to ask, wanted to know him but she couldn't help wondering if what she found would make her hate him more. Was his past what had driven her to these extremes, or would it be the key to understanding and accepting him? Did she want that?

The answer was uncomfortable for her, so she didn't think on it any more.

After a while she did drift off to sleep, surprisingly. She never would have imagined that she could sleep in a car with five werewolves and a vampire. But she did, and no dreams haunted her either.

Seven

WHEN SORCHA WOKE it was to the crunch of gravel and quiet conversation. Apparently, they had arrived at the packhouse. She sat up and rubbed her eyes.

"This is it?" she asked, taking in the large cabin. It looked like it would hold them all comfortably.

Then she remembered that the vampires would be in a basement of some sort, that sounded less comfortable.

Not that it mattered to her. She wasn't going to be down there, She had no allergy to the sunshine thankfully.

"This is the packhouse. We should be comfortable and undisturbed here," Tray said.

Samson waited for Sorcha outside the van. Three other vans stopped and people stepped out. Mostly werewolves.

A wolf she vaguely recognized, one that sent a spike of forgotten memory through her head stepped forward with a look of authority.

"Welcome, Sorcha. Glad to see you made it out alive."

She rubbed at her head where the pain seemed to radiate and grimaced. "Yeah, alive," she agreed.

"That's the memory curse, huh. Ian mentioned that. Okay,

well I am Patrick, I'm the alpha of this pack and I promise you're safe here. I keep my wolves on a tight leash," he said with a laugh. "We don't harm innocents."

She wasn't sure she believed that but she'd try and take his word on it. "Thanks. I would just love a bed where I can pass out for the rest of the night," she said, staring at his feet since they didn't try and dredge up any memories.

"Of course. I am assuming you want one above ground?" he asked with seriousness and no hint of judgment.

"Yeah," she said, and she swore she heard Samson hiss behind her but he didn't say anything.

Sorcha followed Patrick inside, forcing herself not to look back and see Samson's reaction. Was he disappointed in her choice? He had to realize she wasn't going to spend the night with someone she didn't know, not to mention the fact that looking at him made her want to rip out her eyeball and dig a spike through the back of her head.

Worst of all was that she was disappointed she couldn't make that choice. What the hell was wrong with her? It had to be exhaustion, she reasoned.

Patrick led her through the house, pointing out the kitchen which he said was stocked and she was free to take whatever she'd like, then up some stairs. He showed her where a bathroom was and a bedroom she could use. She thanked him profusely then quickly shut the door.

As soon as it was closed, she slid to the floor and put her head on her knees. She tried to steady her breathing and clear her mind of all the confusing mixed messages it was sending her.

Her entire life felt like it was on fire, and she was in the middle of the room with a can of gasoline.

After twenty minutes or more she pulled herself together enough to find the bathroom and take a shower. She was covered in dust and dirt from the house collapsing and the hot water worked to help her let go of a little more of the fear that was coursing through her body.

She'd survived an attack. An attack by Elantra and her witches. That bitch hadn't cared at all that Sorcha might be hurt, didn't give a damn, just wanted revenge. Elantra would tear down entire cities in her pursuit no doubt and that had to be stopped.

That wasn't what a Descendant was supposed to stand for, it wasn't what a witch was supposed to stand for. She frowned as she remembered Tray and Samson's words in the van. Apparently it wasn't what vampires and werewolves were supposed to stand for either.

Samson was right though, a long life could lead to a lot of twisted thoughts and feelings. There were always those who were born twisted or became twisted. No matter what they were supposed to stand for they chose the opposite.

She wasn't sure how Elantra was as a child but she was twisted as fuck now. How the hell were they going to fight that? And could she count on the vampires and werewolves working together for this?

She imagined an army of vampires and werewolves facing down witches and Descendants and she shivered. It would be a bloodbath. And it would all be because of one twisted witch.

There was a good chance that Elantra had blinded the witches to what her end goal was or what she's willing to do to get there. Sorcha couldn't imagine they would all sign up for a high chance of death for someone's revenge plot.

The missing piece was what Elantra had in mind as her end goal.

Just total destruction of the vampires and the werewolves, or was her goal taking over Atlantis? Could she hold the monsters in Atlantis the same way the vampires did? There had to be a reason vampires were created for the job instead of having the witches or the citizens of Atlantis themselves do it.

Sorcha was certain that wasn't a risk worth taking. The world couldn't handle the release of all those monsters. The vampires couldn't just give themselves or Atlantis up to appease her bloodlust.

Sorcha gave a frustrated sigh. It would be easier to work against Elantra if they knew her end goal.

Or even her next steps.

When Sorcha emerged from the bathroom, she wasn't at all surprised to find Samson hovering in the hallway. The sight of him half in a shadow looking menacing as hell sparked less fear than it should have even as a spike of pain lit through her skull making her cringe.

"What do you want?" she asked a little more gruffly than she'd intended, but he knew he caused her pain to look at. If he cared, he'd be staying far away.

"I wanted to talk to you about what happened, and what might happen next."

"Seems fair," she said. "Though you could have sent someone else you know. It would have been less painful."

His face twisted into a grimace and he turned away. "You're right, I'll send one of the others to speak with you."

"Wait," she said before she could stop herself.

He froze. His back to her still but he didn't move.

"Just, follow me into the bedroom and sit facing the wall. I think I'd rather have a conversation with you." She felt safer with him than the others. She wished she knew why.

He nodded but didn't turn around. When she went back into the room Patrick had shown her to, she went to the bed and sat facing the window. She heard his footsteps follow and the bedroom door shut. After a moment of silence she turned to check and saw he was sitting on the floor facing the door and she turned back to the window.

"So, what did you want to discuss?" she asked.

"Obviously we don't know everything, but it seems reasonable to assume that Elantra has gone off the deep end. She's enslaved the Descendants with the Stone and she is coming after the vampires, maybe the werewolves too."

"Right," Sorcha said.

"You know why you weren't enslaved?" he asked carefully.

Sorcha took a deep breath. "Sort of," she said as a spike of pain lanced through her head. "You saved me? You and Tray?"

"Yes."

"But there's more, more I chose to forget?"

"Yes," he said quietly.

"Will you tell me?"

"No."

"No?" Sorcha snapped and turned around, glaring at his back.

He didn't look at her, just shook his head as he continued staring at the wall. "No, it isn't safe. It could do damage to your mind or cause you more pain than necessary. I'm not willing to risk that. The best thing to do is remove the spell."

"Sure, but how? I don't even know where I got it."

"There is a powerful witch in Atlantis. I would like to take you to her, see if she can reverse the spell and return your memories."

Sorcha was torn. She hated this not knowing, hated these vague memories and half-formed dreams. But she also knew with a hundred percent certainty that she'd done this by choice.

Was it better to live with knowing something terrible, or live with knowing you'd chosen to forget it?

She didn't have an answer. "Can I tell you tomorrow night?" she asked shakily.

"Yes, of course. Sleep on it and tomorrow tell me. I'll be just downstairs if you need anything," he hesitated. "Sorcha, this is my fault and for that I am sorry beyond measure."

She didn't say anything, and he stood then, leaving and shutting the door behind him.

Sorcha fell back on the bed and stared up at the ceiling. Somewhere outside a wolf howled and she heard voices float up from inside the house. It reminded her of the compound in a lot of ways. Happy voices, familiar with each other like one big extended family.

It was less feral than she'd have expected of a packhouse, and it was really a very nice place. Clean, and although it had a masculine flair to the decorations, it was comfortable.

She'd really hate to have to admit she was wrong about so many things. Maybe not all werewolves were monsters, maybe not all vampires were evil incarnate, and maybe not all witches were looking out for the best interest of the Descendants.

Maybe there was more room for individual desires, morals, and circumstances than she'd given credit for in all these not-entirely-human beings.

With a grunt she rolled over and stared out at the darkness, trying to get comfortable in dirty clothes. She wasn't going to strip down though; she didn't trust everyone that much.

She thought about what Samson had said. He wanted to take her to Atlantis, wanted to take her to a witch who could possibly return her memories.

She already knew she would do it no matter how terrifying. She felt at such a disadvantage not knowing everything that had happened to her. Like she wasn't whole, a piece of herself stripped away leaving her half formed.

She thought of the passionate dreams and wondered if they would be replaced by whatever betrayal had caused her to want to erase Samson from her memory.

She hoped not. Sometimes it seemed that those dreams were the only good thing she had in her life.

* * *

Samson sat in the living room of the packhouse trying not to think about how close Sorcha was, how easy it would be to slip into her room once she was asleep and pull her close and hold her tight until the sun threatened to burn him beside her.

He would risk the sun to hold her for even a moment.

"Samson, are you sure?" Ian asked with annoyance in his tone and Samson wondered if he'd asked the question more than once.

Samson was having a hard time keeping his mind on the round and round conversation that they'd been having.

Tray wanted to take his entire pack to Georgia right then and end Elantra's reign of terror. Ian wanted to bring up an army from Atlantis and wait for her to come to them.

"Am I sure that Sorcha needs her memories back? Fuck yes I'm sure."

Beltar gave him an empathetic look. Beltar knew the whole story, Samson had confessed it when he'd returned to his coven an absolute mess ready to walk into the sun. If it wasn't for Beltar's support and the knowledge that as long as he was alive he could at least try and keep protecting her, he probably would have done just that.

"Then it's settled. We go for Atlantis when the sun sets. I will speak with Sparah and we will decide how best to deal with my mother. If you decided to go after them in the meantime then I can't stop you, Patrick, but I would ask that you wait. That you let us get all the information possible before jumping in hotheaded," Ian said.

Patrick looked annoyed but nodded. "We will stand in Miami as a pack and be ready if she comes, but we won't go after her. I won't allow more humans to suffer, so if you are fine with the way she's treating the Descendants right now, then we wait," Patrick snarled.

Ian's jaw clenched and Samson could see the tension in his hands as they clutched his Descendant mate's hand. Katherine put her other hand on his arm and his body relaxed some, but his glare didn't waver.

"I would do what is necessary to keep them from harm, but they are not in danger. Sorcha described them as happily working alongside the witches. There's no reason to assume that would change now. Elantra needs them and they don't have the mind power to push back. It's not right what she's doing to them, but they will be safe until we can free them."

"You're doing the right thing," Katherine said, looking up at him with a soft smile.

Samson couldn't help looking at the couple with jealousy. It had been so easy for Ian to convince Katherine to fall in love with him and accept his vampiric life. Seeing that some part of acceptance still clung to Sorcha's mind even though she'd erased every loving thing they'd had together gave him hope of doing it again.

It would just be harder this time because this time she'd have proof of his monstrous side from firsthand knowledge.

Did he have any right to ask her to look past that?

The room cleared out, the werewolves heading to bed as the sun was going to be up soon and they weren't entirely nocturnal like the vampires. Ian took Katherine downstairs to find the semi-private bedroom that Patrick said was down there, and that left Samson with Beltar as Laric and the twins headed outside to do one last security sweep before sunrise.

"When you tell her why you did it, she'll understand. She isn't without reason. If she were, then she never would have rearranged her prejudices to fall in love with you the first time."

"Making her forget preconceived notions is easier than making her let go of a personal betrayal," Samson hissed and walked up the stairs. He just wanted to check on her once before he had to hide out in the basement.

He listened at her door and heard nothing but the almost silent sound of her deep breathing. He let himself in and crept over to stare down at her in the bed. She was so small, curled up on her side and gripping her pillow like it was a lifeline. He leaned closer and caught a glint of metal.

He straightened and smiled. She was armed. Smart woman.

He had to clench his fists to keep from reaching out and

running a hand through her red hair. The color was so brilliant in the moonlight, so full of fire, just like her soul.

He stood there until it was almost dangerous, then raced down to the basement as light began to filter over the horizon. He knew he would lay awake and count the seconds down until he could leave the basement and be with her again. There was no hope of rest for him this day.

Eight

SORCHA SLEPT through the night with no dreams. She wasn't sure if it was exhaustion or stress, but she was thankful when she woke up in the afternoon and felt rested. She was also thankful for the pile of clean clothes she found on a chair in the room. She wasn't sure if they belonged to Lilly or Katherine, but she was happy to take off her dusty and rumpled clothes and slip into the leggings and t-shirt.

Then she followed the smell of bacon and eggs to the kitchen.

"She's awake," Lilly greeted her with a smile.

"Where is everyone?" The place was quiet, but the evidence of the pack was there in the pile of dishes Lilly was currently scrubbing through.

"When we heard you moving around, I kicked them out. Of course the vamps and Katherine are downstairs, but the pack is out running. I figured it was safest if you woke up just with me in the house. We never met, so you shouldn't be triggered seeing me."

That was thoughtful. Sorcha gave the werewolf woman a smile.

"Here, you are probably starving," Lilly handed her a plate piled high with bacon, fresh venison steak, eggs, and fruit.

Sorcha sat at the counter and dug in; she was hungry.

"I did see you once, I think. Your red hair is pretty memorable. You were in the window of the Florida compound when the guys and I came for some books. It was right after the vamp attack that Ian's brother, Jovi orchestrated. We were after some werewolf lore books your sister had. The place was a bit trashed, Julie was pissed, and scared, I think. She'd just been under the influence of the Descendants' Stone, all of them were, except you and Katherine I guess because of the vamp blood thing."

A little spike of pain shot through Sorcha's head and she groaned. She couldn't wait for this to be over. How the hell could anyone decide to just live with this kind of reaction to a spell?

There was no way *knowing* could be worse than this.

Could it?

"Coffee?" she asked, hopeful that there would be a hot pot somewhere.

"Over there, sorry I don't know how to work it," Lilly confessed.

Sorcha went to the pot and found everything she needed, getting the coffee going. "How is it you don't know how to make a pot of coffee?"

"I was held captive in wolf form for a hundred years by the Aristotle Society, up until recently."

Sorcha nearly choked on the bite of bacon she'd taken. "What?"

Lilly shrugged with a frown. "I know, it's a long story, sort of... most of it was just me in a cell. But Tray helped get me out and now the Society is no more. I have him and this pack and I am happy."

"Wow, that must be quite a story."

"The story of the last Aristotle Wolf," she said with a half-smile. "A weapon for destroying vampires, but like I said, most of my time was spent in a cell alone and pissed off when I wasn't disassociating. I was a dusty, unused weapon waiting for death before Tray. Like all werewolves, I grew up knowing that vampires were the enemy and I hunted and killed them to protect innocent humans. It was hard for me to not be doing that."

"But not now?" Sorcha asked, thinking of the sleeping vampires below their feet.

"Patrick trusts Katherine and by association, Ian and Beltar, so I am trying to let go of my prejudice. It's just difficult when it's all I knew for so long, vampires bad, kill on sight. I guess you understand, you grew up fearing them too."

"Yeah, and more recently werewolves."

Lilly paused in her cleaning and gave Sorcha a sad look. "I get that. I was taken by the same pack that attacked you. Not the same werewolves, Tray and Samson killed all of them when they found you. The same pack though. We killed their leader, so don't worry about them. I don't think the remaining werewolves will come over into Patrick's territory again. Patrick is in charge of everything East of the Mississippi and Weston used to have everything west, mostly his pack was all the way over on the west coast. Now it's up for grabs, I'm sure we'll hear from a new alpha over there soon. Hopefully it's someone who enjoys peace."

"Peace sounds nice," Sorcha said. She'd grown up with an ever-present feeling of looming danger. What would it be like to live without that?

"We stopped Weston. We can stop Elantra," Lilly said confidently.

"Elantra is more powerful than a simple werewolf," Sorcha pointed out. "She's a witch with an enslaved army."

"So it might take more than a pack of werewolves to take her out, I think that's why Patrick agreed to wait for the vampires to get back from Atlantis with reinforcements and some more information."

Sorcha thought about that as she finished up her breakfast and tried not to think about the sexy vampire asleep just below her. She'd almost been disappointed he hadn't made an appearance in her dreams, especially now that she had a face to put on the mysterious figure who brought her pleasure.

She must have made some kind of noise because Lilly suddenly smiled her way.

"So that vampire Samson seems alright."

"I don't know," Sorcha said honestly.

Lilly shrugged. "He may have done something stupid but that doesn't mean your body has changed its mind about who it wants."

"And I should listen to all the things my body tells me to do?" Sorcha asked with a snort.

"No, but when it comes to choosing a partner that fits, sometimes our body speaks louder than our brain because it's not so full of the what ifs."

Sorcha wasn't sure the werewolf was wrong so she didn't answer.

When the sun went down the vampires came up and they were all set to head out. The plan was to make it back to Miami and down to Atlantis before the sun rose again. Ian told her that if she went with them, Sparah would certainly at least try and reverse the memory spell. Sorcha didn't love the idea of entering the vampire's lair, but if she wanted her memories back, she didn't think she had a choice. And she definitely wanted her memories back. She thought maybe Lilly was right about her body knowing something her mind was too full to recognize, but that didn't matter much if she was shocked with pain every time she laid eyes on the man in question.

She was a reasonable person, had always liked to look at a situation from all sides with all the information, which is why it shocked her that she'd make such a drastic decision like giving up some of her memory in the first place. She needed to know, good or bad, she had to see it all before she could decide if her body was just a horny slut, or if it was telling her something her mind was too prejudiced to accept.

She rode in a car with Lilly and a couple of werewolves whose faces didn't send spikes of pain through her mind. The choice was an obvious disappointment to Samson who had begun to argue with her but when she'd turned away, flinching at the pain just looking at him sent through her, he relented and grumbled as he got into a van to follow behind them.

Even in the short time it had been since leaving the mall she'd already accepted that not every werewolf was going to attack her. She didn't need Samson to keep her comfortable through this ride.

See, I'm not unreasonably prejudiced! She wanted to scream at herself. She wasn't without reason; she could grow and change.

The drive was long and tiring, they stopped only when necessary and by the time Miami showed in the distance, Sorcha would have agreed to anything to just get out and stretch her legs. They drove straight to the beach which was thankfully deserted at this time of almost morning. Aside from a few sleeping bums anyway.

"We will stand guard in the city," Patrick said when their group was gathered around the parking lot.

"My coven is staying as well," Beltar said.

Sorcha had to keep herself from reacting. She had assumed Samson would go, wanted his reassuring presence as she walked into the land of blood suckers that had been the star of more than one nightmare as a child.

"Not me, I'm going with Sorcha," Samson said, and she let out a relieved breath.

"Of course," Beltar agreed, "I was expecting as much."

"Fun," Katherine declared. "Another girl in Atlantis! It gets a little boring, just me and Sparah down there with a bunch of guys."

"No other women?" Sorcha gasped.

"They all left before the sinking," Ian reminded her.

"No female vampires," Sorcha said with a nod, remembering that little fact. What the hell was she about to walk into?

"I will protect you," Samson said fiercely behind her.

Sorcha pulled a blade from her belt. "I can protect myself, thanks," she said without looking at him, afraid that everyone would see how terrifying this adventure was for her.

Samson didn't respond.

"Get a boat, we need to move this party below the waterline," Katherine ordered Ian.

Ian hurried off to do as she bid. It was endearing the way he hovered over her, watched her with lust and protectiveness. How he seemed to care more for her needs than his own.

Sorcha envied them their relationship. It seemed so easy and smooth. She dared a quick glance at Samson, whatever they had had in the past, there was no way it had been like that. If it had, she wouldn't have tried to forget it.

"How exactly does this work?" she asked Katherine as their small group headed toward the water where Ian was apparently going to bring a boat.

"Well, since I'm not as strong a swimmer as vampires are, we *borrow* a boat of some kind to take us out to the triangle. There's a vortex sort of deal there. We swim down and it sucks us in and spits us out in the water of Atlantis."

Sorcha gave Katherine a look that clearly expressed how crazy she sounded.

Katherine just laughed. "I know, it's hard to believe, and even after experiencing it, you'll have a hard time wrapping your brain around it. But I promise you you'll survive. Just hold your breath and let Samson pull you along. There's another entrance but despite Ian's claim that it's a shortcut, I still almost drowned," she said with a frown.

"I will not let you drown," Samson assured her.

"And there's just a bunch of male vampires down there, that's it?"

"Sparah too, and the monsters in the prison," Katherine shivered. "I don't go down there though. Ian said that mermaids show up sometimes, but he warned me they can't be trusted. Shady dealers apparently."

"Evil things," Samson agreed.

"Mermaids?" Why was that surprising, she knew of the existence of witches, vampires, and werewolves. Why not mermaids? "I don't think they are in any of our books."

"Mermaids don't deal with anyone on land. It's why they come to Atlantis at all, it's the only place for them to interact with others. They were hunted to near extinction way before the sinking of Atlantis by a group of Viking warriors who prized them for their beautiful scales. Or so the legend goes," Samson added. "I've never met one, but I heard the stories when I lived in Atlantis."

"Why didn't you stay there?" Sorcha asked.

"I didn't like Ian telling me what to do," he grunted.

Ian arrived shortly with a small rowboat he'd found along the beach and the women got in while the men remained in the water to push them out to the spot. Sorcha tried not to think about what she was going to do, just concentrated on the hope that this would help her save her sister and the other Descendants. She couldn't fight a battle with half the information missing.

She couldn't make life decisions about who she might love with half the information missing.

When they stopped the boat at a seemingly random point, Katherine jumped in without hesitation then promptly disappeared under the water with Ian.

Sorcha frowned down at the dark depths. "I think I have that thing, that fear of water that you can't see the bottom."

"Thalassophobia," Samson said with a smirk.

"Yeah, that's it," she grumbled.

"Just close your eyes and jump, I won't let anything happen to you, Sorcha. I have already spent too long without you by my side, I would never let something as silly as death come between us."

"What *did* you let come between us?" she asked, but instead of waiting for his answer she closed her eyes as he'd directed, and she jumped in. She felt his arms catch her and bring her head up above water.

"Never again," he promised. "Now take a deep breath and don't panic. You are going to swim as hard and as fast as you can straight down. The vortex will pull you where you need to be and you'll be breathing air again before you know it."

"Okay," she said and did as he instructed. She took a deep breath then dunked under and forced herself to swim down, going against every instinct. She felt a push every once in a while and knew he was helping her, he was there. Then soon she felt the pull he was talking about. It was like being sucked into a drain and she wanted to panic, wanted to open her eyes and her mouth but she managed to not do either as it rushed around her and then when her lungs were burning with the need for oxygen and her mind was starting to go fuzzy, she felt hands pulling her up and her head burst through the surface of the water.

She gasped and sputtered and embraced the hard solid body in front of her as she realized she hadn't died. He swam with her until they were both laying on a warm sandy beach.

"Welcome to Atlantis," Samson whispered in her ear when her breathing was once again calm and even.

Sorcha sat up and looked around, gasping at the beautiful sight. They were on a white sandy beach that stretched out in both directions and the clear blue water in front of it was smooth as glass and seemed to stretch to the horizon line. She knew they were under the ocean and this must be a spell. A wonderful spell. When she turned to look up the beach, she saw a line of palm trees and grass. There were flowers blooming in vibrant colors, deep blood reds to bright pink, brilliant yellows to deep oranges and every shade of purple. She wanted to smell them all, she had a feeling they would fill her lungs with scents that hadn't been on earth in centuries.

It was barely morning above the waterline, the sun just about to come up over the horizon and down here it looked the same when she stared at what was a fake sky, apparently. It was as if she were seeing morning just about to break. "How is this possible?" she wondered.

"It's breathtaking, isn't it?" Katherine said nearby. "I still can't believe how beautiful this place is, the magic here has to be incredibly strong to create this for the vampires."

"It was meant to keep the Descendants happy here," Ian said. "The vampires don't need the fake sky and sunlight to do their job."

Katherine scoffed. "You're telling me you wouldn't have had half these men walking into the daylight to get out of a dark, depressing, underwater tomb?"

Ian shrugged and gave her a half smile. "Maybe you're right, but it wasn't the original intent."

Sorcha felt bad for Beltar and his coven above the waterline with only night to greet them. They hadn't been born vampires, they had to remember the sunshine and light. How did they manage to stand it up there in only darkness?

"Why did you give this up to be above the waterline?" she asked Samson.

"I didn't fit here with Ian and his people. Nowhere to go, not enough room to roam and so many damn rules to keep me busy."

Sorcha wanted to ask him to explain but stopped herself. She had no right to demand he reveal himself to her, not when he probably had already and she'd given it up. She'd given him up.

The realization made her heart ache, would he ever be able to forgive her for erasing him from her memory?

She went back to examining the surroundings and gasped when she caught sight of a pyramid popping up beyond the palm trees and something resembling the Parthenon next to it.

"Wow," she whispered and a nerdy part of her couldn't wait to go explore this piece of perfectly preserved history.

Nine

SAMSON ITCHED, being back in Atlantis. He hadn't enjoyed his short stint in this place the first time around. When he'd escaped the hell he'd been living in and ran across Beltar's coven he'd thought leaving the land of the living would be great. Get as far from humans as possible. But Ian was too controlling, and the place was too small. He needed room to run and roam, hated to be chained to one spot.

It was different this time. He wasn't planning to try and stay and he would endure anything because Sorcha needed to be here and he refused to leave her side ever again. No matter what happened from here on out, he knew that he would stay by her side, as close as she'd allow. He would watch over her whether she wanted him to or not until she perished from natural old age.

Then he would embrace the sun and join her in the next life. Maybe then he would deserve her because there was no way he would in this life.

"You'll want to keep her close if possible. The others will be anxious to meet her and since she isn't attached to you, I can't tell them to stay away," Ian said in a low tone so that the women nearby wouldn't hear.

They were wringing out their clothes and brushing sand off. Samson had discarded everything except his underwear back at the beach and Ian was looking comfortable in his traditional leather kilt.

Ian's words irked him, but he couldn't deny they were right. He had no claim on the beauty and even after her memories were returned, he likely wouldn't be able to claim her as his own. "Are there clothes we can borrow?" Samson asked, he wanted to provide every comfort he could for Sorcha.

"Oh yes, we will find something. Come on girls," Ian called to them, and they all started up the beach. A path cut through the jungle there and led to the gates of the city.

Samson watched Sorcha's eyes widen as she looked around and made sounds of surprise and delight as they passed by flowering plants. He ached to take her hand and enjoy the sights with her, ask her which was her favorite.

"Do my eyes deceive me? Is that Samson come back to what he described as an underwater hellscape prison for eunuchs and idiots?"

Samson hissed under his breath as Thorn strode forward from his post as guard at the gate. He was a good man, a little too jovial for Samson's taste though. A good strong warrior, even now he had two swords hung at his waist to protect the city.

"Fuck, you brought another one," Thorn said then, his gaze finding Sorcha.

"Mine," Samson hissed and moved to stand in Thorn's line of sight.

Thorn darted his eyes to Ian who just shrugged. "She's not here for a social call. We came to see Sparah and I need to talk to my warriors about a possibility of battle."

Thorn nodded. "I'll call everyone together."

"Give me a couple hours, I need to see Sparah first, then spend some time with my wife," Ian said.

Thorn rolled his eyes. "That means we won't see you again

until sunset," Thorn laughed and slapped Ian on the shoulder. "I will tell them to be ready then."

Ian laughed back. "Unfortunately, we may need to be on the move at sundown, so be ready in three hours."

Samson was surprised at the light teasing interaction. Ian had changed since meeting Katherine.

"Will do," Thorn said and with a final wave to the women, he turned and hurried off.

"Mine?" Sorcha snapped and pushed Samson away from her. "I am no one's, asshole."

Samson just grunted, he couldn't argue with her, no matter how much he wanted to. But he could continue to warn off anyone who even glanced in her direction, she really couldn't stop him from doing that. She might not even notice the glares he was giving out, since she still refused to look at him.

They continued through the gate and toward the pyramid where Ian kept his home. Below the pyramid was the prison holding the monsters. Sparah lived there as well, and Samson was glad that's where they were headed first.

The vampires did come out to stare and Samson glared at all of them, baring his teeth and walking as close to Sorcha as he could get while she remained in conversation with Katherine. It worked; they didn't try to approach, but they showed more than curiosity about the woman.

"I have uncovered so many wonderful artifacts here," Katherine was saying to Sorcha. "Ian and his men used to take down whole ships, it's what gave this area such a bad reputation as you know. They collected so many things from the wreckage."

"Yeah, like dead bodies," Sorcha said.

Katherine nodded, her lips in a thin line. "Yeah, I am glad they found a different way."

"Sea animals, yum," Samson grumbled.

"You'd prefer what?" Sorcha challenged and he looked away,

unable to meet her accusing eyes. So much disdain and she didn't even know the half of it.

Katherine quickly changed the subject. "But also some things that were brought down with the city are still here, things unlike anything found anywhere else. It's an archeologist's dream."

"And all so well preserved," Sorcha pointed out. Obviously noticing the great condition of everything around them from the pyramid itself to a stack of pottery outside someone's cottage and a rack of swords set up outside another.

"Oh yes, something to do with the spell, Ian says. Nothing ages here, including me," Katherine said brightly.

Those words struck Samson. Katherine wouldn't age as long as she spent most of her time here in Atlantis. Sorcha either. He could live a life of eternal happiness with her here. Would she ever agree to that? Could he handle it?

That was a dumb question, he could handle anything if it meant having her.

"Another one," a vampire nearby whispered, watching their small group make its way through the little village toward the pyramid. Ian greeted some with a shout or a wave. Most just stood watching and were only interested in the new Descendant among them. He'd been caught up in their conversation and forgot to be glaring at the vampires.

Samson hated how vulnerable she was right now. He wanted to ask her if she was okay, she seemed okay but was she really? This had to be like a nightmare for her, walking into the heart of the vampire's territory. He knew his concern wouldn't be welcomed though. Not only did she resent him for what he was, she knew that he had done something terrible, something that had forced her to make the drastic decision to erase memories.

Was it possible that she was imagining something worse than the reality? And when her memories returned, could she decide to forgive him because it wasn't so bad?

He didn't have much hope.

"No way, we are going *inside* the pyramid," Sorcha squealed as Ian held a door open.

"Oh yes, you have no idea, it is so cool," Katherine agreed, grabbing Sorcha's arm excitedly. "It's so nice to have another woman from above the waterline to share this all with."

"I don't know how you can stand to be down here all alone," Sorcha admitted and shivered slightly. "Gives me the creeps, honestly. All those hungry eyes."

"Oh, I am rarely alone. Ian is like a second skin most of the time and I have grown fond of a few of the others here, consider them my friends. No one here would harm me, or you, Sorcha. They aren't like that, I promise. Besides, I am in heaven among all the artifacts I get to dig through and anonymously send up to my friends at the museum."

"Katherine is always busy with something when I let her out of the bedroom," Ian agreed and pulled her in for a deep kiss.

"Dear Goddess it's true," a feminine voice called from down a hallway.

Sparah walked toward them, her long black hair flowing freely down her back. She had a streak of grey at the temple hinting at her age, which Samson knew was ancient despite her youthful golden-brown skin. Hidden behind that streak of grey was a missing ear Samson had caught sight of once or twice, she liked to try and keep it hidden and he had no idea what it was from. He didn't dare ask, she'd likely turn him into a toad or shrink his dick for the audacity. Her blue eyes were shrewd as they took in their group and her black lips pursed. She stared with particular interest at Sorcha and he wondered if she'd predicted their arrival. She seemed genuinely surprised, so he doubted she believed it to be a strong possibility even if she had seen it. "We have someone who needs your help. This is Sorcha," Ian said motioning to Sorcha.

"This is Sparah," Ian said to Sorcha.

"The cursed Descendant," Sparah whispered when she got to the group. She pushed Ian and Katherine aside to get close to

Sorcha who was standing just behind Samson now, intimidated by the small witch. "Move big man, I am not afraid of you or your glowers. Come child," Sparah beckoned Sorcha forward. "I can't help you from a distance."

Samson stepped aside grudgingly and Sorcha moved in front of him. Sparah held Sorcha's face and looked into her eyes as if she were searching into her soul. "Yes, I have been waiting a long time for you. A sign I wished would never come."

"What the hell does that mean?" Sorcha hissed.

"Sparah can see the future," Samson pointed out.

"I can see possibilities, but only some, and only sometimes. This is something I saw and hoped would not come to pass. But here you are." Sparah shook her head. "A little gift from my sister no doubt."

Sorcha stepped back, breaking the hold Sparah had on her face. Samson could see Sorcha's face now clearly and she was wary, confused, and underneath, he thought perhaps frightened.

"You don't have to do this," Samson reminded her.

"Yes, she does. We might need the information she's locked away and you," Sparah turned her knowing eyes on him, "you need her to know what you've done."

Samson stiffened.

"I want to know what I was running from," Sorcha said before Samson could argue further.

"Yes, come with me. Katherine fetch something dry for her to wear and Ian, I will need you to keep the big man out of my room while I work."

Sparah grabbed Sorcha's arm and dragged her down the hall. Samson moved to follow and found himself up against Ian's chest.

"You heard what she said, Samson. She doesn't need you disturbing the magic. You are welcome to wait here in the hall or outside, and if you can't handle either option, I will have you taken to a cell and locked in until it's over. I want to be in bed with my wife, not babysitting you."

Samson met Ian's glare with his own and debated his ability to take Ian out or get past him. But the witch was more than capable of fighting him off on her own and what if he did interrupt and disturb the magic, it could harm Sorcha.

"Fine," Samson said and sat down against the wall. He was only a few doors down from Sparah's chambers, he would wait right there until Sorcha was fixed.

Then he would see if he had a chance at a life less tortured by grief and regret.

Katherine moved past with a bundle of clothes and when she returned from Sparah's room, Ian grabbed her arm and pulled her along and up the stairs. No doubt they were about to spend a few hours in carnal delight.

Samson envied Ian the happiness he'd found.

* * *

Sorcha's mind was spinning. Not only was she in the sunken city of Atlantis, in a *pyramid*, but she was here willingly. The way Katherine seemed comfortable here eased her a lot and although the vampires they'd passed on their walk had looked at her with open curiosity, none had tried to attack her.

That could have been because Samson was walking close to her looking like he wanted to tear them all apart. She knew he was being overly protective, and she should stop him, but she appreciated that no one else tried to approach her. The last thing she needed were multiple vampire suitors.

She already had one too many.

She had changed into the clothes Katherine brought her, a sundress and dry underwear. She'd squeezed most of the water from her hair and braided it loosely as she gazed around the room she was in. It wasn't a bedroom, more like a living room space. There was a small table with half burned candles and wax dripped down to the wood. A couch of sea green velvet and dark wood that looked like it should be in a museum. Paintings that showed varying degrees of water damage and rows and rows of shelves holding bottles of herbs, rocks, shells, stones, and what she was fairly certain were bones.

She didn't look close enough to be certain if they were from humans or animals. Some things were best left alone.

The room smelled strongly of incense and herbs, and Sorcha wondered if Sparah had a garden somewhere to keep fresh herbs in supply.

Sparah was hunched over a book at a podium scanning it with her finger and mumbling to herself, completely ignoring Sorcha and her wandering investigation of the room. Sorcha took a moment to study the witch. There were definite similarities between her and Elantra, a bit of sisterly resemblance. But where Elantra had a look of stone cold control, Sparah looked—dazzled —that was the only word Sorcha could put on it. Like her mind was so full she was thinking a million thoughts at once all the time.

It didn't trick Sorcha into thinking she wasn't paying attention to everything though, almost as if her superpower was to be able to pay attention to everything everywhere all at once. The now, the past and the possible futures all rumbling around in her brain.

"I wrote this down, when was that?" She flipped through pages and frowned, then flipped back. "Was it before World War Two, or after? No, it must have been before. Was it during the whole Roman debacle?"

Sorcha tried to understand what the hell the woman was talking about but gave up when she started mumbling about the British monarchy. She went back to investigating the room. She walked over to an altar with a carved stone image of a woman with a pregnant belly and the head of a wolf. She had claw-like hands and human feet. Her breasts were large and hung halfway down her belly and there was a swirl that circled the belly with images of life etched inside.

"The original earth mother," Sparah explained. "Mother of all earth has, even the dark things," Sparah said. "They were all born of her. My father was a werewolf, the first werewolf, born of my grandmother's ferocity and my mother was born of her desire for control, the first witch."

"Gross," Sorcha said before she could stop herself then slapped a hand over her mouth hoping she hadn't just pissed off this powerful witch.

Sparah just laughed. "It's not mother like that," Sparah explained. "She didn't create them the way we create now, it's not a genetic or sexual thing. She created through her magic and brought to life all the things, so she was mother to all she created, and her creations went on to breed and create their own things."

Sorcha nodded. She supposed that was as good a creation story as any.

"So you really are that old?"

"Yes, and lucky for you, that powerful. I actually saw you so long ago I almost forgot. I predicted a red-haired beauty who would seek refuge in my magic. Self-cursed and holding the key to stopping my sister's insanity once and for all. The cursed Descendant."

"I don't know about that, I just—"

Sparah held up a hand and stopped Sorcha's words. "Don't worry about all that, it will reveal itself in its own time. Right now you are here because you want me to lift the memory curse. I will do that. I warn you that it won't be pleasant, you will relive all you have forgotten and then you will awake with memories restored. I don't know how long the reliving will take, not as long as they took to create in the first place, but depending on how much you've lost, it could be a little while before you wake up from the spell."

"That's fine, that's what I want. I need to know. The good and the bad."

Sparah nodded. "It is what makes life, good and bad. If you were meant to only have the good your people would have stayed under the influence of the Descendants' Stone and served the vampires for eternity as happy blood slaves. Now lay on the couch. I will be here when you wake as will that big hunk of vampire you tried to forget."

Sorcha nodded and did as instructed. Fear almost had her running for the door but more than fear, the need to know held her in place. She closed her eyes as Sparah laid a hand on her forehead and started to mutter.

A warmth spread through Sorcha and a scent, something like cinnamon and vanilla filled her nose. Then it changed, pain and smoke, blood and bile.

Ten

SORCHA STOOD NEXT TO A CAMPFIRE; bodies strewn around her feet. So much blood, some of it her own. Half the bodies were in wolf form and a werewolf turned human form was nearby dragging a still living beast away. He had saved her; he had been the distraction she'd needed to stop them.

She'd been so stupid, hunting this far away alone, but she'd heard rumors of people being attacked and she had to see if she could help. Had assumed it was vampires. Julie wasn't going to tell others to help unless Sorcha could prove it. So she'd come for proof.

She'd stumbled on a pack of werewolves. They'd wasted no time in tearing through her clothing with teeth and claws, some human, some not at the time. They'd been merciless in their desire to take and destroy and she would forever bear the scars if she lived through this.

She was nearly falling over now from blood loss; the pain had numbed and she thought that was certainly a bad sign.

Her mind was spinning toward total blackness, but she was going to kill this last one. She used the axe they'd had in the campsite, bringing it down to the man's throat ending his worthless existence.

The effort was too much, she closed her eyes as she began to collapse. She braced herself for an impact that never came. Strong arms caught her, and she was pressed against a hard chest, that's when the blackness finally overwhelmed her.

Sorcha woke two days later in a dark room with a funny taste in her mouth. Her entire body ached and when she remembered why, she jolted up to a sitting position and stared around her, expecting to see angry werewolves ready to use and destroy her. One of them had survived, snuck up behind her and taken her here.

Why hadn't he just killed her and gotten it over with? What terrible plans did he have for her now?

Her gaze landed on a large man watching her from across the room with a blank expression. He had short black hair and amazing purple eyes. She couldn't look away, he was gorgeous, all muscle and gold skin. He wore a pair of jeans and no shirt, leaving a lot of golden skin for her to lavish her gaze over. Something about him attracted her unlike anything she'd ever felt, and it didn't make sense because she knew the instant she laid eyes on him what he was.

Vampire.

The immortal enemy of her people.

"You have the Stone, or you are enchanting me. You are going to make me your blood slave," she gasped, a fear unlike anything she'd ever experienced filled her. The thought that she was going to have her will, her choices, and her ability to want to fight, taken away from her was more terrifying than anything the werewolves could have done to her.

His eyes widened and his mouth opened a fraction at the accusation.

"I would never make anyone a slave to anyone. I have lived the life of a tool, a slave, a worthless being except for use at the disgusting whims of my owner. I would never do that to another," he declared.

His voice was deep and smooth, and it sent a shiver through her. Inexplicably, she wanted to believe him.

"Then what is going on? Why do I feel..." she didn't know how to explain it and her cheeks reddened a bit because she didn't want to say she was turned on, attracted to him, looking at his stomach like it needed to be bathed with her tongue. "Not terrified," she finally settled on.

He was frowning slightly when her gaze darted back up to his face, having stared too intensely at where his pants met his bare stomach.

"That is the vampire blood in your system."

She gasped and touched her neck, which is when the blanket dropped, and she realized she was completely nude under the thin thing. "What?" she hissed and pulled the blanket up again. "What did you do to me?" she demanded.

"What do you remember?" he asked gently, still sitting across the room. He hadn't made a move to get closer and his face was once again a calm mask.

Sorcha wanted to snap at him to just talk, to tell her what he had done and what he planned to do next, but as she stared at his calm face and unmoving body she got the feeling she might not be in immediate danger from him. She tried to relax, tried to take his actions as proof he wasn't about to harm her. She wouldn't trust the situation in the long run, but maybe he wasn't hungry right now and if she played along, got some information, she'd be able to escape.

"The last thing I remember?"

"Yes," he said.

"Werewolves attacked me," she whispered and frowned as her mind brought up image after image of the terror, pain, and death that had surrounded her in those moments. A human face with glowing eyes, he was about to turn and he was stalking toward her. She was already bleeding. She had already been harmed but they weren't done, they wanted all of her. Her breathing became frantic, her body shook, and she heard a scream from somewhere. Hands grabbed her and she fought against it.

"You are safe little one," a calming voice broke through the panic, and she realized it was herself screaming, and the hands on her now were the vampire's. He was stroking her back, soothing her with his gentle voice and she began to relax against him. She wasn't there with the beasts anymore, she hadn't died at their hands, she couldn't believe it.

Then most horrifyingly, the tears came. She sobbed and sobbed against his chest, clinging to the blanket between them as her face leaked embarrassingly all over his bare chest.

He didn't move though, didn't stop his gentle stroking or his mantra of telling her she was safe now.

When the tears finally settled to gentle hiccups, she pulled away enough to wipe her face with the blanket, then his chest where she'd blubbered all over it. His arms fell away from her and hung limp at his sides as he watched her with a curious look while she wiped the snot and tears from his beautiful chest.

His muscles were so firm, so much harder than anything she'd ever encountered. Her hand brushed over a taut nipple and it felt like a small pebble under her palm. She bit her lip as her mind brought up a very specific fantasy of that nipple and her mouth. Her cheeks heated and she looked away from him, scooting back slightly and holding the blanket tight to her body once more.

"You don't have to tell me. I saw your injuries. I saw them dead. You never have to speak of it if you don't want to." He must have taken her move as one of shame over what had happened to her rather than the forbidden fantasies running through her mind.

"Thank you," Sorcha whispered, unable to look up at his face. This man, this monster, knew what had been done to her. Somehow it was comforting, to have someone to share in her grief without explanation. She didn't think she'd ever want to speak of the horror of that night, but it was a burden she also knew she didn't want to bear alone. She looked up into his purple eyes and saw a sympathy there that made her chest ache.

"I took you from there and brought you here to help you heal. I had to give you my blood to aid in the healing. It can have some temporary effects on your libido, but I promise I did not, I would not, take advantage."

Sorcha nodded, staring down at her lap at the mention of how she felt towards him. It was nice to know it wasn't insanity, just the effect of his blood in her system, that made her want to jump the bones of her enemy. Not enemy... he had saved her, healed her, and now said he had no intention of taking advantage of her. She believed him too; he seemed so earnest. There was a deep pain behind his words that spoke of personal trauma.

"Thank you," she whispered again.

He put a gentle touch to her chin and forced her eyes up to his. "What is your name?"

The realization that this man had seen her naked, had fed her his blood and done who knew what else. Judging by the lack of dried bloody wounds on her body she'd guess he'd bathed her at the very least. Yet didn't know her name, struck her as funny.

She laughed and he looked concerned, as if her mood swing was indication of an addled brain. "Sorcha," she said as she tried to regain her composure.

"It is nice to meet you, Sorcha. My name is Samson."

"Samson. Where are we?"

"Near the border to Georgia, but on the Florida side. This is an abandoned farmhouse I discovered a while back. A safe space for both of us."

A safe place for both of them, and miles from where she'd been when she'd run across the werewolves. Never would she have imagined a vampire doing such a thing. Shouldn't the smell of blood have whipped him into a frenzy of uncontrolled animalistic desire? Shouldn't he have torn through her and the others? Sorcha was so confused. She should hate this vampire, she should be in danger with him. But he had saved her life and he had taken her somewhere safe where he could take care of her while she'd been passed out and healing.

Why hadn't he just taken her to a hospital or left her in a town to be discovered by humans and cared for?

What did he want from her?

She couldn't help the suspicions from rising up. They were far too ingrained for her to ignore.

"Are there any clothes here?" she asked. If he denied her clothing she'd know his true intentions.

"No," he said with a frown.

Her body stiffened, this was it, this was where he started demanding things from her. She'd have to fight her way out. Her eyes darted around for a weapon.

"But I will get whatever you need. Clothes, food, anything," he continued quickly, shocking her. "I was afraid to leave you while you slept. If you woke up alone and confused you could have harmed yourself or if someone stumbled upon you helpless like that..." he trailed off clearly knowing the horrors that humans posed in this world as well as the monsters.

"Oh, okay, a phone would be good too, I'm sure my sister is freaking out by now since I didn't show back up at the compound."

A flash of disappointment crossed his face, but he quickly covered it with stoicism. "The sun won't rise for a few hours; I'll go get what you need." He stood and looked down at her. "Stay there," he said with a firm tone.

"I'll stay, but not because you told me to, asshole. I'm staying because I'm naked and don't feel like being arrested for indecent exposure." No shoes, phone, or weapon either, she wouldn't make it far and had no desire to explain any of this to the police.

"Good," he said, and left the basement. She felt his absence like an ache and had to shake the feeling away. It didn't make sense; she didn't even know the man, but she wanted to keep him nearby.

It was probably the blood he'd given her. It must cause some kind of tie between them. She wondered how long it would last and hoped it wasn't a lifelong connection she'd have to deal with.

She leaned back against the wall and thought about how she felt about the fact that she had vampire blood swimming around inside of her body. Did she hate that? She didn't feel sick, she actually felt pretty good and surprisingly not hungry or thirsty even after a couple days of being passed out recovering. That was pretty amazing.

Her hand lifted to her neck wondering if he'd taken from her as well, but she didn't feel anything there, but would she? How did she know he hadn't spent the last two days sipping from her whenever he felt like it?

Something told her he hadn't, something told her he was trustworthy, but she was afraid to believe too hard in that. She was obviously attracted to him; he was a specimen from a romance novel and she wanted to believe he was good. But unlike the men in romance novels, he wasn't hiding from a tortured past that had turned him cruel. He was an actual monster who enjoyed hurting and taking.

She moved the blanket off of her body and inspected her skin. She ran her fingers across various scar lines that looked aged even though they were days old.

He hadn't taken advantage of her passed out body, he hadn't left her for dead. What kind of vampire was he?

She knew what her sister would say.

He's tricking you; all blood suckers are the same. He wants you to willingly give yourself to him then he'll take everything from you. You'll never be the same, you won't survive it and he'll live forever, with you as just a blip on his life story.

It was the story they'd been fed all their lives. Every Descendant understood the evil intentions of vampires.

Sorcha carefully stood and wrapped the blanket around her body then walked around the room. They were in a basement. It looked as if it had been cleaned up recently, swept floors, dusted empty shelves that probably once held canned fruits and vegetables, now holding some stacked blankets and wash cloths and towels. Had he cleaned it, or was this the way he'd found it? Had he killed off a family upstairs so he could hide her here?

She looked at the staircase and knew that she had to answer that before he came back. It would tell her what kind of monster she was dealing with. She snuck quickly to the stairs and rushed up but she stopped at the door, hesitating with her hand on the knob, afraid to find the crack in what felt like a fairy tale beginning.

The dark prince saves the damsel in distress and they live happily ever after...

Sorcha snorted, she'd never been a fan of fairy tales, stupid princesses just letting life happen to them. She opened the door with confidence and looked around expecting blood and death.

She sighed in relief when all she saw was dusty floors and a broken kitchen window. The place looked dated and definitely abandoned.

"Thank fuck," she said and closed the door, heading back down to the impossibly clean basement. He had done that.

She was shocked to find a sword and dagger leaning carelessly against the wall as she finished her inspection of the place.

He had left his weapons here? Where she could easily take them and use them against him?

She shook her head, it must have been a mistake. He probably was in a hurry to leave and come back. He hadn't thought of them, or he thought she was still too weak to use them.

She found a door and pushed it open to find a bathroom. As with the main room, this had been cleaned. Swept, wiped, and stocked with toilet paper and hand soap.

He may not have wanted to leave her alone and vulnerable but he obviously had, at least once, and she was thankful as she realized how full her bladder was.

This wasn't all for him, she knew, so that meant he'd done this so she'd be able to use it when she woke. Why would he care if she had a clean place to relieve herself? She tried to reason through it as she used the bathroom and then walked back to the main room. She needed proof that he wasn't kind and thoughtful. She needed to hold on to what she knew about vampires.

Uncaring, heartless, bloodthirsty monsters.

She sat down on the cot and looked around, hoping for some sign that would show her the truth of what he was.

She saw nothing to indicate what he could be nefariously planning. Did that mean she could trust him though? Her chest was tight with worry but as she thought through what she knew about him so far, it eased a bit. He had saved her, he had prepared this space for her to safely heal and wake up. He'd watched over her while she was at her most vulnerable and was now out getting her what she'd asked for.

She had to admit that it seemed like she was perfectly safe with this vampire.

But for how long?

She laid down and stared at the stairs as she thought about what she was going to tell her sister.

Eleven

WHEN THE DOOR at the top of the stairs opened, she sat up. His footsteps were hurried as he descended, and his gaze snapped to her immediately as if he hadn't believed she would still be there.

His arms were full with all the items she'd asked for. She wondered where he'd stolen them from since they didn't look brand new; but she figured it didn't much matter in this situation. Emergencies were meant for bending the idea of right and wrong.

He approached her slowly and held out the items.

"You brought clothes," she said because she wanted to break the silence and wasn't sure what else to say. It felt like the *I carried a watermelon* moment in Dirty Dancing though and she wanted to rub her face in awkwardness.

"You asked for clothes," he said in confusion.

She shook her head and took them. "Yeah, thanks."

He turned around and walked to the far wall, offering her privacy. She stood and dressed quickly. He'd brought her some loose fabric pajama pants and a comfortable black t-shirt.

"They're great, thank you again. I guess I owe you for a lot, don't I?"

He turned back to her. "You owe me nothing, Sorcha. Now eat, you need your strength." He came forward again and handed her the food he'd brought, and the phone.

Sorcha grunted agreement and opened the bag of chips he'd brought her while staring down at the phone. She wasn't sure what she was going to tell Julie. If she told her she was here holed up with a vampire, Julie would probably send assassins to take him out. But she didn't want to repay Samson's kindness with a stake through the heart. At least not until he proved his intentions were what she'd been told to expect from a vampire.

In the end she decided to gloss over it all. She called the compound and assured her sister she was safe, relayed most of what had happened with the werewolves and said she was recovering and would be back on her way home soon.

Julie demanded to know where she was and said she'd send someone for her but Sorcha just blew her off and said she could take care of herself.

"I'll see you soon," she huffed and hung up.

Samson eyed her the whole time as if he were waiting to hear her beg her sister to come kill the monster who held her captive. When she hung up without mentioning him, he looked surprised.

"You lied to her."

"No, I just omitted what she didn't need to know."

"Why?" he demanded.

"Because she would have sent someone for me and to kill you," Sorcha said with a shrug, popping another chip in her mouth.

"Then I guess you've already repaid me."

"How's that?"

"You have saved my life from your sister's assassins."

Sorcha laughed, "You could probably get out of here before they arrived even if I did tell her."

"I won't leave you," he said fiercely making her stomach do a funny flip.

"Why?" she asked, a little afraid of the answer. Did he think she was his now that he'd given her some blood, was it some kind of weird vampire ritual she didn't know about? Claim your very own blood bag by shoving your blood down its throat.

Samson frowned and looked uncomfortable. He was sitting against the wall opposite her, and his already stiff body became stiffer as he avoided looking directly at her.

"Why, Samson?" she demanded.

Guilt filled his face. "I am attracted to you. You smell sweeter than anything I have ever encountered, and my body reacts to you in a way that I haven't felt for a human in a very long time."

"Oh," Sorcha said because she had no other idea how to respond. Attraction, and spoken with a blush and uncomfortable whisper was nowhere on her list of possibilities. "Is this a vampire to Descendant thing?"

"I don't know, I have never met a Descendant other than you."

"But you've run across plenty of humans."

"Yes."

"Is that why you saved me? Because you were attracted to me?"

"When I saw you standing over a decapitated man, I thought you were a witch. I thought you were sacrificing him for a spell and I was about to kill you. Then I saw the mark on your neck, and I recognized the destruction around you. I saw what had become of your body because of them and I decided to help you. It wasn't until I had you in my arms and the other's blood washed from your body that I recognized the sweetness was all you and my instincts became something more than to just save your life."

Sorcha's breathing started to sharpen, her heart was beating fast and her entire body warmed at his words.

"I didn't take advantage," he said fiercely, misinterpreting her body's reactions.

"I know." And she did, she could see in his eyes that the idea repulsed him. "You're nothing like those other bloodsuckers, are you?"

"I wasn't raised the same way that they were. I never saw Descendants as a god given food and pleasure source. I knew nothing but suffering and pain all my life and it's likely what I deserve, for what I am," he whispered the last and stared down at his clenching hands.

His words made Sorcha's chest ache with empathy. She stood and crossed the room before she could stop herself. She knelt down in front of the vampire. He looked at her with surprise but didn't move as she reached out and grabbed his face. Forcing him to meet her eyes.

"You are a good soul, Samson, I can see it in your eyes, and I can feel it in your blood that runs through my body. I know it because you took care of me when you didn't have to, and you haven't once lied to me about who you are." She knew she was probably making a mistake, but she didn't stop herself from leaning forward and pressing her lips to his. He didn't look like an enemy vampire sitting there with a despondent look on his face, he looked like a lost soul, a victim of circumstances beyond his control and Sorcha knew all too well what we could be forced to do when our backs were against the wall. Survival sometimes came at the cost of blood.

She wanted to comfort him. He had admitted he was attracted to her, and she was definitely attracted to him. In that moment she wanted nothing more than to make the tortured look in his eyes disappear. She wanted to replace whatever terrible memories he had with good ones.

She wanted to replace her own awful memories with good ones as well.

He didn't respond at first and she almost pulled back, her lips pressed to an unyielding mouth but just as she was about to give up in shame, he started to press back and his hands tentatively touched her sides, she didn't hold back a soft moan of encouragement.

He answered immediately, lifting her in a smooth motion and

settling her in his lap. His tongue darted between her lips and swept through her mouth, claiming her.

"You don't have to do this," he said, pulling away, his purple eyes searched hers, full of confusion and passion. He would stop. He would let her change her mind and that knowledge made her even more certain about what she was doing.

"I know," she assured him and pulled his head down until their lips met again. She'd never been good at denying herself what she wanted, and right now she wanted him even though a part of her mind knew that this was a step she'd never be able to come back from. She would forever be branded by his touches, his kisses.

She wanted that though, wanted to walk away from this experience with memories to fuel her dreams for a lifetime.

He stopped holding back. His hands roamed over her body leaving a trail of fiery need behind. The clothes she'd just put on were suddenly in the way and she pulled from him long enough to strip her shirt over her head and shimmy out of the pants. He hadn't brought her any undergarments, so she was quickly naked in front of him.

His groan set off an explosion of need in her belly as he looked at her.

She held out a hand and he took it, standing with her. She led him to the bed then unbuttoned his pants, shoving them down his legs. He had already been shirtless, and she'd loved the sight, but this, his entire body exposed to her, was breathtaking.

He stood still as she gazed at him then reached out and ran a hand over his muscled chest and abs, down his thighs and back up just to the edge of where she most wanted to touch him, afraid to go too fast.

"You won't hurt me?" she asked, looking up at him, suddenly shy.

"I could never," he said, his voice rough with emotion.

"Will you want to bite me?" The thought sent an odd thrill

through her mixed with fear and she wasn't sure what she wanted his answer to be in that moment.

He turned his head and closed his eyes. "No, not ever," he said.

Something in those words stung but she didn't have time to look too closely because he grabbed her and pressed their naked bodies together. She was soon lost in his kisses and caresses again. He laid her gently on the bed, pushing a knee between her thighs and settling there, giving her plenty of time to adjust to the idea of what was about to happen. Plenty of time to change her mind.

She didn't want to. She lifted her hips, urging him on, already ready for him. He grabbed her hips in a bruising grip and thrust.

She cried out and grasped his shoulders as he moved. Pushing their pleasure with an urgency she'd never experienced. Racing her toward release. His body was perfect, and she gloried in the way he felt against her. She watched his face and when he opened his mouth, his fangs showing sharp and long, she trembled with anticipation of what they would feel like, piercing her.

"Yes," she moaned and turned her head, offering her neck like a wanton blood slut.

But he didn't take it, he only moved faster, harder. He gripped one leg and held it up to get deeper. His other hand moved between them to touch her where she needed it and she was too soon crying out with her release, unable to hold back as he touched her in all the right places. He followed quickly with a shout that echoed in the small room and she wondered if there were any neighbors around to have heard him.

He collapsed on top of her with a long drawn out groan, his body shivering.

Their bodies were covered in sweat and she was trembling with little lightning bolts of pleasure. The aftershocks racing through her body a reminder of the most amazing and fastest orgasm she'd ever experienced. She wondered how much of that had to do with him and how much was the blood that ran through her body like an aphrodisiac.

She trailed her fingers up and down his back, loving how it felt to be under him. How protected and warm, she never wanted to leave this cot. "I thought you were going to bite me," she finally said.

"I don't bite for pleasure," he said gruffly.

"Just for survival?" she asked.

"Something like that." He moved off of her and rolled, pulling her against his side.

She missed his full body contact but this was nice too. She laid her head on his shoulder and cuddled up against him. She couldn't believe she was pressed against a vampire, naked and satisfied. Her sister would freak.

"This feels unreal," she admitted with a giggle. A drip of reality seeping in to make her wonder how big of a mistake she'd just made.

"This feels perfect," he corrected.

She snuggled closer against him, throwing a leg over his thigh and an arm across his stomach. She closed her eyes and pushed away thoughts of anything beyond this moment. Perfect was the right word, too bad it couldn't last. Descendants and vampires were not meant to be together like this, like partners in pleasure. Vampires dominated and destroyed. Descendants had fought against that because no one deserved to be owned.

Twelve

THEY SPENT three days in that basement. Samson provided for her every need and pleasured her as often as she'd allow. But he never took blood from her. Even in the throes of passion when his eyes darkened and his fangs seemed to beg for a chance at breaking her skin, he held himself back.

Sorcha wasn't sure if it was the sex or the being taken care of, something she'd never had in her entire life, but she wanted to return the favor. Wanted to provide for him, take care of him and the only way she knew how was with her blood. He brought her food and water and whatever else she asked for, like more clean clothes to change into and shoes. She only gave him orgasms, which honestly was selfish because damn, that man made her fly to heights she'd never imagined in those moments.

She wanted to give to him selflessly, more than pleasure, she wanted to give him sustenance.

But every time she brought it up he told her the same thing. "I would never do that to you. I don't bite for pleasure."

And every time he said that, every time he denied her offer, she felt rejection. He didn't want her blood; he didn't want what she could give him. Was she not good enough, was her blood tainted?

Was it because he'd given her his blood, did that make it less attractive to him?

It hurt, and she hated that it hurt because she shouldn't want him to take her blood, but she desperately did. Sorcha imagined him putting his mouth on some blonde slut's soft white neck and slipping his fangs into her skin and she wanted to scratch the imaginary bitch's eyes out.

It didn't help that every story she'd ever heard of vampires contradicted what he said. Vampires took blood from anywhere, all the time, without care.

Of course every story she'd ever heard of vampires contradicted *everything* he had done for her so far. And with every lovingly provided orgasm and every time he caressed her back while she fell asleep in his arms, she started to feel her heart open more and more to him.

Could she, a Descendant of Atlantis, be falling in love with a vampire? Could this be more than a weekend of passion to give her masturbation fuel?

It wouldn't be her first couple night's stand that she used to satisfy an itch and moved on from. But she had a feeling moving on from him wouldn't be as simple as losing his number. His touches, his looks, his tongue, were burned into her memory.

Her sister would kill her if she ever found out, though. There could never be a happily-ever-after for them, she was certain. She knew she should let it go, she should just accept what this was and enjoy it while it lasted.

She should cut and run before she got any more ideas about liking him.

Sundown on the fourth day Samson prepared to go out. Usually he asked if she had any special requests, usually he offered to bring her back anything her pretty little heart desired.

Tonight though, he seemed agitated. He kept rubbing the back of his neck and glaring around the room as if he thought an answer to whatever problem he had was suddenly going to appear.

"I'll be back," he hissed and rushed up the stairs without his usual kisses and promises to return as soon as possible.

"What the fuck was that all about?" Sorcha wondered. The phone he had snatched for her tinged with a message from her sister.

When are you coming home?

Sorcha sighed. Yesterday her answer had been *I don't know, when I'm ready I guess. Don't worry about me.* Today though, with the way Samson's attitude had turned from fire to ice, she thought maybe she'd be returning sooner rather than later. She couldn't help but wonder if she was overreacting though. Maybe whatever had him irritated had nothing to do with her. Maybe he had an annoying brother somewhere texting him about getting home.

She knew that wasn't true, they'd talked about his life, and though he'd been very closed lipped about anything far in the past, she knew he now lived in Miami with a small coven of vampires.

She knew about them, it was why the Descendants didn't dare enter that city.

Samson said they were alright, but he would often wander for days to weeks so he could clear his head from the bustle of the city and the annoyance of the others, apparently living in close quarters.

She could understand that. It was why she'd been happy to travel north and check out the rumors on her own, sometimes the compound and Julie's nosiness was too much to handle and she needed some breathing room.

Sorcha stared down at the phone. She knew her sister cared, and that's what was behind her aggressive need to be involved in Sorcha's life.

Maybe soon, I'm feeling well and about ready to travel.

Julie responded immediately.

I'll send a car to pick you up, where are you?

No car, I'll find a ride when I'm ready.

Sorcha turned the phone off then, she didn't want to continue arguing with her sister about it. If Julie thought she could pressure Sorcha to agree, then she'd push and push until she got what she wanted.

Sorcha wasn't ready to pull the plug just yet on her and Samson though. She'd see what was up his ass when he got back.

Sorcha pulled out a book he'd brought her recently and started staring at the page without really reading it, ears perked for the sounds of him returning. It was longer than usual before she heard him and she pulled the book closer to her face, hoping to appear as if she hadn't been sitting there meditating on his absence.

When he walked down into the basement Sorcha looked up with a casual smile, expecting the usual gifts of food and water. His hands were empty and she was confused, worried something had happened, she looked up at his face. A new calm was there, different from the hyper irritation he'd had when he left. Stoic now, his eyes were empty and when he stepped close she could smell cheap perfume on him, and there was blood on his shirt. She sucked in a breath to try and remain calm about it and that's when she noticed another scent. Maybe it was because of his blood that her senses were heightened, she wasn't sure, but she knew it the moment it hit her nostrils.

Sex.

And it wasn't because they'd had a romp before he left.

White hot anger, jealousy and hurt that she didn't want to think about filled her.

"What the fuck! Are you fucking kidding me right now?" Sorcha screeched. She threw the book and hit his chest. He didn't move or speak so she threw the next thing in reach, which happened to be the cellphone. This time it hit the wall beside his head and smashed into pieces.

"Sorcha," he said calmly, "Let me explain."

"You went out and fucked someone, explain that to me. I actually thought I was falling for you and you went out and stuck your dick in some whore? You fed off someone too. I can see it. You fucked and sucked and you come back here to explain! Why?" She hated how her voice cracked on that last word, how she was about to cry in front of him, how her heart was tearing into pieces and everything she knew about him was second to what she knew about vampires.

Selfish monsters, ready to destroy and take whatever they wanted.

Why the hell hadn't he wanted *her* blood?

She pushed that thought away and glared. "You're a fucking asshole," she snapped and stood, pushing him.

He let her, taking a step back even though there was no way her push could have moved him if he hadn't wanted it to.

A flash of pain crossed his face. "No, it's not like that. I had to feed."

Sorcha thought her head was going to explode. "Fuck. You," she said slowly then pushed past him.

"Where are you going?" he asked, desperation in his voice. He grabbed her arm and forced her to turn.

She did, and she swung. He wasn't expecting that, so she landed a fist to his jaw and shocked him enough to let go of her arm. She shook her hand, wondering if she'd broken something, but the adrenaline was pumping so fast right then, she didn't feel more than a slight sting.

She didn't wait for him to grab her again. She was out of the basement as fast as her legs could go. She thundered through the abandoned house and out to a front lawn that was brown and overgrown where it wasn't just dirt. A car was parked there, and she jumped in not caring whose it was, she just needed away from him. The tears were starting to fall and if he saw her cry she'd hate him even more because he didn't deserve her tears, he didn't deserve any part of her.

He was just a fucking blood sucker who had taken what he wanted from her without a thought to her as a person.

"You'll need keys," he said as he slid into the passenger seat. He didn't look at her, just held out the keys.

Sorcha grabbed them. "You fucked someone and took their blood," she accused, tears streaming down her face.

"Yes," he said.

"I don't want to ever see you again, vampire."

"Let me make sure you get home safe, I just want to keep you safe," he said, still not looking at her.

"Fine," she hissed and started the car.

They didn't speak another word to each other as she drove to the Florida Descendants' compound. She cried silently the entire way and he didn't look at her or react at all. The sun was about to come up when she got out of the driver's seat outside the gate.

"I just want to take care of you," Samson whispered as she stood there with the door still open. He finally looked at her and his eyes were desperate, his body stiff and his mouth pressed into a thin line.

"And I just wanted to believe you were something else, something different than I'd been told. I just wanted to love you," she whispered back then slammed the door and ran to the gate that he couldn't see. Tears streaming down her face as she called for them to open and embrace her in their familiar safety. As soon as she got close to it, she'd disappear from his sight, wrapped up in the safety of the spell hiding the compound.

But she knew he would never disappear from her mind, or her heart. She couldn't run far enough to forget what she thought he could give her. What he had done to betray her.

"Sorcha, what the fuck happened to you?" Chase asked as she

passed through the gate. "You've had your sister in a pissy mood for days."

"Fuck off, Chase," she snapped and stormed into the house and to her room. She didn't want to face her sister yet. She was afraid she'd tell her everything and she couldn't handle the response of *Well duh, that's what asshole predator vampires do!* Because she'd thought Samson was different She'd let him convince her he was something more.

She'd been desperate to believe he was something more. She'd been such a fool.

Life went back to normal after that, normal except for the fact that she dreamed nightly of the passionate embrace of a vampire and the kisses and caresses that had brought her so much pleasure. She woke up in tears because she wanted him even after the betrayal. She wanted him and she hated that she did. Knew she could never forgive him and that meant she'd never be truly happy.

The torture was made even worse when she was confronted with the relationship of another Descendant and the vampire who loved her. When her clan became aware of an unknown Descendant in Miami they brought her to the compound. Every Descendant thought they were saving Katherine from Ian who had her stuck away in an apartment, but Sorcha could see the truth there. Could see what she had once felt and hoped for with Samson.

So when Sorcha knew that her sister was sending werewolves after Samson, Ian, and the rest of the Miami clan that was coming toward the compound, she convinced Katherine to help her warn them. It ended with them all stuck in the compound's basement cell where her and Katherine had saved the vampire's lives. Because no matter how mad Sorcha was at Samson, she couldn't let him die. But being faced with Katherine and Ian who were everything she'd hoped to have with Samson and knew she couldn't have only made her ache more for the loss.

Why hadn't he wanted her blood?

It hurt so much and she wished it would just stop.

So when the opportunity presented itself, when a powerful witch offered Sorcha the escape she needed, she was willing to pay any price.

She gave Elantra the Descendants' Stone in exchange for a memory curse, to forget Samson and everything they'd had together. She knew she couldn't go on living with the memory of what they could never have. The knowledge that the one being she truly wanted to give her soul to, hadn't thought she was worthy of him.

Thirteen

SORCHA'S EYES flew open and she sat up with a gasp.

She remembered everything.

"Welcome back to the present," Sparah said with a smile. She was sitting in a chair across the room sipping a cup of tea. "How do you feel?"

"Like I regret every decision I've ever made in my entire life."

"Sounds about right. No one takes on a memory spell like that without a real good reason to forget."

Sorcha nodded, she definitely had a good reason. It just hadn't turned out like she thought it would.

"I don't know what is between you and Samson, but if you want my advice—"

"I don't," Sorcha snapped, interrupting her. She was full of anger, all the hurt that his rejection had caused her feeling raw and fresh. She wanted to punch him in the fang right now and her fist clenched.

"You get it anyway," Sparah said with a smile. "He has a history that made him the way he is. If you care, find out what that history is."

Sorcha wanted to tell the woman to shove it, but a part of her knew Sparah was right. Even if Samson was an asshole who didn't deserve her forgiveness, she knew she wanted answers. She deserved an explanation and she may not have been ready to hear it a year ago, but she was now. She needed to know why he'd done what he did. Maybe then she'd finally be able to let it go.

Let him go.

"What are you going to do about your sister?" Sorcha asked to change the subject.

Sparah frowned. "That is a good question. Her heart has grown black, her hatred has not eased with time, but grown and festered." Sparah gave Sorcha a pointed look. "She is someone who has never cared to hear the other half of the story, but kept to her own hateful conclusions."

Sorcha rolled her eyes.

Sparah continued. "She risks too much now and has taken advantage of the people she wanted to protect. Did she tell you why she wanted the Stone?"

"How did you know I gave it to her?" Sorcha gasped.

"I saw it."

"Right, you see the future."

"I see possibilities," Sparah reminded. "It would be much less complicated if I saw certainties." Sparah frowned and seemed to lose herself for a moment, eyes fixed on some distant space above Sorcha's head. She shook herself and snapped her gaze back to Sorcha. "I knew when I saw you here that you'd done it, it was your destiny. So did she tell you?"

Sorcha was annoyed by that answer, like, even if it had only been a possibility, couldn't Sparah have given her a fucking heads up? "She said she would keep it safe, never let a vampire use it on us ever again. I figured that was safer than my sister keeping it locked up under her bed. No guarantee another vamp and his pet monster weren't going to walk through our defenses again."

"And I suppose my sister thinks she's keeping that promise,

because if she destroys the vampires, they can't use the Stone against the Descendants."

"Tricky," Sorcha said.

"Witches tend to be that way," Sparah said with a wink. "Here drink this." She handed Sorcha a cup of tea.

It smelled like mint and honey, Sorcha took a sip. It was good, so she quickly finished the whole cup. "Thank you."

Sparah smiled. "It's nice to have company other than the men. Katherine of course is here now, too, most of the time. I miss the days before. I had my sister and so many other Descendants to keep me company."

"It's got to be interesting, living here with a bunch of vampires and monsters." Interesting wasn't really the word Sorcha wanted to use, *terrifying, stupid, awful*, all crossed her mind but she didn't think Sparah would appreciate those.

"A life I chose. I knew when Elantra escaped that day that I was going to be lonely. I just couldn't put my loneliness above the good of those on land. The monsters can't be contained above the waterline. The spell holding them is sealed in by the ocean above."

"A noble sacrifice," Sorcha agreed.

"I was in love," Sarah said. "I would have done anything for Ian's father." She shrugged. "Sometimes love is one sided."

That statement made Sorcha's heart ache. She'd been falling in love, apparently it hadn't been reciprocated. "Were you ever with him?"

Sparah gave a wide, wistful smile. "I was, though it was never more than scratching an itch for him. I was a willing body but he didn't feel for me. I think after Elantra left he realized that he had betrayed the love they might have had, and finally saw things from her point of view."

"He was in love with Elantra?"

"In a way, yes I think he was. But despite that love he couldn't see how he was hurting her by controlling all of the Descendants.

His idea of love was owning her body and soul. He wanted her willing to give him everything."

Sorcha stared down into her empty cup. None of that sounded like what she now remembered having with Samson. He hadn't been trying to possess her body and soul, and when he was with her, it hadn't felt like he was using her to scratch an itch.

Did that mean it was love? Or had he just been really good at hiding the truth from her. Was he using her for an itch, or was he trying to manipulate her towards something more, some kind of live-in blood bag?

She didn't know, couldn't, not without talking to Samson.

Sorcha stood and thanked Sparah again.

"Samson is waiting outside for you," Sparah said with a wink.

"Oh, good," Sorcha said.

Sorcha walked out of Sparah's room and into the hallway.

Samson was there, sitting on the floor staring at the door with a contemplative look on his face. When she emerged, she was almost afraid to look at him. Afraid of the pain. But there was nothing, just an ache of loss, a desire to know and an anger at his actions.

"Are you alright?" he asked quietly, his purple eyes searching deeply into hers.

"Yes, and you owe me an explanation," she demanded.

"I suppose I do," he said with a sigh. "Walk with me?" Samson stood and held out his hand to her.

She didn't take it but started walking down the hallway. When she emerged from the pyramid she paused. Samson stepped out beside her and then started heading down the path. She followed. He led her back out of the little city to the beach where they'd emerged from the water.

It was a beautiful place and Sorcha wished she was here to enjoy a tropical vacation instead of this crisis she was in the middle of. The water begged to be swum in and the sun, or what seemed to be the sun, was warm on her skin, making her wish she could lay down and let it soak in.

But that wasn't what she was here for, so she sat next to Samson, not close enough to touch, but close enough so that their conversation would be relatively private.

"You remember everything about our time together?" Samson asked without looking at her. He gazed out over the water looking resigned.

"Yes, you saved me, you healed me, and then you made me start to fall in love with you, Samson. You used me and betrayed the trust I had given you."

Samson's face twisted with regret. "I had already fallen in love with you, Sorcha. I fell during those two days that I fed you my blood and begged you to come back from all your injuries. Before you ever looked at me with those amazing green eyes, before I heard your angelic voice. I was in love with the tiny helpless being that was completely dependent on me for survival. When you woke up and you didn't run, when you didn't react the way I expected, with hate and fear; I allowed myself to fall further. Then when you gave your body to me." His voice hitched, he closed his eyes and took a deep breath. "I knew I didn't deserve what you were giving me, but I took it anyway, that wasn't right, I know. But I couldn't stop myself. No one in my life had ever given themselves to me freely and completely. I was lost then, completely powerless to the spiral of loving you and I would have done anything to keep you."

"Why did you betray whatever it was growing between us? Why did you deny what I was offering to give you? Why did you need to go to someone else, why didn't you want my blood?" The question hurt, but she couldn't go on not knowing. Ignorance was not bliss as she'd found out the hard way.

"I—" he took a steadying breath. "I wasn't born to this. I wasn't raised in Atlantis and given the choice of honor that being a vampire is. I am not like Ian and Beltar and the others." His body was stiff and his hands were clenched. His face filled with a past anger that she wanted to soothe away.

She didn't touch him though, didn't dare distract him from what he needed to tell her. "Tell me," Sorcha pleaded, wanting more than anything to understand this man who still held a piece of her heart.

"I was born the son of a maid. She had been impregnated by the master of the house and when I was born looking far too much like the man, his wife, Charlotte, sent my mother away but kept me. Maybe to punish my mother, as if it was her fault that the master of the house took advantage of her. Maybe because she was unable to have children of her own and she thought in the beginning that I could replace that. I don't know. All I remember was her cruelty. Maybe it would have been different if my father had lived, but he died when I was quite young leaving Charlotte and me alone. She inherited everything of course, a little queen of all she saw around her, and she loved that. I would have been better off dead at that point or given off to a poor family to raise."

"Oh, Samson," Sorcha whispered and grabbed his arm, her heart aching for the child he was.

"That part isn't important, it was a long time ago," Samson insisted but she could see the tightness in his body, the stiff set to his mouth.

She could see the pain that his upbringing still caused him and she instantly hated Charlotte. "Everything you've suffered through is important, Samson," Sorcha insisted.

Samson gave her a sad smile before turning back to stare out at the water.

"As I grew into a young man, Charlotte realized that my handsome face and muscled body could be used to her advantage. She started sending me to the beds of visiting friends, people who she wanted to gain favor from. I went willingly, I figured why not? It made her happy, something I strived daily to do and I found pleasure there that I hadn't ever experienced before." He laughed bitterly. "I didn't see anything wrong with what she was asking me to do, didn't consider a parent could ask their child to do something so inherently harmful. I didn't know then that she wasn't my mother. She held that piece of information from me. Keeping me from even considering leaving her with a promise that someday I'd inherit what my father had left to her."

Sorcha wanted to kill this woman who was probably long dead. She wanted to rip her apart piece by piece for what she'd done to an innocent child.

"And then one day I stumbled upon a man in the woods. It was late at night and he had a young woman with him who looked dazed and pale, sick. I invited them to the house so she could rest, thinking they were weary travelers. Charlotte allowed them to stay, though she wasn't happy with my presumptuousness in offering our hospitality. They wanted a dark room; the woman was suffering from an ailment that made her sensitive to the sun he said. So Charlotte gave them a room under the house, near my own quarters. I woke that night to the man standing over my bed. He was a vampire, the girl his blood slave. He'd already drained her too much, he couldn't feed on her for a while and so he took me that night. But he took too much. He was out of control, half crazed, I realized many years later. It happens sometimes to vampires, usually they're taken care of by the coven at that point, not allowed out to harm humans. But somehow he was wandering alone in the world. Perhaps he hadn't gone down with Atlantis, or maybe he'd escaped after it sunk, I don't know. I never saw him again after he left my room. He left me for dead that night, disappeared with the girl before sunrise. Three days later I was a vampire. I had no idea they existed, I had no idea what to do and I was so scared. I confessed to Charlotte all that had happened and she threatened to tell the authorities if I didn't do exactly as she instructed me. She told me I'd become a monster and no one would allow me to live if they knew. I depended on her for survival more than ever, or so she convinced me. I became her personal assassin. I spent years doing her bidding. I never bit a single person that I didn't intend to kill. I didn't know another way. Feeding was killing for me. I learned no control from another vampire, no finesse in my powers. I was a baby vampire walking the earth like the most dangerous of monsters. And she held my leash, I still wanted her approval, her love and protection."

Samson paused there and took a shuddering breath.

"One day she sent me to kill a woman who had traveled into town, a nobody, a poor woman just passing through. I didn't understand. She usually sent me out after people who threatened her in some way, but I wouldn't dare question her. When I approached the woman on the dark street she gasped and touched my face. She smiled at me like she couldn't be happier. *My son*, she whispered and cried. I was so confused, who was this woman? She threw her arms around me, giving me perfect access to her neck and I couldn't stop myself. I had been given an order and I did what I was told to do. I always did what I was told to do. As she lay dying at my feet she whispered it again. *My son, you look just like your father. I am sorry I left you with her.*"

Sorcha felt tears roll down her face. She wanted to grab him and hold him. She wanted to stroke his back and tell him that it was okay, that she forgave him. But she couldn't, not until she heard it all. A traumatic childhood didn't excuse bad behavior as an adult, it didn't heal the wound he'd torn in her when she realized what he had gone out and done. So she stood there staring at him as he stared out at the sea and she cried for him silently.

"When I returned to Charlotte and told her what the woman had said, she admitted everything with a laugh, no remorse. I snapped and killed her. Then I was on my own, still no idea how to control myself, no idea how to be a vampire. I didn't want to be a monster and without Charlotte telling me who needed to be killed, I was afraid to eat. Beltar found me hiding in a cave, half-starved and ready to walk out into the sun. I didn't know there was another way, and I didn't want to be what Charlotte had made me."

"You're not," Sorcha whispered.

Samson gave her a weak smile, clearly not believing her. "When he tried to teach me how to handle being a vampire, I couldn't do it. I drained and killed over and over... I don't know why he didn't just kill me then. But one day, actually it was after watching the twins interact with a victim, I started to take advantage of the sexual feelings my bite induces. If I let my body take them as I drew their blood, I was able to hold back. I was able to stop before I killed them. But I hate myself after. Sex, feeding, killing. It's all Charlotte ever wanted from me. She ordered me to do all three over and over and all I wanted was for her to look at me and say she cared for me. That she'd raised me, and she cared. I was nothing to her."

"*She* was the monster, Samson. Not you," Sorcha said grabbing his face and forcing him to look at her. "You saved my life, you cared for me, and you are a good person."

"I wanted to bite you, Sorcha. I wanted to taste you," he whispered, his purple eyes sweeping down to her neck briefly. "Every moment we spent together, I worried that I wouldn't be able to stop myself and when you woke up and you offered me your body, I took it even though I knew I didn't deserve it. I couldn't use you like the others. You deserve better."

"I *want* all of you, Samson," Sorcha said firmly. "But I still don't understand, if I was giving you my body, if I was offering you my blood; why did you go out and fuck and suck on some random whore?" Sorcha couldn't keep the anger and hurt out of her voice.

Samson looked at her with eyes so open to his emotions that she felt like she would drown in the sorrow in their depths. "Because, if I treated you like I treated them, I didn't know if I could still love you. I didn't know if it would destroy my feelings. If you would become nothing more than Charlotte's orders in my brain." He slammed his eyes shut and gripped his head. "She's still in there," he whispered. "She's there every time I do it and I can't turn her off. I don't want her to touch what we have."

"Was she there when we made love, Samson? Was she in your head when you cared for me? Was she telling you her poisonous lies when I laid in your arms?"

"No," he admitted.

Sorcha reached out and took hold of his hands, pulling them down away from his face. "She was hatred and poison. She was the closest thing to a monster that a human could be, evil. She can't touch something as pure as love. And *that's* why she wasn't in there when we were together, Samson. That is why you could forget her memory, because that's all it is, her memory. She isn't hiding out in your mind."

She leaned forward and pressed her lips to his. She meant it to be a quick reassuring kiss, a promise that she wanted to see where this relationship might take them now that she knew him.

He grabbed her and pulled her against him and deepened the kiss. His groan of desperation started a fire in her belly and she was soon running her hands up into his hair before she even realized what she was doing. She felt him harden between them and couldn't stop her hips from rocking forward and she smiled against his mouth at his groan. His hands gripped her hips and moved her against him as he thrust his tongue deep into her mouth.

"Woah, get a room, you do realize this isn't a private beach, right?"

Sorcha squealed and Samson hissed as she scrambled to put a little distance between them. The vampire who'd interrupted was a tall, lanky, redhead wearing a pair of leather leggings and a white button up open halfway down his chest revealing an intricate patterned tattoo.

"Felix," Samson said.

"I was sent to make sure you weren't devouring virgins by the shore," he said with a wink at Sorcha. His voice was soft, almost feminine and the way his gaze traveled over Samson sent a short burst of possessiveness through her. His eyes swept back to her and he smiled. "I think they have the devouring part right but not the virgin bit."

Sorcha's face heated and Samson gripped a dagger at his side. "Rude," Sorcha muttered.

Felix laughed, a high and happy sound. "I'm just teasing. Ian said he wants you two in on the meeting we are about to have."

Samson grabbed Sorcha's hand, pulling her close once more. He kissed her quick and sweet before turning her to face Felix. "This is Sorcha," Samson said.

"I know. Everyone's talking about her. Same as when Katherine showed up. I think Ian's going to have to reevaluate the way things are run with so much sex being thrown in our faces. It's been ages since I've had a strong man throw me around."

"I thought Saul was happy to throw you around every once in a while," Samson said as they began walking back up the trail.

Felix laughed. "Only on the training field," he said with a sigh.

Fourteen

SAMSON WANTED to grab Sorcha and whisk her away, he wanted to stay in a cave with her for as long as possible. He wanted to deserve the forgiveness that she'd offered so sweetly. Wanted to believe her when she said that their love could overpower Charlotte's voice in his head. But what if it wasn't possible, what if he was destined to hurt her because he was an undeserving monster?

He was almost thankful for the interruption of the meeting so he didn't have to make any decisions yet.

The meeting room was in the base of the pyramid and obviously used for nothing other than this sort of thing. It had a large table in the center with a variety of mismatched chairs around it. The walls were bare except for a few weapons that had seen better days and a map of Atlantis from before it sank. Back when it was just another part of what is now Florida.

Ian and Katherine were seated at the head of the table looking a bit more rumpled and satisfied than they had earlier. Sparah was to Ian's right and Thorn on his left. Saul sat next to Sparah so Samson pulled out a seat for Sorcha next to Thorn and took the one on her other side. Felix remained standing but surprisingly, he didn't leave the room. Apparently guarding the door in case anyone tried to disturb them.

"Sorcha, I take it you have regained all that you lost," Ian asked.

"Yes, unfortunately I was the one to give Elantra the Stone," she admitted. "I wanted the thing safe from ever landing back in the hands of a vamp, I thought she would be able to do that better than anyone."

"She probably is," Thorn said. "I never would have guessed she'd use the damn thing though."

"She's become unpredictable in her old age," Sparah agreed.

"What does that even mean? How do we possibly prepare?" Sorcha huffed in frustration.

Samson grabbed her hand under the table, knowing she was likely feeling responsible for the current situation. But he knew no one here blamed her. It didn't matter if she had been tricked into giving Elantra the Stone, it wasn't what had set Elantra off on this crazy path.

"I will go up and meet with her, try to find out what she is after and I will try to get her to change her mind," Ian said.

"Fuck no, you aren't!" Katherine snapped. "You promised me forever, you are not going to be a sacrificial lamb to your psychotic mother."

"I have to agree with Katherine on this one," Sparah said. "She stopped seeing you as her son as soon as you decided to follow in your father's footsteps. You meeting with her will not make her change her mind, and I don't think you're prepared to kill her, are you?"

Ian looked uncomfortable at the assumption.

"That's what I thought," Sparah said to his silence. "So I think we have two clear choices. We can wait and see what she does from here, then react as necessary. She might stay in her little compound for the next hundred years, plotting and festering, breeding an army. Or she might come after us like a banshee without a moment's thought."

"And the other choice?" Thorn asked when Sparah paused for what had to be dramatic effect.

"We go after her, she wants a fight, you take one to her." Sparah spoke to Ian but the words were for all of them. This wasn't a one person fight and it shouldn't be a one person decision.

Everyone sat silent, mulling over her words.

"I suppose you have a preference. Some kind of intuition or prediction that leads you to choose one over the other?" Ian said.

"Unfortunately not. She's worked some spells around herself that make it difficult for me to see her in my predictions of futures. Ian, you're not the only one she cut ties with. She blames me for a lot of awful things that came to pass. I chose to make sure Atlantis sunk and kept the monsters safe. In order to do that I had to take with me the magic that helped the werewolves stay in control. As the daughter of the first powerful witch and the original werewolf, I have the ability to shift into the creature of the night. I couldn't be doing that down here so I took with me the original magic, locking the rest of the werewolves to their feral nature controlled by the full moon. When that happened and my father was forced into an uncontrolled shift, he killed our mother. I knew the risk, and so did they. They understood this had to happen anyway, but Elantra couldn't forgive me for what she saw as another selfish act on my part. She didn't understand that to turn werewolf down here with nothing to hunt, I never would have survived. I could have attacked the vampires and they would have had no choice but to kill me. That would break the magic holding this place together and the monsters would have been unleashed."

"We aren't talking about the Blood Moonstone, this is something else?" Katherine asked.

"No, the Blood Moonstone was a gift, a creation I made and sent up many years after the sinking. I wanted to help. I wanted to offer a way for the werewolves to have a more normal existence and continue their protective nature of humans. I was worried their species would die out because who would want to become a monster?" She laughed as if it were the most ridiculous thought, and maybe in a room of vampires who had chosen to become them, it was a bit ridiculous.

Samson looked at Sorcha and realized that for the first time in his entire life, he didn't regret what he was. He didn't regret that he was a bastard child raised by a woman who hated him, or an unloved monster used to kill for her. He had a woman who willingly held his hand, pressed her body against his without the enticement of his bite, who arched against him in pleasure and begged for more. She wanted all of him and knew him, really knew him now.

He would take the years of abuse over and over to end up sitting next to her and holding her hand.

"The magic I took is something older, something that was created along with my father," Sparah continued. "The first mother wanted him to have all the benefits of shape shifting and the ability to protect without any negativities. But she had to attach his magic to something, so she chose the moon, then gave them magic to keep the moon from completely controlling their shifting. That is what I took down here, what I broke that night for the greater good."

"Everything was ripped away from her that night," Sorcha whispered. "Her sister, her children, the man who loved her... even if she didn't love him. Her home and then her mother. It's no wonder she blames you and hates the vampires and werewolves."

"Yes, and after all this time, something has set her on this path now—I don't know what—and I don't think she'll wait to attack." Sparah's voice was strained with worry.

"I think I know," Katherine said. "I think it's me."

"What are you talking about?" Ian asked.

"I am the first Descendant in how long to be a willing victim to the vampires?"

"*Willing* means not a victim," Ian spat.

Katherine laughed. "True, I feel very unvictimized by you, love. But in her mind, a victim of the king vampire. She must have been triggered by it. She must think that the vampires are going to try and come for the Descendants again. She's trying to keep them safe in her twisted way."

"Perhaps, but does it really matter what set her off? The fact is she has made some extreme choices and has to be stopped. We still don't know what her next move is going to be. Like you said, Sparah. She could sit in that damn compound for a hundred years, it would be a blink for her. Or she could be sitting in Miami now," Ian said.

They had talked in circles and it was grating on Samson's nerves, he was a man of action. "I will go back up; I will find out what she's planning."

"Not alone," Sorcha snapped. "I want my sister and the others safe and out of her spell as soon as possible. You can't do that by yourself."

"I'm going," Felix said firmly, surprising everyone in the room. "I deserve a vacation," he said with a wink in Katherine's direction. "And a night out dancing."

"This is war, not a fucking holiday," Samson hissed.

"I will go," Saul and Thorn said in unison.

Ian nodded around the table. "I trust this group; it is why I have you all here. We will go and figure out what she's planning, how best to interfere. Hopefully we can stop her before she can make any more moves against us. I will keep my people safe," he insisted and looked at Katherine as if he were going to consume her. She looked back at him with love in her eyes and a soft smile.

"I'm always safe with you," she said.

"The sun sets in a few hours, we will go up then," Ian said.

No one argued with that order. Everyone was quiet as the room cleared out, mentally preparing for the trip and the fight that would likely ensue.

Samson stood and pulled Sorcha up with him. "I think Sorcha should rest before we go."

"I'm fine I—"

"You need to rest," Samson insisted and looked at Ian.

"Of course, I'll show you to a room you are welcome to use."

Samson pulled Sorcha along behind Ian as he led them up some stairs and then into a small bedroom obviously meant for guests. It had a bed and a chair and that was about it. A few random looking decorations on the walls and a thick rug on the floor. Samson didn't care about any of that though, he was only interested in the bed and picking up where they'd been interrupted on the beach. Knowing that they might be heading into danger soon only amplified his desire to find a way to be with Sorcha.

"See you in a few hours," Ian said and then shut the door.

Samson turned to Sorcha, nervous. His heart was beating wildly, and his palms were sweaty. She was staring at a painting of a castle on a cliff, water crashed below it and a small boat looked like it was about to capsize.

She turned to him suddenly and frowned.

"You have to bite me."

Samson stepped back until he was pressed against the wall. He hadn't expected that. His eyes strayed to the soft skin of her neck and his fangs suddenly ached to pierce that flesh and hear her moan.

"Not now," he whispered.

"I won't have you any way except fully, Samson. If we are doing this, whatever this is," she said motioning between them. "Then I will be your only. I want what Ian and Katherine have. I deserve to be your everything."

"You *are* my everything," Samson insisted. "It is because I value you that I hesitate."

She shook her head and stepped slowly toward him. "No, it is because you were twisted by an evil woman that you hesitate. You are not a monster or a weapon, you are a man, and you are a vampire." Each word had brought her a step closer until she stood directly in front of him, craning her neck to look into his eyes. "If you stick any part of you inside of someone else ever again, I will fucking gut you, which means you either starve, or you take from me when you need. There is no other option and I won't continue this relationship until the deed is done and we know it works."

"I don't want to harm you, or use you." He closed his eyes and whispered, "Or lose you," he admitted.

"You aren't using me if I'm offering. I more than trust you not to harm me and you will lose me if you don't do this."

Samson opened his eyes and met her determined gaze. "I'm afraid," he admitted.

"Jump in with both feet, it's the only way to conquer fear."

Samson had no arguments that she would accept, he knew that, knew he was only buying time. He was so scared that he wouldn't be able to treat her the way he wanted if he bit her. He couldn't let go of the fear that she'd become nothing more than food to him if he took her blood. He could fuck her and bite her, he knew he wouldn't kill her. Thanks to the twins, he'd figured that one out. But that's not what he wanted. He didn't want to take from her, blind her with fake pleasure and then walk away like he'd learned to do with the others. He didn't know if he was capable of anything else though. Didn't know if his twisted brain could separate her from the others.

Her face was full of determination as she watched him struggle through his thoughts. Her words made perfect sense though. If he wanted to keep her, he would have to do this. She would never accept him going out and taking from someone else, he realized that now. And after seeing what Katherine and Ian had, he understood what he could have with Sorcha.

But could he do it? Could he keep his mind on her while he filled his belly with her sweet blood? Could he keep her from being more than just a tool for his own needs?

Samson reached out and ran his hands down her arms, delighting in the shiver he felt flow through her body.

"What if I lose control?" Samson whispered, one last effort to change her mind. Maybe he could frighten her enough to say no.

"I trust you, Samson. You are not a blood-crazed monster. If you were, then you would have destroyed me that night you found me bleeding and broken in the woods, you wouldn't have been able to nurse me back to health."

He leaned forward and kissed her softly, tasting her lips slowly. He gave her mouth the time and attention he felt it deserved. Until he felt her hands on his shoulders, sliding up into his hair and heard the sweetest growl in her throat as she pressed her lower body against his, begging for more than he was giving her.

She was an enthusiastic lover.

He deepened the kiss then, sliding his tongue between her lips and caressing hers. He walked them back until the bed was behind her, then he laid her gently back, never breaking the kiss. When she was on the bed he pulled back and stood over her. She was panting and her eyes were glossy with desire. She was the most beautiful thing he'd ever seen.

And she was his.

He pulled a dagger from his belt and pressed it into her hand. "Take this. Stab me, kill me if you have to. Do *not* let me hurt you."

"I don't nee—"

He pressed a finger to her lips and scowled. "Just take it, I won't do this if I know you can't protect yourself."

She flicked her tongue out and licked at his finger, then opened her mouth and took it between her lips. He groaned when he felt her blunt teeth scrape against his skin.

"You are going to make me lose my control," he warned.

"Maybe that's my plan," she said with a wicked grin. "You are too in your head about all of this. Just be here with me, just feel what's right."

Could he do that? Could he let go of all the past memories that held him back? Just be here with her now?

It sounded wonderful, and he wanted it. But he couldn't get Charlotte's voice out of his head, even now her words slid around there like a snake. *Worthless bastard, better off a monster, you have been destroying lives since you were born. At least now you're useful to me.*

He couldn't destroy Sorcha; it would end him if he ever harmed her. He would give her what she asked for, prove to her that he wanted their relationship to work, but he would not let go of his control, he couldn't.

"Undress for me," he demanded, his voice rough with emotion.

Her smile was wide, and a look of triumph filled her eyes. She thought she'd won the argument; he wouldn't disillusion her.

She sat up and quickly discarded her borrowed clothes. Her body was perfection, slightly marred by the attack she'd survived but it only added to the overall sense of strength she exuded. She had lived through something terrible, and she'd welcomed him into her arms after. She'd been able to let go of her trauma and trust him.

And he had betrayed her.

"I'm so sorry for what has passed between us, Sorcha," he said as he ran a hand from her neck between her breasts, stopping at her belly where a deep scar ran from ribcage to hip bone.

"Don't be sorry, just show me you can make it right."

"I will spend the rest of my immortal life showing you," he promised.

Samson stripped, then laid on the bed beside her, his body

pressed close to her side. He wasn't sure how to do this, how to be with her in this way. It scared and aroused him.

He kissed along her neck and nibbled at her earlobe until she was squirming and giggling. Then kissed his way down to her breasts, lavishing them each with attention, making her arch off the bed and offer herself up for his use.

She wasn't a patient lover. She wanted everything fast. She wanted to be consumed by passion not lavished with love.

He would accommodate her. His hand slipped down between her thighs as his mouth moved back up to her neck. She turned her head exposing her flesh as she parted her thighs in invitation. Such an offering should be served to the gods, not him, and he marveled at the fates that had brought her into his life.

He licked the spot on her neck where her blood pulsed and then sank his fangs in as his fingers dipped inside of her. The first taste was explosive, better than he had expected. To be honest he hadn't let himself think too much about what she'd taste like, far too afraid that it would drive him to act on the forbidden fantasy.

She moaned and lifted her hips as he pulled on the wound again. He started to move his fingers in her, wanting to take advantage of the pleasure he knew the bite would induce. While still holding himself back, making sure he was in control. His cock pulsed, hard and angry at being denied a place in her body.

A spiral of darkness, familiar and loathed started to spin through his mind.

Take, kill, this is your prey and I want it dead. Fuck it and kill it.

"No!" Samson shouted and pulled away from her. He rushed back from the bed and pressed his body against a wall. He slammed his eyes closed and balled up his body as he tried to push Charlotte from his mind.

Worthless, weak bastard. Fuck or kill, that's all you know.

"No," he whispered.

"Samson? Samson what is it?" Sorcha's voice jolted him, and

his eyes opened. She was crouched on the bed, one hand on her bleeding neck, eyes wide and frightened. There was blood, lots of blood, gushing between her fingers, too much. He'd already hurt her.

"Shit," he hissed and leaped at her, ripping her hand from her neck and pressing his mouth to the wound.

Fifteen

SORCHA WAS FRIGHTENED. She'd been experiencing a pleasure unlike anything she'd ever imagined and then he'd ripped himself away. She'd felt a tearing at her neck and as she'd watched him shake against the wall her head had become dangerously light. Confusion filled her as she stared at him in the fading light of her eyes. Had she really misjudged his abilities so much, pushed him too hard, too fast? Had she been so wrong to trust that his feelings for her could outweigh his past trauma?

His wild purple eyes met hers and he leapt at her. She was certain this was how she'd die. She had a vague wonder of where the knife had gone and felt bad that she had failed him, failed to do the one thing she'd promised she would do. She wouldn't protect herself against him.

She was going to let him kill her.

Then a wetness pressed against her lips.

"Drink, love," Samson commanded, and the tangy warmth of blood filled her mouth.

She swallowed and as the warmth hit her belly, she began to tingle all over and strength rushed back into her body. She grasped his arm, weak at first, nothing more than a touch. Her tongue darted out at his skin, trying to actively take in more of the hot liquid. She swallowed again and another rush of strength moved through her body like an electric pulse. Her hands gripped his arm with strength. Her fingers dug into the skin afraid he was going to take it away. She pressed her mouth firmly to his arm and began to willfully suck at the wound he'd opened there.

"Yes, that's it, love," he groaned and stroked her hair.

She fell back as her body spasmed near orgasm just from ingesting his blood. "Oh fuck, that is good," she groaned and looked up at his face, smiling like a fool. She wondered if she looked like some kind of demon with blood all over her face and neck. His face was only a bit bloody, apparently he wasn't a very messy eater.

She giggled at the thought and he frowned.

"What about this situation do you find amusing?" he demanded. "I almost killed you." His face was filled with rage, but she knew it wasn't directed at her. He was beating himself up over what happened.

She leaned up on her elbows and cocked an eyebrow, not allowing her face to show anything other than calm. "But you didn't, what you did do is manage to bring me so damn close to the edge of orgasm that a soft breeze is going to push me over."

Shock washed over his face and she smiled, loving that this vampire could be shocked by something she said.

"I would much rather you do it though," she said, her voice a little husky.

He shook his head. "You don't mean that. You are under the influence of my bite and my blood. You should hate me right now. I'm a monster, a worthless monster. I'm nothing, I'm—"

She pressed a finger to his lips and stopped his words. "You are a fierce vampire, a predator, a protector, and a damn good lover. Samson, I offered what you took, you didn't coerce me. Maybe it didn't go exactly as planned but you didn't harm me, not really. Now get your cock over here before I get out of this bed and find another vampire willing to finish what you started." She didn't mean the threat, but it did what she meant it to.

Samson's face went from shock to anger, and he pounced with a possessive growl. "You are mine, only mine," he hissed as he slid between her thighs.

"Prove it," she hissed back.

As soon as he penetrated her, she was over the edge, arching her back and riding the wave as he moved over her with slow steady strokes dragging out the pleasure as it consumed her. When she settled, he was still moving in her, looking down at her with a possessive stare that would have befitted any stalker.

"Mine," he groaned and then his mouth was on her neck, his fangs in her as he pumped faster, and the mix of sensations brought her racing back toward a quick second orgasm. Her body loved him, it wanted everything he could give her, and she knew she'd never be the same after this. How could anyone experience this kind of pleasure and ever want something else. She had a brief thought of wondering how Elantra had given this up, but she quickly pushed it aside. No one belonged in this moment with them.

Samson licked her neck clean and lifted his head to stare into her eyes. "I love you, Sorcha," he whispered and kissed her lips. The taste of her blood there was surprisingly erotic, and she lapped at his mouth, tasting as much as she could.

He started to move faster, pistoning his hips with deep, fierce strokes that hit where she needed it most. "Fuck yes," she groaned and grabbed his ass, digging her nails in and encouraging him to give her more. "So close, fuck, I'm already so close, Samson."

He laughed darkly and ran one hand between them to touch her perfectly. It pushed her over the edge and after a few more thrusts they were both crying out with orgasm.

He rolled off of her and pulled her to lay on top of him as they panted and shivered and came down. He stroked her back lovingly and she kissed his neck.

"That was perfect," she whispered.

"Yes, it was," he agreed.

She leaned up and looked down at him. His lips were still a little bloody and she ran a finger over them. Her blood had tasted bland compared to his.

"What does my blood taste like to you?" she asked.

"Like sweet fire," he said without hesitation.

"Fire isn't a taste," she said with a laugh.

"Oh, it most certainly is," he said with a grin. "What does my blood taste like?"

"Musky and male, sweet and spicy, I guess. I can't even believe I'm saying this, but it tastes good."

"That's because I'm a vampire. Don't worry, you aren't about to start craving human blood. It won't taste good to you."

"That's a relief," she said with a laugh. "I did enjoy tasting my own blood on your lips though. It was erotic," she admitted, and her eyelids fluttered half closed.

"Everything about you is erotic," he said and grabbed her ass, thrusting his hips up. He was still buried inside her, half hard and making her feel delicious.

"How do you know I wouldn't like a human's blood?"

He pulled his gaze away, his hands dropping from her body and stared up at the ceiling. "Charlotte, she made me feed her a human once, convinced that it would strengthen her. She said it tasted dull and metallic. She retched it up almost immediately."

"Did she ever taste yours?" Sorcha asked, jealousy raging through her. That bitch didn't deserve to know what Samson tasted like, didn't deserve to feel the pleasure of consuming a piece of him.

"No, she was too afraid she'd turn into one I think, so she never asked. I don't know what I would have done if she had."

"You would have done it, because you were desperate for her to love and accept you," Sorcha whispered and grabbed his face, forcing him to meet her eyes again. "Samson, you belong to me. I love you, which is why your past actions hurt me so badly and why I couldn't forget you despite the strong spell. I love you and I want to be your everything forever."

He reached up and tucked a red lock behind her ear. "Sorcha, I don't deserve what you're offering."

"Yes, you do," she assured him.

She cuddled against him and breathed in the scent of sex and blood. It was soothing and she let her eyelids close, drifting off to sleep knowing that Samson would never let anything happen to her.

* * *

"Oh sister, what have you brought upon the world?" Sparah grumbled as she stared down into her spell pot. She dripped in three drops of her own blood, a link to Elantra. The mixture began to bubble, purple smoke drifted up from the center and a green spiral spread from it slowly until it met the edge, then the entire pot stilled, the water became like glass and through it, an image appeared.

Elantra, surrounded by her witches and the Descendants she'd enslaved. She was visible by the light of the full moon in a clearing surrounded by trees. She was confident, she was prepared to do whatever she had to in order to win, no thought to consequences, no care for anyone or anything outside of herself.

Elantra faced an army of familiar faces and she was ready to take revenge at the expense of those around her.

"Sister, I thought you'd never come," Elantra said smoothly and Sparah gasped as she watched an image of herself walk into the picture.

"No, it can't be," she whispered and the image broke.

Sparah fell back into a chair, her body shaking. She looked around the room she'd been in for so long, the evidence of the life she'd made for herself here, a sacrifice to the mission.

Was it really her destiny to meet her sister on a battlefield? Was she going to have to risk undoing what she'd done to save the earth?

There was only one place she could find the answers she needed. She left her room and headed down under the pyramid. Down to where the monsters were kept. She stopped outside the door to the prison where the image of two lovers embracing in the crashing waves was carved. Their fingers twined in each other's, a reminder of their eternal love. It was meant to go on even as they'd sacrificed themselves for this place. Maeve's bones had become the bars for the prison cells, and her lover, Peleseus, had given his soul to become the bubble that surrounded the entire city. All had been sealed by Sparah and her spell.

Elantra had betrayed them all with her actions that night. And for what? She'd obviously never found happiness outside of these walls. The vampires had suffered without willing blood donors and their mother had died anyway. Now Elantra was bringing war to the gates of Atlantis, no matter that it could destroy the earth as humans had come to know it, that it could release the monsters that so many had sacrificed to imprison.

"Maeve, first mother. I don't know what to do," Sparah whispered at the shrine. She reached out and touched the carving, she'd always felt a strength here and a boost of power. She needed it now.

Sparah closed her eyes and opened her mind, listening for the voice of the first mother.

"The full moon strengthens my lover, plan your actions for that night and keep the innocent safe. You must face your sister for victory, you must be the one to take her from her suffering. Early action will lead to tragedy."

Sparah's eyes popped open and she took off at a run. She had to stop them from leaving Atlantis.

Her feet flew under her as she pounded up the stairs and burst out of the pyramid, she rushed down the paths to the beach.

"Stop!" she yelled at the group gathered there. "You can't go up!"

Everyone froze and looked back at her. Ian stepped in front of the group with a confused look on his face.

"Sparah, we talked of this already," he said, more like a question than a statement. He had always trusted her implicitly, she knew he would now, too.

She shook her head and panted a bit from the run and the worry that she'd be too late.

"I have to be there, but we can't go up until the full moon. The shield will hold under the full moon, it strengthens him," she panted.

"You saw this, in a vision?" Ian asked.

"Yes, well, partially and the other was revealed to me by Maeve herself."

The group mumbled and looked at each other with uncertainty, then at Ian for a decision.

"What did you see, exactly?" Ian pushed.

"Full moon night, we will meet in battle. She will bring all the innocents to sacrifice, she doesn't care for them, the witches and the Descendants. But we all have to be there, we have to meet her with an equal force and we have to be willing to spill blood to keep her from her goal. She will release the monsters if she has to, she doesn't care for the consequences, only revenge."

"We will stop her now," Samson said fiercely, and the others grumbled their agreement.

"No," Sparah shook her head sadly. "I have to be there, I have to stop her. That's why we have to go at the full moon. The plan will certainly fail if I am not there."

Ian's face told her he didn't like the idea. "I have always trusted your judgment, but if we can stop her first, if we can take her unawares…"

"No, it won't work. I know that I was given this vision for a reason, the fates want this outcome and I'm afraid it's the only one where Atlantis survives."

Ian looked ready to argue. "We will prepare now, and when the full moon rises in two nights we will be ready for that battle."

Sparah sighed in relief and she felt a tingle of destiny. "Thank you," she said quietly so only Ian could hear. "Thank you for trusting me."

Ian nodded and turned to the group. "Someone will go up to warn the others and gather what knowledge we can. We will meet her when it's time and we will stop her."

"*I* will stop her," Sparah said firmly. "I let her go once and it is a mistake I regret."

Ian stepped forward and embraced Sparah. "No, you could not have been expected to harm your sister, Sparah. And we both know that letting the Descendants go that night was the right thing."

Sparah looked up at his face and smiled shakily, "A right decision doesn't mean it doesn't have negative consequences."

"A truer statement has never been uttered," he said and squeezed her shoulders before turning back to the group. "Who shall go up to inform the others and gather information?"

"I will," Samson said, stepping forward. "You know I hate being down here," he muttered.

"Take Thorn with you."

"I'm going. I want to see something other than your ugly faces," Felix said with a laugh.

"I'm going, obviously. Sorry if I don't want to hang with a bunch of bloodsuckers," Sorcha said, grasping Samson's arm.

"As if I'd leave you behind," Samson grunted and kissed her

deep enough that when he pulled away her cheeks were red and Katherine was giggling.

"Glad to see you two worked things out," Katherine said.

"Me too," Sorcha agreed.

"We will meet you at sundown of the full moon with our army," Ian said. He looked at Samson. "You are in charge of these two. Make sure they understand how to behave up there," he said, indicating Felix and Thorn.

Samson's eyes widened slightly as if surprised by being given a responsibility over the other vampires. Sparah thought for a moment he was going to rebel against it, but he just nodded.

"Great, see you all soon, ready for battle," Ian said with a grin, he'd never been one to back down from a fight.

With that send off, the others entered the water.

"Well shit, I was hoping for a little vacation," Saul said as they disappeared under the surface.

Ian turned to Sparah. "What is going to happen?" he demanded.

Sparah straightened her back and arched a brow. "You trying to make demands of me? I'm your elder, boy."

Ian's chest rumbled and Katherine grasped his arm.

"Sparah, please. I may not understand everything about this place, but if you leave doesn't that mean the spell is broken?" Katherine said.

"If I go above the waterline, the city will rise," Sparah said matter-of-factly.

Katherine looked at Ian with worry. "People are going to freak out."

"Yes, but it's that or they die at the hands of the monsters Elantra is willing to let free. Her revenge knows no consequences and cares nothing for others. Atlantis will rise with the full moon, and if we don't fail, it will sink again before the sun rises again. The prison walls will hold under the strength of the full moon.

Everyone will just have to get over it up there, forget about it again. No one will believe it ever occurred in a couple thousand years."

Sparah walked off before Katherine could ask any more questions that she wouldn't like the answers to.

Sparah had to prepare.

Her sister was a powerful witch, and it wasn't going to be easy to kill her.

Sixteen

SORCHA CRAWLED out onto the beach and lay panting as Samson and Thorn discussed something she couldn't make herself care about. She hated that trip. "How the hell does Katherine put up with doing that over and over?" she grumbled.

"Well she doesn't like being stuck in Atlantis full time and if she doesn't go back she'll age and die," Felix laughed.

"Katherine mentioned something like that," Sorcha said.

Felix nodded. "We don't age, you humans do, unless you're down in Atlantis, then the spell preserves you same as it preserves the rest of the stuff we have down there. Katherine keeps calling our stuff, *artifacts*, as if we don't use that shit every damn day. Woman tried to send my favorite blade up to a damn museum last month."

"Great," Sorcha said, her gaze landing on Samson. Tall, wet, and gorgeous. Even now she wanted to crawl over and lick the drips of water that were slipping down his legs. He would always look exactly like that. Perfect, young, strong and tight. She'd age and sag and turn grey. She'd look like his goddamn great grandma.

No way would he still want her then. But was she willing to

live in Atlantis like Katherine so they could get that real happily ever after with the ever after stretching into unknowable eternity?

She thought she might. Even if they saved her sister and the other Descendants, even if they returned to the Florida compound and continued on like before. What was there for her really? A life of one night stands caught from time to time but mostly just training for a war they likely didn't actually have to worry about now that she knew the vampires and werewolves were less monstrous than they'd thought. Farming and living off the grid?

Fuck all that. She wanted passion, she wanted a partner.

She wanted Samson.

But could he live in Atlantis?

He hated it there.

Were they still doomed despite working out what had been a pretty large hurdle in their relationship?

Depression threatened to take over and she looked at Felix who was standing now, looking around the beach like a kid on Christmas. There were people around, humans. It was still early evening and of course just beyond the trees that lined the beach were lights brightening up the sky.

"When's the last time you were on land?" she asked him.

"When we sank. I wasn't allowed out after that. I wasn't one of Beltar's chosen ones." Felix rolled his eyes. "And I did well following orders below, unlike Samson. I wasn't brave or stupid enough to run away like Jovi and a few others over the years."

"Well, you're in for a treat," Sorcha said, standing up and trying to let go of the worry of her relationship. Nothing else would matter if they all died.

"Shall I carry you to the bunker?" Samson asked, coming to her side as she wobbled a bit on her feet.

"No, the swim was intense but I'm fine. You carried me half the swim anyway," she reminded him. "Should I offer to carry you?" she asked with a laugh.

"You couldn't carry my leg," he teased. "I on the other hand am capable and willing to carry you anywhere," he whispered against her ear and kissed her neck.

"Let's go find some dry clothes," Sorcha said, pushing him back playfully.

"There will be clothing at the bunker. Ian stashed some things there for Katherine as well so you can pick from that," Samson said. He put a hand to her lower back and they started walking up the beach. More than one person had stopped to stare at them looking like drunken fools who'd jumped in half prepared. Samson was in just underwear, Thorn and Felix in leather kilts, none of them had shirts or shoes. She was wearing a bathing suit she'd borrowed from Katherine. If it wasn't for the weapons strapped on to the men, they might look like the average 'partied too hard and went for a swim' type. The shine of swords and daggers caught a lot of notice and wary looks.

Luckily no one approached, probably because of the weapons, and people mostly moved on quickly after taking a moment to gape and wonder. There was nothing outwardly vampiric about the men, at least not to the untrained human eye. But they were still something to look at with their muscled bodies.

"Let's move quickly, we are far too exposed right now," Samson said. "Humans don't walk around with weapons strapped to their body very often."

"How do they protect themselves?" Felix asked.

A flash from a phone camera and the giggle of a group of teenage girls caught the group's attention and Sorcha sent them a death glare. "Social media, it ruins lives faster than anything ever invented," she said and grabbed Samson's hand. "Let's get out of here."

Thorn and Felix whispered behind them as they moved quickly along the beach, commenting on what the hell kind of weapon social media is, and if they could get one.

Felix's gasps of amazement and joy made Sorcha smile as they made their way through parts of the city. Thorn had apparently been up recently enough to be less impressed but he still had wide eyes, Sorcha noticed. It made her a little sad for all the men stuck down in Atlantis. They had missed so much being down there and they were so isolated, she wondered if she could do something to bridge the gap. Maybe set up little fieldtrips to Miami for the vampires, supervised visits up to the land of the living.

She laughed at the thought, feeling like Ms. Frizzle, she even had the red hair!

"What is it?" Samson asked, looking at her like she might be losing it.

"Oh, nothing, just excited to be back on this side of the water."

He frowned and nodded.

They avoided people as best they could, and Sorcha was actually impressed that humans weren't more curious about the vampire men. How did they not sense at least something different and dangerous about them? They got looks from some, mostly lascivious, but they quickly passed on, no more interested than they'd be in anyone else.

"Such easy prey," Sorcha mumbled.

"I was just thinking the same thing, how do you resist the temptation of so many warm bodies," Felix groaned and Thorn grunted agreement.

"Once we are at the bunker and you know where it is, you can go out with the twins and satisfy your needs. Once you've done it, you'll find resisting the urge much easier," Samson explained.

Sorcha darted a look at the two vampires behind them, they both looked a bit strained, and she pressed herself closer to Samson.

"They are not interested in your blood," Samson whispered, clearly sensing her discomfort.

"Why?" she asked, trying not to sound offended, what was wrong with her blood? Why the hell didn't anyone want it?

"You smell too much like me, for one. But also, the temptation of blood for them is a willing partner, they don't seek to take and destroy. You are not a willing partner, you are my wife."

Sorcha's head reared back and she looked up at him like he'd just grown a second head, "Excuse me?"

He shrugged. "It's an old custom. If a vampire shares his blood with you and you are sharing your blood with him, it elevates your status from blood slave to wife. Ian explained it to me, and I decided I like the term very much."

"Didn't even get a ring," Sorcha mumbled and decided it wasn't something she could think about or argue about at the moment. If it kept her off limits to the others, she'd call herself whatever Samson wanted her to.

The walk was long, since she refused to let Samson carry her. She was almost dry by the time they arrived outside what looked like an old barn, the salt dried on her skin was itching like crazy. She wanted a shower and food.

"Shit, is there any human food down there?" she asked.

Samson frowned. "I doubt it, we will find you something though. I will care for all your needs."

She smiled at him because she knew he would, he had before. "Shower first, clean clothes, then feed me," she demanded.

Felix and Thorn laughed.

"Are all females so demanding?" Thorn asked.

"The good ones know what they want," Sorcha said. "And we don't appreciate being called *females.*"

Samson grunted and led them into the building and through a trap door in the back, down a staircase and into a bunker hollowed out of the earth beneath.

For being underground it wasn't bad, Sorcha decided. Wooden planks on the floor kept the dirt to a minimum and electricity had been installed so it was bright and almost cheery.

"Do I smell a delicious treat?" The twins, Prat and Trenton walked out of a hallway into the main room with wide smiles, eyes raking over her.

"Back off, idiot twins. Get them some clothes and take them out to eat," Samson demanded, pointing to Thorn and Felix.

"Never any fun," Prat said.

"I see you must have gotten your head fixed on right, but you still haven't decided he's too much work?" Trenton teased.

Sorcha wasn't sure if these two were harmless flirts, or sexual demons so she stayed close to Samson but met their gazes without hesitation.

"He's mine," she assured them and patted his chest possessively.

Prat and Trenton both laughed.

"Yep, she's as crazy as you, Samson. You're obviously a good match," Trenton said.

"Come on, get some clothes and we can go have fun. I know all the best places for debauchery," Prat said and motioned Thorn and Felix forward.

"Where are Beltar and Laric?" Samson asked Trenton when the others had disappeared down the hallway.

"Out scouting with the wolves. They are running a loop around the city making sure Elantra doesn't get in unnoticed."

"Any sign of her?"

"Not yet, but the wolves did get word that there's been some activity at the Florida compound, a few witches showed up the other day, no Descendants."

"I have news, but I'll share it when everyone's back at sunrise. I need to attend to my wife now and you need to make sure Felix and Thorn don't cause a scene."

"We know how to be subtle and still have fun," Trenton said with a wink.

Sorcha wasn't sure she wanted to know what they were going to get up to, but she had a feeling she knew exactly.

"Just make sure the partners are willing and having a great time," she called over her shoulder as Samson ushered her down the hall.

Trenton gasped and put his hands over his heart. "We always leave them satisfied. We love them!"

Sorcha actually believed him.

"This is all so weird," she said.

"What's that?" Samson asked as he led her down the hall.

"Vampires. You all are nothing like what I expected."

"I would agree, most are not what the Descendants believe we are."

Sorcha was reminded that he'd been bitten and changed by a real monster, the kind of vampire that haunted nightmares.

"*You* are not what they think you are," she reminded him and stroked his arm lovingly. "I'll reserve judgment on the others."

He gave her a sad smile and pushed open his door.

She vowed then to spend her life making him realize what a wonderful being he was and making him believe that he deserved love.

She stepped into the room and he flipped the lights on. She looked around with her jaw hanging open in shock.

"You are a Wolverine fan?" The walls were covered in posters depicting the character and a floor to ceiling bookshelf was stuffed with comic books. There were smaller shelves with figurines and the bedspread was a plush blanket with an image of Wolverine showing off his claws.

"More like obsessed," Prat said as he passed the doorway in the hall. Thorn was behind him and tried to poke his head into the room, but Samson slammed the door shut in his face.

"I might have started getting his comics a few years ago."

"Are you kidding me? This is a *collection*!" Sorcha said with a laugh. She spun back to face him and smiled. "I love that you are a big dork."

"What?"

"You, are a big, soft dork under that hard vampire exterior."

"Soft? I am anything but soft," he rumbled and stepped forward.

She giggled and took a step back. "Soft, a little nerdy even. Do you have a costume somewhere that you like to put on, maybe some jammies with little Wolverine heads all over them?"

"If you're lucky, you just might find out. But right now, I think you challenged my hardness. Take off those wet clothes."

"Oh, you want me to lay naked on top of Wolverine?" she asked with a shimmy of her hips as she slipped her bathing suit off. She quickly hopped onto the bed, petting the blanket. "Are you jealous that my ass is currently on Wolverine's face?"

"A little bit," he admitted and stripped quickly, then leaped onto the bed taking her in his arms and rolling until she was straddling him. "Now *my* ass is on Wolverine's face, but he's used to that."

Sorcha laughed and leaned down to kiss her vampire lover. The joy she felt in this moment was more than she'd felt since she was a child.

An hour later they emerged, clean, from the bedroom, and Sorcha wearing some borrowed clothes from Katherine—a skirt, tank top and flip flops. Samson was dressed in jeans and a t-shirt, his usual style of dark and casual. They both had a few weapons strapped on and Sorcha was starving.

"This is awkward, but do you have any money?" Sorcha asked as they stepped into the main living area of the bunker. She'd lost her purse back at their hideout in Georgia when Elantra had attacked.

"I do. I will provide for you whatever you need."

"How do you get your money?" she asked, genuinely curious. It hadn't occurred to her that the vampires would need money, they certainly weren't buying food and they could convince a human to believe almost anything. The Descendants were into investing and had made some smart moves that grew their wealth to the point they didn't have to worry about working other than that. Many of them chose to attend college and before they had been so heavily into investments, they'd been known for being the best hired goons around. Some still chose to go down that path for the right price. But none of them had to work if they didn't want to, they just had to train for the possibility of vampire attacks and work to keep the compound running. What were they going to do when they realized the vampires weren't a threat?

"Ian pays us for our service to Atlantis. We take the Atlantean coins and melt them down. Laric is artistic, he makes the gold into jewelry, and we sell or pawn it."

"Wow, that's really cool."

"It keeps us from having to steal everything," he agreed.

They made their way to the nearest store where she was able to purchase a few essentials and some basic food. There was no kitchen back at the bunker so she picked up things that needed neither refrigeration nor cooking, then they hit up a burger place and she indulged with a groan while Samson stared at her mouth with what could only be described as jealousy.

"Like what you see?" she asked as she wiped a bit of sauce from her lip.

"I've never wanted to be a hamburger before in my life, but right now I'd give my soul for the opportunity."

She laughed and finished off her food in a rush then grabbed his hand and they hurried back to the bunker.

Sorcha felt free and happy and... guilty. What the hell was she doing? She was on a date. She was having sex. She was falling madly in love. All while her sister sat under the influence of Elantra and the Descendants' Stone, nothing more than a puppet having its strings pulled.

"Whoa, what just happened?" Samson asked, stopping and pulling her to face him. "It's like your body suddenly became a block of ice and your face looks like you're watching someone being gutted right in front of you."

She shook her head and met his gaze. "I am just so worried about Julie and the others. It isn't right what Elantra's doing to them and I'm so afraid they are going to be harmed, that they will be used as a shield. It isn't fair."

"No, it isn't," he agreed and hugged her tight. "Let's see if everyone's back yet so we can tell them what we know and see if they know anything more."

The spell of their couple hours was broken, they were back to reality, and it sucked, a lot.

Seventeen

WHEN THEY GOT to the bunker there were a few werewolves milling about outside in wolf form while Lilly and Tray stood in human form with Patrick. They were talking with Beltar and Laric but all conversation stopped when Samson and Sorcha approached.

Their eyes ran all over the couple, taking in the possessive way Samson gripped her hand and the way Sorcha leaned into him for comfort and protection.

"Glad to see you got your memory back in the right place," Lilly said with a smile.

"Me too," she said and smiled up at Samson.

"Is everyone here? I have news," Samson said.

"Yes, let's all go down and hear your story. I can share what Patrick and I have found as well," Beltar said and ran a frustrated hand over his mohawk. "It seems a confrontation is on the horizon."

They settled into the living area. It was cramped with the five vamps who lived there, the additional two Atlantis vamps, three Werewolves and Sorcha. The Werewolves opted to stand near the entrance, for a quick retreat perhaps, and Samson pulled Sorcha onto his lap in a chair, which she couldn't really complain about since that still left Felix and Thorn standing, while the vamps who lived there took the other seats.

"Sparah foresaw a meeting between her and her sister."

"She can't leave Atlantis," Laric gasped.

"Atlantis will rise, but she thinks that if she leaves during the full moon that the spell holding the imprisoned will stay in place until sunrise, any longer though, and things could get bad."

"That's already bad, what the hell are the humans going to think?" Patrick growled.

"Not our problem," Thorn said.

"She is the only one who can stop Elantra. Without her magic we won't stand a chance, Elantra is too powerful, and we would have to risk killing the Descendants she has under her power," Samson continued.

"Not an option," Sorcha hissed, and the rest of the room rumbled agreement.

"We will need all the help we can get; will the Werewolves stand with us?" Samson asked Patrick.

"We will stand with you," Patrick said without hesitation then turned to Samson. "We scented some witches near the city limits tonight, they didn't come into the city, they came to the line and headed back. We don't know what they were doing, but it can't be good."

"Why would they come to the city limits and then leave, did they sense you out there?" Samson wondered aloud.

"Doubtful, the trail we scented was hours old, no wolves or vamps had been near there when they were there," Tray said and his mate nodded agreement. "And we scented it at a few different spots, all the same, hours old and a touch then gone."

"What the hell?" Sorcha frowned, then a thought hit that made her panic. "Oh shit, did you check the area thoroughly?"

"They weren't hiding in a nearby bush," Beltar huffed.

"Not for the witches," Sorcha snapped. "For runes, for spells?"

"We—" Patrick began and then snapped his mouth shut and looked at the other two werewolves.

"That's what I thought. Those bitches are planning something," Sorcha said.

"We will go back and check it out and report back here at sundown. Enjoy your daylight rest, vampires," Patrick said with a friendly wink, then the three of them headed out.

Sorcha was stiff on Samson's lap as her mind tried to figure out what the witches were planning.

"Would they risk exposure to humans?" Laric asked.

"Elantra would risk anything at this point. I don't think she has a shred of humanity left in her. And those witches follow her like a god, they'd do anything she asked of them," Sorcha said.

"We will need to report back to Ian," Thorn said.

"Let's wait until we hear back from the wolves, we don't know for sure that the witches are trying to set a spell and besides, the sun is about to come up, we can't do anything else before sundown again," Beltar said.

Prat and Trenton yawned obnoxiously. "Well, with that settled we are off to bed, see you all in a few hours. And hey, Sorcha, try to keep the screams to a minimum, I need my beauty sleep," Prat said with a wink.

Samson glared daggers at the vampire who just laughed and headed down the hall.

"I'll show you to our extra room, you two can fight over the bed," Beltar said to Thorn and Felix as Sorcha tried to ignore the fact that her face was beet red.

"Goodnight, love birds," Laric said and then he too disappeared down the hallway.

"Such close quarters," Sorcha complained as Samson scooted her off his lap and stood up.

"Would you prefer something more private, love?"

"No, it's too late for that. Just keep to your side of the bed."

"No way," he said darkly and put a hand on her back, leading her to his room.

* * *

Elantra dipped the bones into the blackened liquid. When she pulled them out, they dripped red and she smiled. She threw them onto the silk covering her table, lines of salt crisscrossed it in a deliberate pattern and each corner was held down with a large black onyx stone that radiated power.

She stared down at the pattern the bones had landed in, interpreting the meaning that the spirits were giving her. She'd stopped asking the goddess for help a long time ago, abandoned by the first mother perhaps, or perhaps Elantra had forsaken Maeve when she'd walked in on the mangled carcass of her mother, her stepfather standing over it once again in human form. The sun had just been rising and Elantra had been too late.

"What have you done?" she whispered, tears filling her eyes.

"I thought I was strong enough," Gilead said, his voice cracking with sorrow. He was naked, covered in blood and his face was twisted in agony at what he'd done.

Elantra had no sympathy. She saw only her own anger. This is what they do. This was the fate of women who loved monsters. Monsters that deserved to die.

She walked calmly to the wall where she knew weapons were kept. She heard him drop to his knees and weep over the woman he'd murdered. The woman who he had supposedly loved.

Elantra picked out a long, sharp sword, the handle made of pure white stone, etched and inlaid with gold in a delicate pattern. This was a sword meant for her mother's grip. Elantra had seen her use it in practice many times. Why hadn't her mother armed herself with it last night? Why hadn't she fought against this beast, this traitorous monster? Was she so blinded by love that she didn't even have the sense to defend herself?

Elantra walked back to Gilead. He didn't move, he was bowed over Fray begging her to come back to him. Elantra stopped next to him and raised the sword over his head and he looked at her briefly then back down.

"Release me," he whispered. "I want to join her in the afterlife."

Elantra hesitated. "You don't deserve the honor."

"Kill me!" he roared, lifting the lifeless body into his arms and sobbing.

Elantra stepped back, her foot bumping a table and a large black stone rolled there, catching her eye.

And she knew then what she needed to do. She grabbed it up and the spell she wanted filled her mind as if whispered by a demon, a demon she would fully embrace for the rest of her life if she could avenge what horrors she'd endured.

"Gilead, you will suffer," she whispered, then spat out the spell and hurled the stone at him. It hit his shoulder and turned to liquid on contact.

"What is this?" Gilead asked and touched his shoulder, the liquid was quickly spreading, covering and containing as it went. First his arm, then up his neck. When he realized it was immobilizing him he pulled Fray closer.

"Let her go!" Elantra screamed but it was too late, the spell was working too fast and it spread to Fray. Moving until it covered them both and then with a flash and a snap it retracted and rolled, and Elantra stared down at a smooth onyx stone the size of her fist holding the soul and power of her mother and her mother's murderer.

She bent and picked it up, gazing into the stone and there she saw *the contented face of Gilead, pressed against the mangled remains of his wife trapped forever together.*

"I hope you suffer for your sins for an eternity and I will use you to power my revenge," Elantra vowed.

A spark of lightning hit outside from the clear blue sky and Elantra knew that her vow had been sealed into existence, promised by a demon that would forever whisper in her mind. She was no longer a witch of Maeve's creation. She forsook the original mother. She was the witch of something darker and she liked that very much.

Pocketing the rock, she left that house and thought a strike of lightning into existence, exploding the place into flames. Whatever wasn't rock would burn, no memories of their life or love would remain.

Elantra shook herself out of the memory and tore her gaze away from the stone that to this day held those two. Her most powerful stone. She focused back to the predictions she'd just cast.

"Knowledge here," she said as she motioned to a particularly spattered section where the bones crossed each other, one balancing precisely atop another. "Betrayal," she sneered as she motioned to a broken line of salt where a round bone had landed and slid.

"But does it predict our success?"

Elantra glared at the demanding twit, Devon. She'd forgotten she was there for a moment. She was only useful because she had a particular aptitude for magic, she was annoying as hell though and Elantra constantly wanted to crush her.

"The goddess doesn't speak in such terms. She shows a path. They have knowledge and we will be betrayed."

"What the hell is that supposed to mean?" Devon snapped then bit her lip, obviously realizing the mistake in questioning Elantra.

Elantra shot her a glare. "It means that we have lost the element of surprise. It doesn't mean we won't still succeed."

"Who betrayed us?" Devon asked.

"No one yet," Elantra hissed. Which meant it could be anyone and she hated to have to kill them all before the battle. Would an army of Descendants be enough?

Elantra picked up one of the heavy onyx stones and stared into its dark depths. She saw a shadow move inside, the ghost of someone she'd taken from their earthly form so many years ago she couldn't recall the name, or the way.

"Do you know why these stones are so powerful?"

"No, you never tell me anything," Devon said sullenly.

"I trapped a poor soul in it and have been slowly draining it's life force to fuel magic like this ever since." She had discovered that using the magic in them would slowly release the soul, so she used Gilead's sparingly. Although it held the most powerful magic, she didn't want to release his soul, didn't want to give him the satisfaction of it. She wanted him trapped with that dead body for eternity.

Her hand was clenched around the stone she held and her eyes darted to another, that one filled with a more recent soul, Stephanie, a powerful and willing witch who she'd taken just after the attack on Ian and that bitch Sorcha. She'd needed the boost, and now she wanted another.

"Y-you, what?" Devon said, eyes wide. She stood and took a step back.

"Want to see how I did it?" Elantra asked, looking up at the frightened girl. She loved the smell of fear, loved the power that she could wield over these witches.

"N-no, thanks, maybe another time. I need to help in the kitchen," Devon said taking another step back.

"Oh, but you said you wanted me to show you more magic," Elantra sneered. "You, the one I've trusted the most, the one who knows the most. The one who could betray me the most," she snarled the last and threw the onyx stone at Devon. It seemed to move in slow motion as it hit her between the eyes. It became like liquid on impact and enveloped her face first, stifling the screams quickly then the rest of her head as she fumbled around looking for escape or help. The liquid moved down her neck, over her shoulders, immobilizing her arms and then quickly down the rest of her body until she was cocooned in black.

Elantra snapped her fingers and with a flash of light the liquid began to shrink back to the size of a lemon, Devon completely contained within.

Once it was done, Elantra walked over and picked it up, looking into its depths and seeing the screaming face within, this time she knew its name. "Devon, you will still be an important part of this plan. Your power will fuel my spells well past what your simple lifetime would have been, count yourself lucky. It's the closest to immortal you could have gotten."

Elantra dropped the stone into a box along with the other three and then swept the bloody bones and salt into a cleansing bath of honey water. She laid the silk over the stones and as she closed the lid, she was sure she heard a tiny scream of despair that made her smile.

She left her room and called to the nearest witch.

"What is your name?"

"Bethany, ma'am," she said brightly, eager to please.

Elantra touched Bethany's shoulder and assessed her ability to perform magic. Not as strong as Devon or Stephanie had been, but not a poor showing. She would do.

"Bethany, tell everyone to pack up. We are moving out before nightfall."

"Of course, ma'am," she said and hurried to do Elantra's bidding.

Elantra went back to her room and laid on her bed, magic like she'd just performed took something out of her. "Will you meet me, sister? Will you continue to try and defend the monsters and what they've done to our family?"

You will destroy her. The familiar voice whispered through her mind. A voice she'd become so used to since that day she'd taken Gilead into the stone. She didn't know its name, but she knew it was right. It had never lied to her yet.

Eighteen

SORCHA SLEPT EASILY through the day and woke up before the sun set to Samson's head between her thighs. Eyes barely open, she groaned and rolled her hips against his face. Her hands gripped his hair and urged him on.

There was no better way to wake a girl up, she decided. For this, she'd take an early morning any day.

His tongue worked her at an inhuman speed and when he added a couple fingers to the mix she was sitting up and crying out as she tried her best to shove her body ever closer to the source of pleasure.

"Fuck," she groaned as she fell back on the bed, the orgasm still rippling through her body.

"Yes, that's next," he agreed and kissed her inner thigh. "May I bite you here?" he asked, licking her inner thigh with a deep groan that made her tremble.

She looked down and saw pure desire swirling in his purple eyes. "Yes, please, anywhere," she said without hesitation.

He groaned at her words and bit into her flesh. The sting was so quickly replaced by a pleasurable warmth it was hardly worth mentioning. Her other leg wrapped around his back and hugged him closer, unable to get enough of him.

His fingers went back to work on her wet core as he sucked until she erupted in a fast second orgasm—the pleasure unreal.

"Your turn," he said huskily as he moved up her body. "I want to feel your teeth enter me as I enter you, Sorcha."

"I might need a minute to recover," she answered honestly. Her body was vibrating, and her head was cloudy.

He only laughed, "That's what my blood is for," he said and pressed his arm against her mouth.

She opened and bit down as hard as she could. It wasn't easy to get through his skin, but she managed, and even as she worried she was going to hurt him he groaned in pleasure and pushed inside her with a slow deliberate stroke.

"Such a good girl," he said as his hips moved at a slow pace and her mouth worked at his arm, taking in his blood eagerly. Its warmth spread down her throat, clearing her head, and strengthening her body just in time to feel the building of a third orgasm.

"Fuck, how is this possible?" she said, tearing her mouth from his arm and looking up at him with wide eyes. Her hands gripped his hips, and she arched her back. She felt like she could do this all day with his blood in her body. She had a moment's wonder about how Ian and Katherine managed to ever get anything done if this was an option, all day every day.

Samson leaned down and captured her mouth in a deep kiss, mixing their blood as his hips increased their pace at her demanding grip. She wanted more, she wanted harder, and he was willing to give it to her.

One of his hands gripped the headboard and the other grabbed her leg under the knee and lifted so he could get the angle he wanted.

"Yes!" she screamed as he hit her perfectly.

"You're so perfect," Samson whispered as he kissed her sweetly, never stopping his strokes. "All mine, forever."

"Yours," she agreed and dug her nails into his ass. "And you are mine," she added, meeting his gaze and licking her lips, tasting his blood, her blood and a hint of her own pussy juices mixed in. It was explosive.

Her orgasm set his off this time and with no care for anyone who might still be asleep in the bunker he shouted out her name as he came deep inside her.

When he rolled off of her and pulled her body against his, he buried his face in her neck, and she stroked her hands up and down his back.

"I think I could get used to this kind of morning," she said shyly.

"We can have an eternity of these mornings," he said and nipped gently at her neck.

She wasn't ready for that conversation, so she pushed him away and demanded a shower.

They rushed naked to the bathroom after Samson peeked out into the hallway and declared it all clear. They were both a bit bloody and she was feeling like a drug addict wanting more and more of him despite the three great orgasms she'd just had. Luckily, he seemed to feel the same because he pressed her against the shower wall and took her again before Prat was banging on the door demanding they fuck somewhere else and let him get in there to wash his own balls.

"Someday, we can go somewhere, just you and me," Samson promised as he dried her off and then carried her, bridal style, back to his room.

Prat gave her a wink as they passed and he hurried into the bathroom. The vampire was wearing only a pair of boxers and she couldn't help sweeping her eyes up and down the toned body. She may be falling in love with Samson, but she wasn't dead, and all these men were something to look at.

"You eyeballing my coven mate? Do I need to kill him?" Samson said with a tone serious enough that Sorcha wasn't sure he was joking.

"Can't a girl appreciate a view?" she teased, and he growled. "Don't worry, he's not my type."

"Oh and what is?" Samson asked as he kicked the door to his room closed.

"Comic book nerd with the body of a god," she answered honestly.

He laughed and dropped her on the bed.

She dressed in a pair of pants and a t-shirt he'd bought her yesterday, then ate dry granola and a banana as Samson tried to explain his favorite issue of the Wolverine comic.

She didn't care one bit what he was saying, she just loved the look of pure joy on his face as he shared this with her.

When she'd eaten, they went to the main room to meet with the others. Everyone was there already, and they eyed her with a knowing that made her blush. She tilted her head up, challenging any of them to comment on her relationship. No one did.

"I'm heading out as soon as we hear from the wolves," Thorn said. "I'll let Ian know what is going on and be back up before sunup to relay any messages back."

"I think it would be pertinent to check out a few social clubs," Felix said brightly, and Prat and Trenton whooped agreement.

"Insatiable," Beltar murmured.

"One must find joy where he can," Prat said. "This life is anything but easy."

Sorcha looked at the happy vampire and saw a look of sadness pass briefly across his face. There was a story there that she would like to know someday. She couldn't blame anyone for trying to find happiness within the chaos that was existence.

Wasn't that what she'd decided to do with Samson?

It's what she saw between Ian and Katherine too, and from

what she knew of Lilly and Tray, they were looking for a piece of happiness in a fucked up world as well.

But not Elantra, she was looking for more destruction. Revenge and hate were not things that led to happiness.

The wolves howled outside, and they made their way up into the new darkness.

Patrick, Tray, and Lilly stood in human form surrounded by twenty wolves.

"What did you find out?"

Tray dropped a rock at their feet. It was a regular stone, nothing special about it except for the rune carved into it. Just looking at the thing made Sorcha shiver.

"That's a ward stone, they are trying to separate the city from anything outside of it," she said.

"We collected ten of them spread out around the city. Their plan won't work, but that doesn't mean they don't have a backup," Patrick said.

"I'm sure Elantra has a backup, in fact this could have been a distraction from something else entirely," Sorcha said with a frown.

"It won't matter. We will be prepared," Beltar said firmly.

"We also have a report from a wolf on watch that they've all arrived at a place just outside the city, the whole crew of Descendants, witches and Elantra."

"That's not surprising. It's almost the full moon," Sorcha said, giving the werewolves a wary look.

"Will the lifting of Atlantis be enough to help the werewolves keep their control during the full moon change?" Samson asked.

Patrick looked thoughtful. "It certainly might. Legend says that before the sinking, we weren't controlled by the moon."

"I'll let Ian know what you found and see if Sparah has any new insights," Thorn said. "Enjoy your night, boys." He clapped Felix on the back. "Try to stay out of trouble."

"Always," Trenton said.

"What do *we* do?" Sorcha asked, not sure she expected anyone to answer. "How do we prepare?"

"We need to remove some of her power. I don't think we can separate her from the other witches, they won't go willingly. She doesn't gain power from the Descendants, but they will act as willing shields to run through. If we can get them out of the way, it would be something. Fewer innocents in the way at least," Samson said.

"How the hell would we manage that?" Sorcha grumbled. It felt impossible and she was worried for her sister.

"If someone went in and took the Stone, that would help," Patrick said.

As if it were just that easy, Sorcha wanted to snap, but she knew he was right. It was likely the only thing they could try that would actually help tip things in their favor. "I'll go, I want to make sure my sister is safe," Sorcha said quickly.

Samson hissed beside her and grabbed her to him as if he could stop her from doing what she wanted. She pulled away from him to make a point—they may be in some kind of relationship, but she would never agree to be under his control.

"No way. She'll sense you immediately and she'll kill you on sight," Samson said.

"I will *not* risk my sister. I will do what I can to save the Descendants before the battle Sparah saw," she said.

Samson was the only one shaking his head no, the others looked at her with mixtures of impressed concern.

"I'll go with you," Laric said, "I can fight while you steal."

"As if I'm letting her go in alone," Samson snapped.

"Great, you two can maybe cause some kind of distraction while I sneak in. If I can get the stone, I'll need one of you to use it to release them from the spell. There will be *no* fighting. We are there to get them out alive," Sorcha added.

"If we work fast, we can resolve the issue of the Descendants before sunup and then when we meet Elantra tomorrow night. It will be with one less barrier," Laric said with a bit of hope in his voice.

"I'm ready," Sorcha said, one hand on the dagger at her side. "No reason to delay."

Nineteen

UNDER THE GUIDANCE of Patrick and one of his werewolves who she learned was named Dallas, they found the place where Elantra was setting up a new home. It was a huge house that looked far too well maintained to not have been inhabited previously which made Sorcha wonder what had happened to the people living there.

Their group stood in shadow watching the movement around the place for a while, trying to think up a plan. They saw witches and Descendants moving things from vans to the house and plenty of people seemed to be milling about both inside and around the yard.

Behind the house was a large yard that led to a well-maintained orchard.

Was this where the battle had been predicted?

"How do you plan to get in and find the Stone?" Samson asked, no doubt hoping he was going to be able to talk her out of it, still. He'd been not so subtly arguing with her the entire way, but she hadn't changed her mind. No vampire or werewolf was getting in there unnoticed. No way.

"I have an idea but it's going to be a little morally grey," she admitted. "We need someone on the inside and the only way to do that is going to be to wake up one of the Descendants."

"You mean feed one of these random people my blood," Samson scowled. "It is an honor I only wish to bestow on you."

She smiled at him. The look of absolute horror on his face made her heart squeeze. He really was just one big hunk of love despite his usually scowling face and overall disdain for humans. "Thanks love, but this is an extenuating circumstance. Don't think you can go around doing it willy-nilly. I own your blood and whatever the hell passes for semen in a vampire." She'd wondered, and planned to investigate when they had time. She knew she wasn't getting knocked up, vampires had never bred with their Atlantean slaves. She assumed the only reason Elantra had gotten pregnant from Barnabas was because of some spells. But he definitely ejaculated something similar, she was guessing it was just a shooting blanks situation. Katherine was a science type of gal, she probably had figured it out already or would at least be as curious, maybe they could find out together when things settled.

If things settled that direction.

"How do we lure a Descendant out here to wake up?" Samson asked. He didn't look convinced but couldn't argue with her reasoning. They needed information about what was happening inside and someone to help them get in there.

"I don't think it will be too hard. It looks like the witches are mostly doling out orders and the Descendants are doing the grunt work of taking things out of the vans. We will hide over there," she pointed to a small thicket of bushes near the driveway. "When the next one comes out to grab a box we take them, then you shove a bloody arm in their face. I'm guessing as soon as they wake up and realize what's been going on, we will have no trouble getting them to cooperate."

"Sounds easy," Samson said.

"That probably means it won't be," Sorcha whispered but she didn't know what else to do. They had one shot at removing the obstacle of the Descendants and making sure they were safe from the fight.

"We will watch from here unless there's a problem. Then we'll do our best to make a distraction," Patrick said.

Sorcha and Samson crept forward in shadows to the bush. There were five witches on the porch as Descendants passed every few minutes. The van they were near had a side door open, and Sorcha could see boxes and suitcases inside.

Beth, a small woman Sorcha knew very well, a Descendant she'd grown up with, was the next to come to the van they were staking out. She was young and adorable, blonde hair in a high ponytail that swung when she walked and big blue eyes. She reminded Sorcha of a doll and even now she was dressed in a bright pink tank top and white shorts, with little gold sandals on her feet. She was far from evil, barely ever even trained to fight and Elantra was going to sacrifice her to the vampires.

It twisted Sorcha's gut and she was hoping like hell they could save her right now.

From where they were, the van blocked the porch, so she was sure she'd be able to get the girl without the witches knowing. But if Beth screamed, they would be found out too quickly.

Her heart beating fast and her palms a bit sweaty, she watched as Beth leaned into the van, hands reaching out for a box.

Samson moved lightning fast. He grabbed Beth from behind, crushing her body against his and his arm went directly in front of her face, already bleeding. Not only did it cut off the scream that was no doubt building, but also forced his blood into her open mouth.

Sorcha got close to the woman's face, looked into her eyes, and hissed, "Drink damnit. All our lives depend on it."

The woman struggled against Samson's arm and his face had a look of grim determination on it.

Sorcha couldn't help being thankful that he didn't seem to be enjoying the interaction. She wasn't sure what she would do with the jealousy that would erupt inside of her.

Beth stopped struggling and moaned, grabbing Samson's arm. And Sorcha wanted to rip her head off. Yep, there was the jealousy.

"I think that's enough," Sorcha snapped, her hands clenched at her side, wanting to punch Samson and Beth both.

Samson grunted agreement and pulled Beth off of his arm.

The Descendant was glassy-eyed and wobbled on her feet. She blinked and smiled at Samson like he was dessert, and she'd just gotten a taste. "Hi," she said, her voice a husky whisper.

"Hey, Beth," Sorcha said sharply, drawing the woman's gaze to her.

Beth frowned and blinked, her eyes clearing a bit. She wiped her mouth and looked down at the blood, then she threw up.

That reaction made Sorcha feel better. She rubbed her friends back and whispered that it was all going to be alright.

"Oh my god," Beth said and retched again, a spray of blood landing all over her little gold sandals.

"Don't freak out," Sorcha said as Beth finally straightened, and her eyes locked on Samson with terror this time. She took a step back but Sorcha grabbed her arm to hold her in place. "Beth, I need you to stop and listen before you do anything."

"You're hanging out with a bloodsucker, he just, I—" Beth's face went white and she bent over and puked again.

Sorcha met Samson's gaze over the woman's back. Samson looked a bit offended; Sorcha just shrugged her shoulders.

"Beth, you've been under the influence of the Stone," Sorcha explained.

"How the hell did it end up back with *them*," she said glaring at Samson.

"Not them," Sorcha corrected. "Elantra."

Beth looked like she was going to call bullshit but then she seemed to rethink things. "Oh shit, I haven't questioned a single thing she's had me do."

Sorcha nodded. "Yeah, sorry the only way I knew to snap you out of it was to feed you vamp blood. Samson is a good guy. He only did it because I asked him to."

Beth darted her eyes to Samson and quickly back to Sorcha, fear and disgust there. "He didn't take anything?" Beth asked, her voice trembling slightly.

"No, I swear, you've been unharmed by him."

Beth rubbed her face then stopped and pulled it away as she realized her chin was bloody.

"Here," Dallas said, taking off his shirt and handing it to Beth.

Beth's eyes widened on the ripped werewolf and took the shirt slowly.

"For your face and shoes, wouldn't want to ruin those cute things," he said with a wink.

Beth giggled and wiped her face and feet, then looked unsure again. "This is fucked up. Elantra is the bad guy here? Why?"

"She's insane," Samson offered.

"That all doesn't matter right now. I need to get the Stone away from her. Can you help me?" Sorcha said, knowing they had to move quickly.

"I don't know," Beth said, real fear showing on her face. "She'll kill us both. She said you betrayed us."

"I didn't betray anyone. She's the one who betrayed us. She's using the Descendants' Stone to control and sacrifice. She'll let the vampires and werewolves tear through everyone so she can have a chance at revenge."

"No," Beth gasped and shook her head, trying to rearrange her beliefs. "She's a witch. She helps us. She—" Beth bit her lip, her gaze landing on Dallas again who stood shirtless and smiling at her. "Are you sure?" she asked, turning back to Sorcha.

"Yes, and we can't leave the others like that, Beth. We also can't force feed them one at a time."

"I don't know where it is, probably in her room. She had all of her things set up first when we got here, spelling stuff mostly."

"Can you get me in so I can search?"

"Maybe." Beth thought for a moment then brightened. "If you don't mind a tight space, I have an idea," she said cheerfully.

"Whatever it takes," Sorcha said, and Samson hissed disapprovingly. Sorcha met his eyes and gave him a tight smile. "I'll make it back out," she promised.

"You'd better, or I will tear the place down to get you back."

"I'll see you later, Beth," Dallas said and took his puke and blood-stained shirt back from her.

"Okay," she said with a hesitant smile.

Samson grabbed Sorcha and pulled her against him, pressing his mouth to hers in a searing kiss.

Beth took Sorcha's arm and led her away toward the van. "Oh your sister isn't going to like that at all."

"My sister will get over it. The vampires aren't the monsters we all thought they were," she defended. "Or the werewolves," she added as an afterthought.

"I admit that kiss looked anything but monstrous. That boy had love in his eyes like I've never seen! So possessive and consuming," Beth fanned herself and giggled. "That other one is a vampire?" she asked as if she didn't much care about the answer but Sorcha could see the attraction in Beth's eyes.

"Werewolf," she said, and Beth's smile widened.

They stopped, still in cover of the bushes, and looked around, waiting for a Descendant to come and go with a box from the van.

"What's the plan?" Sorcha asked when the Descendant was out of sight.

"Get in a trunk, I'll have someone help me carry it to her room."

Sorcha groaned as she followed Beth to the van and watched her open a heavy trunk, she threw some blankets and books out then motioned for Sorcha to get in.

"Don't fucking drop me," Sorcha hissed as the lid closed and she was settled in darkness. Then she waited.

"Help me take this to Elantra's room," Beth was soon saying to someone.

"Okay," the voice responded and then she was moving. Slid, lifted, tilted precariously and then moving, hopefully straight to Elantra's room and the Stone.

"Where are you taking that one?" A voice Sorcha recognized as one of the witches called out.

"Elantra's room," Beth said.

"No, trunks need to go in the basement, we already got her stuff in. That's just extra junk."

"Elantra said all trunks in her room. Up the stairs, door at the end of the hallway," Beth tried again while obviously giving Sorcha the information she'd need to find the place on her own.

"I know where her bloody room is. She didn't mean the ones from the second van. Take it downstairs," the witch snapped.

They started moving again and the trunk tipped as they apparently headed to the basement.

When she was basically dropped to the ground, she had to bite back a grunt as her head hit the side painfully.

Two sets of footsteps retreated up the stairs. Sorcha waited, barely breathing, for a few minutes listening for any other sound. When nothing came, she cracked the lid and dared a peek out. She was in a dingy, dark basement, no one in sight. She flipped the lid and jumped out rubbing at her head and stretching her limbs.

"Fuck," she whispered. How was she going to get where she needed from here?

Sorcha dug through the boxes that had been stacked down there and managed to find a beanie to hide her hair and a large sweatshirt that she could cower into. It would have to work. She'd do all she could to avoid anyone, but if they saw her from behind or out of the corner of their eye, they'd never recognize her.

She hurried upstairs and listened at the door. She heard voices, but not close, so she risked it. She had to walk through the place like she belonged, and she had to do it quickly. She emerged into a kitchen and then tried to find the stairs without looking like she was lost and backtracking when she saw people in front of her.

There were enough witches and Descendants roaming around the fairly small home that she was easily unnoticed, just another body.

She found the stairs eventually and no one was in the way so she hurried up and rushed down the hall as quick as she could while still retaining her casual appearance of movement. The last door was closed, and she hesitated at it. Listening intently. The last thing she wanted was to open the door and find Elantra waiting.

No sounds inside.

She opened it and stepped in, shutting the door behind her and locking it for good measure, then she flipped the light on.

The room was surprisingly put together for them having just moved in. Elantra was using her little slaves well, apparently. It smelled of herbs and something she couldn't identify but sent a chill down her spine. It was decorated in dark purple and black, colors she knew Elantra preferred.

There was a table set up with black candles and various stones. A bowl of something dark was in the center of the table. Sorcha stepped closer, drawn to the setup. It tingled. The whole room vibrated, actually. There was a lot of power here and it was dangerous.

It was quite similar to what she felt in Atlantis, but this had a bitter taste to it, dark. She took another step toward the table. She didn't see the Descendants' Stone but her eyes were drawn to a black onyx stone that shimmered and seemed to move. She leaned over the table and looked into it.

She nearly screamed and jumped back when the screaming, terrified face of Devon appeared in the stone.

"What the fuck?"

"Useful things, powerful witches. But when they start to get a mind of their own, I like to keep them a little more contained."

Sorcha spun at the voice, coming face to face with Elantra. The door to the bedroom was still closed and locked, how the hell had she gotten in, or had she been lying in wait when Sorcha arrived? Using some kind of magic to hide herself. Had she seen her coming and set this trap to catch her?

Were the others safe?

"You're not going to get away with this," Sorcha said, trying to push away the fear for Samson that had suddenly sprung up.

"Oh, but I already have," Elantra said, lifting her hand and showing the small green stone that had caused so much trouble.

"You betrayed me," Sorcha snapped. "I gave that to you so that we would be safe, not sacrificed for your revenge, not enslaved to *you*."

"I promised that the vampires would never get a hold of it. I'm keeping that promise by destroying them all," she said with an evil smile. "You are unfortunately enamored of one, I can see that." She stepped closer and Sorcha couldn't stop herself from taking a step back. "Even after the way he betrayed you." She clucked her tongue and shook her head. "I saw it all when I took the memories away. I know him as well as you. He used you; he took from you what he wanted and sought another to satisfy his deepest hunger. You'll never be enough for him. They are monsters and they will take and take and take. Do you think the vampire king only laid in my bed? I may have been the only one he gave his blood to, but I caught him sampling other's veins and bodies more than once. It's their nature to take and destroy without care. It didn't matter that I was the mother of his children, that I had sacrificed magic to bear a vampire's children," she scoffed. "He only saw what he wanted and took it. They are all the same."

"You're wrong," Sorcha whispered as every fear she had about her relationship was torn into the light.

"Am I? Poor child," Elantra crooned and reached out to stroke Sorcha's cheek. "So caught up in the danger and fun, you can't see that he's nothing more than a monster."

Sorcha pulled herself away with more force than necessary. She knocked over the table and the contents of the bowl spilled on the carpet. It was thick and as it spread out Sorcha could see it was a deep red like old blood.

"You're fucked up," Sorcha whispered, fearing for her life like she hadn't since Samson had saved her. "You don't follow the light, you follow something darker." The realization sent a new shiver of fear through Sorcha.

"I was given a gift the night I found my mother destroyed. When you're as powerful as I am, it doesn't matter much what peons like you think," she snarled and grabbed at Sorcha.

Sorcha ducked and Elantra managed to grab her hair, pulling her back. She fell to her knees at the woman's feet. Sorcha screamed out but she knew there was no one in the house that would help her. She'd been clear to Beth, she needed to get out of the house and as far away as possible as soon as Sorcha had been delivered. The risk of Beth being found out was too great.

There were others outside who might help her though, so she screamed again, head tilted toward the window in the room, hoping to alert Samson or the wolves.

"Got some friends out there?" Elantra hissed and then she made a quick decisive motion with her hand and a pop sounded in Sorcha's ears.

She knew immediately what had just happened and she wanted to cry.

Elantra had set a barrier. There was no way Samson or the wolves would be able to help her now. Just as Sorcha was coming to that realization, she heard a howl, mixed with a fierce cry of sorrow in the darkness beyond the house.

She was fucked.

Twenty

SAMSON WAS GOING to kill everyone in sight if he wasn't able to get through that barrier. The damn thing had sprung up so close to him he'd felt the displacement of air on his nose.

"Shit, I didn't know she'd already gotten that set up," Beth said, trembling. "The Witches must have set those stones first thing while we were unpacking."

Dallas rushed to them and shifted to his human form. He was naked and Beth's trembling stopped as she stared open mouthed at the man.

Samson rolled his eyes as Dallas grinned at the Descendant. "Hey."

"Hey," Beth managed with a gulp.

"Focus. How can we get in? That bitch has Sorcha," Samson demanded.

Beth bit her lip and reached forward. She hissed as her hand made contact with the invisible barrier. "That's not like what we had at the compound."

"We're fucked," Dallas said.

Samson looked up at the windows of the house where the scream of his beloved had come from. "Fight, Sorcha. Fight for me,

I'll find a way in," he promised. "We can't get through that without some serious magic on our side," Beth pointed out, and Samson wanted to throttle her for the doubt. He couldn't handle that right now, couldn't even consider not getting in, not getting to Sorcha in time.

"And someone to wield it, I suppose." Dallas said.

"It's too bad we weren't a few steps closer when she set it, we'd be inside instead of out," Beth said.

That gave Samson an idea. "Dallas, go back and fetch as many of the stones that were set to circle the city as possible. Maybe we can somehow harness whatever power the witches might have imbued them with."

Dallas shifted and took off at a run. He would be quick, but it still might be too late. It would take nothing more than a thought for Elantra to completely destroy Sorcha, and him.

Samson couldn't think about that now though, he wouldn't survive losing her. He had to believe she was alright, had to believe that he'd get her back. Otherwise his life was pointless. In such a short time she'd become his every reason for breathing. He'd often wondered why he kept going after he killed Charlotte and left her house of horrors. Why he hadn't just ended himself then, ended his suffering and meaningless existence, even after finding the others he hadn't felt like he deserved to be alive, hadn't felt like he was meant to exist. But something inside of him kept saying *wait, there's more to come.* It had been a hope he hadn't thought he deserved and kept telling himself he was weak for listening. Then when he'd been in that basement nursing Sorcha back to health, he'd realized she was that thing. She was the more that was coming, and his destiny was to find her. It was that feeling of destiny that had kept him going after she'd left him, hoping that there was still more to come.

It couldn't end here, not like this.

The house remained active as they waited but no one came outside. Samson watched and ignored the whining and shivering of Beth beside him. He wanted to tell her to go away, but realized she probably had nowhere to go and no way to get anywhere so he tolerated her.

"You really love her," Beth finally said after they'd been staring at the house for about an hour.

"More than anything above or below the waterline," he agreed.

"And she just accepts that you're a bloodsucker?" she asked. Her tone wasn't accusing, she was genuinely curious.

Samson sighed and glanced at her. "I saved her life and nursed her back to health, proving that I am not the monster that the Descendants would make me out to be." He felt defensive, not of himself but of Sorcha's choice. He didn't want anyone to judge her for what she'd done with him, didn't want them to think she was wrong for looking past what he was.

"But she ran from you," Beth pointed out.

"I fucked up," he agreed between clenched teeth. "And I'll spend the rest of eternity making it up to her. Or, if she dies in there, I'll walk into the sun after I destroy Elantra and every other witch I can find."

She shivered at his pronouncement, and he was glad. It would be best if she didn't think he gave a shit about anyone involved in this aside from Sorcha.

Dallas showed up shortly after with reinforcements. Patrick, Lilly, Tray, Beltar, Laric, Felix, and the idiot twins who immediately approached Beth and began smooth-talking her.

"Fuck, give it a rest for one fucking night," Beltar hissed, and they gave him fake looks of contrition.

"We have eight of those stones they had set around the city," Beltar said, holding up a bag. "What's your plan?"

"I don't have a plan, I have hope," Samson grumbled and grabbed the bag. "I want to try and trick the magic into opening up and making a new path around us."

Everyone looked at him with confusion. Except Prat and Trenton who were both staring at Beth like she was a new toy they couldn't wait to play with. Beth kept her distance from the two without being too obvious and Dallas went to stand near her with a big smile on his face but a clear indication that he'd step between her and the twins.

"If these are the same sort of stones they used to set this barrier, we can add these stones to it, drawing the circle to them, reshaping the circle without breaking it." Samson hoped, he didn't really know how magic worked, but it was the only thing he could think to try and not trying wasn't an option.

"Like they are magnets for the magic and they will grab it and pull it in a different direction?" Beltar asked with a nod, starting to see what Samson was planning. "Makes sense."

"Yep. Give me one, there's only one way to know if it's going to work," Samson said.

Samson took one of the stones and directed everyone to stand close together and as near the barrier as they could. He then held the stone out to the barrier.

He immediately felt it respond, like the stone had some sort of suction, it pulled on the barrier and the barrier pulled back, wanting the stone to become part of what it already had set up.

Samson wrenched the stone free, and the barrier popped back in place.

"I think it will work but we may need to work fast. Everyone, grab a stone and hold it out away from the barrier where we want to create the new path for the magic."

Everyone except Beth held a stone and they stood in a curve facing away from the barrier with Beth in the middle.

"Ready?" Samson asked and they all affirmed.

Samson touched the stone to the barrier once again waiting until it was pulling then he slowly drew it near the next stone, which Patrick was holding. When he touched his stone to Patrick's the barrier jumped to it and Samson felt the magic slip around him and back to the original path.

"Fuck me, it's working," he said. "Patrick, slowly touch your stone to Laric's."

Patrick did, and then the next, and next. With each new connection the barrier skipped over, allowing one more of them to be on the inside of the bubble. When the last stone touched, they all set the stones down in one motion and turned to the house.

They were in; but did anyone inside know that their security had been breached? And was Sorcha still alive in there?

"Don't do it," Beltar whispered.

"What?" Samson snapped.

"Don't go rushing in without a plan, Samson. We have to think about how to do this to damage the fewest innocents," Beltar reasoned.

"Fuck innocents. I told Sorcha I would keep her safe always," Samson snarled.

"She knew the risks," Beltar reminded him, and Samson wanted to bite the vampire's head off, but he was right. Sorcha had known going in that she was risking everything. Samson had known it too, so why the hell had he let her do it?

Because she was her own person, he reminded himself. He couldn't control her, didn't want to. But fuck, he wanted to lock her in a room and never let her out more than almost anything right now. No matter if she hated him, at least she would be safe.

He steeled himself against those instincts and forced himself to listen to the others plot an attack.

* * *

Sorcha was surprised that Elantra hadn't killed her, just incapacitated her with some kind of horrific magic that had her unable to use her arms or legs and left her there on the floor of the room next to the growing spread of ooze that had spilled from the bowl and the terrifying onyx near her head that showed the face of her former roommate.

She wanted to cry, throw up, and scream for help despite the fact that her throat was ragged from her screams that had already gone unanswered, likely unheard by anyone outside of the house now that the barrier was up.

She kept herself from doing any of those things though because she knew they wouldn't help. She had to keep her head on if she was going to have any hope of surviving this.

The door opened and Julie stood there. Sorcha was so relieved to see her sister alive and well, until she saw how glossy her eyes were and the way her face remained impassive. A glint of moonlight lit on something in Julie's hand and Sorcha's eyes widened on the knife she clutched there. This wasn't a rescue mission. Julie's eyes landed on Sorcha and there was no recognition, no anything. She was robotic and terrifying.

"Julie! What are you doing? Help me, sister, get me out of here before we all die," she pleaded even though she could tell it would be useless, there was no getting in through whatever spell Elantra had cast on her. It had to be more than the Stone, this was deeper, this was dark magic.

Julie didn't say anything, nothing so much as flickered in her eyes as she stepped forward and shut the door behind her. The knife caught another glint of moonlight and Sorcha felt fear spike up her spine, ice cold.

"Julie, listen. I am your sister and I love you," Sorcha tried again.

Julie stopped when her toes were an inch from Sorcha's side. She raised the knife, clearly ready to bring it down and end Sorcha's life. Still her face was impassive, her eyes unseeing. This wasn't Julie, Sorcha had to admit, this was Julie's body controlled by someone else.

"I forgive you, Julie, I know this isn't you," Sorcha whispered. "I know that all you've ever done is try to protect us all. Too bad you were protecting us from the wrong monsters."

Julie started to bring the knife down, Sorcha could no longer hold back the scream of terror. A word whispered through her mind and released her from the spell that had kept her locked in place. Sorcha rolled away and jumped up to defend herself. As the knife struck the air she'd just inhabited. Is this what Elantra wanted, to see the sisters pitted against one another? She refused to hurt Julie, but she wouldn't let Julie hurt her either. She stepped back and grabbed the heavy bowl to use as a defense. Julie was coming for her, and Sorcha wanted to scream and cry and demand that Julie wake the fuck up.

"I don't want to hurt you," Sorcha whispered as she took another step back.

Julie stepped forward again, knife high and menacing. The door flung open and then Julie was flung away, her body crashing into a bookcase and sliding down limp.

Samson stood before Sorcha with a frantic look in his eyes and gathered her in his arms.

"Love, are you alright?"

"Yeah," she said and wrapped her arms around Samson. "Yeah, I'm okay," she whispered against his neck.

He kissed her neck and put his hands on her face, forcing her back so he could look at her, his eyes full of concern. "She didn't harm you?"

"No, not really. We need to get Elantra. But take Julie out of here." Sorcha looked at the space where books and things had fallen off the shelf. No body. "What the fuck?" she whispered.

"Damnit, we'll find her again, don't worry," Samson assured her. "Did you find the Stone?"

"Elantra has it with her. We need to find her."

There was a pop then, the wards broken, and Samson and Sorcha's gazes met. "She's leaving," Sorcha said.

Samson picked her up despite her protests and hurried through the now empty house with her in his arms. When they got outside there were witches standing around shouting and glaring, all confused.

A few looked like they were debating an attack but the werewolves growling nearby were holding them back.

"Where is Elantra? Where are the Descendants?" Sorcha asked as Samson set her on her feet.

"That's a good question," one of the witches said.

"When the ward broke a moment ago, the Descendants all just disappeared," Talia explained. "Fucking Elantra too," she grumbled. "What the hell is going on? What did you do?" Talia demanded.

"Shit, that's strong magic," Sorcha said and the witches around her nodded agreement. It explained why Julie's body disappeared from upstairs.

The witches all looked nervous. That strength of magic was dangerous and had to come from a dark place. "Why didn't she take us?" a young witch asked.

"You all aren't under her control, maybe the Stone created a connection with her that allowed her to take them wherever she poofed off to," Beltar wondered aloud.

"Which is why I'm still here," Beth added. "I'm not under the Stone's spell anymore."

Sorcha met Talia's eyes. "There's an onyx stone in Elantra's room. Look inside, you'll see what kind of evil you've all been following. I suggest you get your things and get out of here before she decides to come back and harvest you all for your magic."

The discomfort in the group grew. Some looked pissed, some lost. Without their leader telling them what to do they were all going to have to make some quick decisions. Sorcha hoped they'd choose to do the right thing, save themselves and run, hide for a few years maybe even.

Samson put a hand to her back urging her away from the house. There was nothing they could do here now. They'd freed half the possible army from Elantra's control, it just wasn't the half they'd intended.

"Check the onyx," Sorcha called back to the witches as they

walked away. "You'll see, then protect yourselves." She hoped they would listen, and she hoped they'd be able to free Devon and whoever else might be inside those stones.

Samson picked Sorcha up when they were out of sight of the house then moved fast and Sorcha held on, feeling safe. When they arrived at the bunker, he took her straight to his room and laid her on the bed, pulling her clothes off to investigate for wounds.

"Unharmed," she said with a half smile.

"It was too close," he snarled, his voice thick with emotion.

"Hey," she said and reached out, she touched his chin and forced his eyes to meet hers. "You were there in time. You are the only thing that kept her from killing me. I don't know if I would have been able to kill her to save myself," she admitted. "Samson, you saved my life, again."

"Oh Sorcha," he said as if it pained him greatly. He collapsed on the floor, his head on her belly and his hands gripping hers. "Sorcha, the day I found you I was saved from a lifetime of torture. I don't deserve what you've been to me and if you ever leave this earth I will walk into the sun and join you on the other side."

"Samson," she whispered and pulled on him until he reluctantly joined her on the bed.

They made love so soft and tender she almost cried when it was done because she was certain he'd touched her soul with his and it wasn't a dark disturbed mess, it was bright and light and scared. He was a good being, he just didn't believe it himself.

"I love you," she said quietly. "Whatever happens tomorrow doesn't matter because we have found perfection right here, right now. This is what life is meant to be."

"I love you too, Sorcha," he said with an edge of desperation in his voice.

His arms embraced her and she looked down at the one that Beth had put her mouth on. She didn't like the feelings of jealousy that image brought up. She ran a finger over the space and frowned. She pushed him back on the bed and pulled his arm to her mouth, biting into the space where Beth had taken his blood. She wanted to erase the memory of the other girl, maybe she was more than a little possessive of this monster.

His eyes widened and then half closed in satisfaction as she sucked. He liked her possessiveness, apparently.

Sorcha fell asleep then, satisfied, and exhausted.

Twenty-One

SAMSON SNUCK out of the room, he hated to leave her side, but he needed to talk to the others.

He found everyone around the entrance to the bunker. The sun wasn't long from coming up and Thorn had just returned along with Katherine, no Ian surprisingly.

Samson relayed his side of the story, though it wasn't anything new aside from what he'd seen in Elantra's room and what little Sorcha had reported.

They all agreed that Elantra was still a threat. She would regroup with the stolen Descendants and be ready to attack the next night, the full moon as Sparah had predicted. They'd knocked her plan off kilter, and hopefully she wouldn't be as powerful without the witches to back her up but she still had an army of innocents to place between herself and them.

Hopefully they'd stand a chance and not have to harm too many innocent Descendants in the process. Sorcha wasn't going to like the odds, but they didn't have a choice.

"Where's Sorcha?" Katherine asked.

"Sleeping," Samson said. "Why are you here?"

"Ian kicked me out," Katherine said with a shrug. "Apparently he doesn't think it's safe for me to be on Atlantis in case the monsters aren't held back, but he has to be there in case the monsters aren't held back," she said bitterly.

"So he wants you with us?" Beltar asked in surprise.

"No," Thorn said. "He wants her locked up in the apartment that you have in the city with a guard."

"Who the hell is volunteering for that duty? Miss all the action," Laric scoffed.

"He ordered Felix to do it," Thorn explained.

Felix grumped as if he wasn't surprised, but he didn't like the idea. He was a fighter, they all were, but he was the least capable. It didn't mean he couldn't and wouldn't kick ass, and he was capable of protecting Katherine, it just meant he was the likely choice to stay back. Felix knew it too.

"I want Sorcha to stay with you as well," Samson said.

"You really think she'll agree to that?" Laric asked.

Samson hissed and glared at Laric. "No," he frowned, but he was going to do what he could to convince her.

"The plan is set. As soon as the sun sets, meet us at the beach. We'll be following Sparah from there. She thinks she'll be able to sense her sister and find her quickly. The army will march behind us except for a few left to guard the prison and mostly to keep the humans out," Thorn explained.

"My pack will be there to assist in battle," Patrick said.

"You'll all do everything possible not to harm the Descendants," Katherine reminded.

"Obviously," Tray and Patrick said in unison and Beltar nodded. "As Ian has ordered."

All the supernaturals perked up a second later and Dallas took off at a fast pace.

Samson had smelled it too, the little Descendant girl who'd helped them, Beth. She had his blood in her system so he'd known she was approaching before he even smelled her. "She's safe, she helped us and is probably trying to figure out how to stay out of the path of destruction," Samson explained as everyone looked after Dallas in confusion.

When he came back, he was dragging Beth by the hand with a goofy smile on his face. She looked like she'd been wandering around since they last saw her at the witch's house.

"Do you need protection from Elantra?" Beltar asked.

"Maybe, but actually I'm here to make sure you don't fail, and I save as many of my family members as possible. I have nothing without my clan," she said, looking around nervously at the gathered werewolves and vampires.

"Great, come spend the day at the apartment with me," Katherine said grabbing the girl's hand and pulling her away from Dallas.

"I'll come too, for protection," Dallas said with a grin. The twins frowned with mouths open, no doubt about to offer the same thing.

"I'll get Sorcha and meet you there," Samson said and ducked back into the bunker. When he got to his room, he was surprised to see Sorcha sitting up on his bed, awake and angry.

"You're not sending me away."

He sighed heavily. "Sorcha, you know I just want you to be safe."

"And I want to make sure my sister is unharmed, Samson. Don't ask this of me. Give me the tools to help if you're worried."

"I'm fucking terrified," he admitted and sunk to the floor at her feet. "I can't lose you, Sorcha."

"And I can't live with myself knowing I didn't do all I could to save them, Samson."

He didn't understand that kind of loyalty, had never felt it toward anyone, not even the vampires in this coven. But he understood that he couldn't stand in her way on this. "Fine, but you'll have weapons on top of weapons strapped to your body."

"Perfect," she said and grabbed Samson's face, laying a kiss on his lips. "Now come to bed, I'm lonely without my big, soft vampire."

He snorted, "Nothing about me is soft and I'll prove it as soon as I tell the others that you're staying here today."

"Thank you for trusting me, Samson."

"It's not about trusting you, Sorcha. It's about dying inside at the thought of losing you." He hurried out of the room.

Twenty-Two

SPARAH LET her head break the surface of the water at the exact moment the sun sunk below the horizon. She immediately felt the magic shift and the spells break. They pulled at her, asking for her to fix them, but she had to let them go for this. She felt the moon rip from her the werewolf magic to distribute to the werewolves and she felt the tie to Atlantis sever.

It hurt and she cringed but took the pain as payment for the magic.

The monsters vibrated with excitement under the pyramid, their anticipation of release was palpable in the air around her.

She sent out a prayer to the first mother as she set the spell that would hold the world safe from the monsters of Atlantis. She prayed that the prison bars Maeve had made with her bones would hold through the night. "Please hold them steady, Maeve, for just one night I bind the moon to you, come up and feel it's power, drink it in and use it to fortify your bars."

Sparah lifted one hand to the moon and one down toward Atlantis, using her body as a conduit for the magic. Then she pulled—with all her might she pulled her hand up—lifting the city of Atlantis back above the waterline.

All around her the water simmered and bubbled, shifted, and parted for the rise of the great city. It wasn't long before she felt it right beneath her and she continued to pull. She pulled and pulled, feeling her feet in the water touching the tops of trees, and off in the distance the rise of the pyramid already showed.

Above her head a helicopter circled. "Damn nosy humans," she muttered. She had asked Katherine what to expect as a human reaction and this was something she mentioned. News crews Katherine had warned.

Sparah didn't stop until her feet rested on the beach of Atlantis once more. She was surrounded by its vampire inhabitants, all ready for battle. With the monsters, the humans, or with Elantra, whatever was needed.

Nobody breathed for a moment, it was like the entire city was holding its breath and waiting to see what would happen. Would the ground open beneath their feet and explode in escaping monsters? Would the city sink again immediately, unable to hold itself above the water?

A minute passed and then two, the ground held steady and a great roar of disappointment rose from the prison below the pyramid. The monsters knew something had changed, but they were still stuck.

"You did it," Ian said with a sigh of relief as they stared up at the night sky.

"Let's not let it be for naught," she said, and they started to walk across the island and onto the beach of Miami, now a sandy strip of land with a mere trickling stream of ocean cut through to mark the border separating it from Atlantis.

Across the stream stood the coven of vampires from Miami, a pack of werewolves, and two determined Descendants.

"Katherine?" Ian asked Beltar as they stepped across the stream.

"Safe in the apartment. Felix is on guard. She isn't happy but she also agrees she isn't capable of fighting."

He nodded. "The humans?"

"Freaking the fuck out," Laric said with a laugh. "They probably think it's the end of the world. Hopefully they hide out in their homes until it's over and then they convince themselves it never really happened."

"I'm sure the government will step in and cover it up like they do with alien visitors," Patrick offered. "Although it does mean they'll also be trying to get down to Atlantis and check out what's really going on, maybe send down a few probes then bombs."

"No worries there, the spell keeps out anyone uninvited. They can't find it, can't sense it, and certainly can't hit it with a bomb," Ian laughed.

"Great, just another crazy Florida story in the making," Sorcha said.

"Let's just hope that's our biggest worry after tonight," Sparah said. She met Sorcha's eyes and nodded. The woman was dressed for battle in leather leggings and tight shirt, blades strapped at her thighs and swords behind her back. Her red hair was up in a twist and her face was determined. Sparah was glad to see the Descendant ready to fight and she hoped Sorcha would be able to save her sister. She also hoped that Sorcha's sister would be able to accept that Sorcha was deeply in love with a vampire when this was all over. The heartbreak of lost sisterhood, because of love and duty, is something she wouldn't wish on anyone.

"Ready?" Ian asked her, breaking her out of her thoughts.

"Follow me," Sparah said. She led the group along the beach. She was following instinct, hoping that she wasn't wrong. As soon as she'd stepped onto the solid land of the Florida beach she'd felt a pull, the draw of strong magic dragging her forward.

Human citizens stood on the sidelines watching them go with open mouths. A line of Atlantean guards were standing facing them with fierce looks that dared anyone to try them. Yet they stood just out of the way, watching and curious like they hadn't a thought for their own safety in the face of obvious danger.

Lights kept flashing among them. "What the hell?" Sparah grumbled.

"They are taking photographs, pictures," Beltar explained.

"Idiots should be hiding and hoping they see the sun rise," Samson said.

"Self-preservation in humans is often beat out by curiosity and the false idea of immortality, especially in the young," Laric explained.

Sparah was quickly distracted from the humans' hopeless plight of survival as they went by all the things she'd only seen in visions. It wasn't as surprising to her as it was to many of the vampires following her, because she had purposefully kept up on the changes in the world through her magic and relayed these things to Ian and whoever was heading up from time to time.

Experiencing it in person was something else though. The noise, the sights, and smells. It was all so much to take in. She had to keep refocusing on the magic she was following.

Knowing that she'd never be a part of this world again made it easier to ignore. Either she'd be dead after tonight or she'd be heading back down with Atlantis. It wasn't her fate to be a part of the world above the waterline. She was as okay with that as she could be. She liked her little magical place, it was comfortable, if a bit lonely at times and she knew she was keeping innocents safe. She'd never put her discomfort above that.

"That looks like a wolf scratch," a werewolf came up beside her and said, pulling her out of her thoughts.

Sparah gasped and touched the side of her head where she was missing an ear. She usually hid the thing, but going into battle had made her decide a tight braid was smart, leaving her ravaged ear open to inspection. "Rude," she snapped and glanced at the wolf man. He was handsome, tall with short brown hair and deep brown eyes. He was muscled and dark skinned. A scar ran down his neck and disappeared beneath his shirt, she was certain it was a werewolf scratch too.

He shrugged. "I figure we might all die tonight so why not ask. My name is Brighton, by the way." He held out a hand and she took it, not breaking her stride as she led the group at a quick pace. They were all able to move at a speed that would have winded humans quickly. Except for the two Descendants. Sorcha and Beth were being carried.

"Sparah," she said with pursed lips.

He didn't take the hint but kept walking near her and smiling like an idiot, this was a deadly mission they were on, why the hell was he so happy?

"So am I right, werewolf scratch?"

"Seriously? I could boil your blood with barely a thought," she snapped.

Next to her Ian coughed to cover a laugh. He knew it was true, but he also knew she wouldn't do it, she wasn't so driven by emotion as that.

"Like I said, we might all die tonight anyway, so I figured why not ask the pretty girl about her scar."

She looked at him and fought back a smile. "If we live, I'll tell you the story," she said, not sure why she would be possessed to make such a promise.

He grinned back wider and let out a little yip as if she'd just promised him the world. He moved back in line with his pack then and Ian leaned over to whisper in her ear.

"You have an admirer?"

"Horny wolves," she said, her cheeks tinting red. "They can smell the wolf on me, that's all. I am only the second female wolf in existence, although I am only half."

"But you're of the original, you're one of a kind."

Sparah touched her missing ear again and her mind was thrown back to a place she didn't want to go.

· · ·

"No!" Elantra had screamed as the first transition had flowed over Sparah.

Sparah was trying her hardest, barely sixteen and just learning her magic, she was trying to force the change to stop. She didn't want to scare her sister, knew how Elantra felt about her stepfather.

"Sister help me," Sparah squealed, not wanting to be a monster in her sister's eyes. She'd looked up to Elantra since she was old enough to focus and this would ruin everything between them.

"I'll help you," Elantra said with a cold look on her face. She stepped forward, hand behind her back.

Sorcha whined as she felt her face start to tingle, it began in her ears and was spreading. She reached up and felt her ear, it was long, pointed and furred. "Make it stop," she pleaded.

"I will, little sister," Elantra promised. She was standing right above Sparah now. Sparah had crumpled to the floor in terror as soon as she'd felt it start. Now she looked up into her sister's face and knew a different fear. The hatred she saw there, the determination and cold unfeeling was something Sparah had never seen directed at her.

"Elantra?" she whispered, about to stand and run, but Elantra lashed out with the knife. Sparah blocked it as it aimed for her head.

The force of the emotion, the betrayal and fear brought the change further, her hand shifted, it was a clawed beastly thing now and as she pushed the blade away from her, the claws slid as if through butter against the side of her own head. Blood gushed from a wound that stunned both girls.

"Now you'll be as ugly on the outside as you are on the inside," Elantra spat. "Good luck finding someone to love such a disgusting beast." She dropped the dagger and walked from the room, offering no help to her bleeding, half changed and confused little sister.

"Sparah?" Ian's voice brought her back to the present.

"I'm fine," she snapped, and he nodded. No one knew what had happened that day. She'd never even brought it up with

Elantra. She'd told her parents she'd freaked out and scratched herself during transition, something her father had been so proud about, had praised and celebrated that his daughter would be like him. Her mother had approved as well, wanting her to help create the line of werewolves to inhabit the earth and protect the innocents. Her father's first born, a son of a human woman, Weston, had already been biting and changing humans, guiding them but without luck for any females successfully turning.

The werewolves would be guardians of the innocent, protectors of the people. It should be a wonderful thing.

Elantra's words had never really left her though. And it was true, she'd never found anyone to love her.

Sparah had always wondered if that response from her parents had been what had originally driven Elantra to seek out her own father and then fall into the hands of the vampire king. Elantra had been young and trying to figure out where she belonged in this quickly changing world.

When Sparah had been fully grown she'd sought out her sister in Atlantis, had taken one look at King Barnabus and fallen head over heels for the strong and powerful vampire.

Her sister had already been his by then of course, had already seen through the glamour and turned against him, one child in her arms, another on the way and hating life.

Sparah couldn't understand how Elantra could hate such wonderful things, family, husband, love, and power.

Sparah hadn't felt an inkling of shame or fear for the Descendants at that point. Hadn't understood what they were going through being held under the control of the Stone. She'd stayed there willingly for years, working as the witch to the king, doing anything he asked of her for so many years. She watched her nephews grow and choose the life of vampires. She'd watched her sister's love for them die at that same time.

And when the last monster was caught and Maeve came to her with the solution, Sparah hadn't hesitated, hadn't thought twice and went running to Elantra with the good news. They would do the right thing, clear the earth of its monster invaders. She felt that her parents would be proud, that she was doing her duty as a werewolf as well, protecting the innocent.

Sorcha had been the one to alert Elantra to the plan, King Barnabus never would have. Sparah now knew that. He was too caught up in the old way, the all encompassing rule of vampire. He couldn't see that he asked too much of the Descendants, couldn't conceive of another way.

Elantra hadn't told Sparah of her own plan that formed after that, but Sparah had known that day as she'd prepared the spell. She'd seen more than one Descendant make their escape and watched for her sister to as well. She stopped none of them, she believed in free will and choices.

A part of her had been happy to see Elantra go, had thought perhaps this would lead to a happy ending for her and King Barnabus. But he'd never seen her as anything more than an occasional willing body.

Sparah truly believed he'd loved Elantra in the only way he'd been capable, it just hadn't been enough. It had been too tainted by power and control. Maybe he realized that at the end, but it was too late by then.

Sparah glanced over at Ian, her nephew and the son of the man she'd loved so deeply. Elantra had gotten everything Sparah had wanted, but her twisted mind couldn't see what kind of life she'd had at her fingertips. How she could have tried to change everything with a few words.

Certainly the vampire king would have listened to Elantra's concerns and changed the way they treated the Descendants. Certainly there could have been a peace that served them all and kept the humans safe. Elantra hadn't even tried, she'd just run away same as she had as a young woman, running from her family because it hadn't been what she'd wanted. A stepfather who was a werewolf and a little sister who was half. She'd run trying to find a place she fit.

Sparah would have found a way. She never would have given up everything like Elantra had.

Her eyes traveled to the two Descendants in their group. One happily cradled in the arms of a vampire, the other being carried by a werewolf. New love blooming around them in a palpable rush.

The Descendants weren't meant to be separate from this world. But they weren't meant to be mindless servants either.

Balance. Everything in life was about balance.

Sorcha stopped just shy of the clearing she'd seen in her vision. She could smell her sister's magic on the other side.

"This is where we battle," Sparah said, and the group vibrated with a new energy.

Twenty-Three

SORCHA WAS SCARED, no way around it. She was terrified of what would happen when they stepped out into that moonlit field. All around her the werewolves were commenting on the feeling of not needing to shift as if it were a breath of fresh air.

It made her feel a little sorry for them. No one should be forced into any action.

The vampires around her were vacillating between awe at the human world they'd stepped into and an eagerness over the coming battle.

Overall, the group had a feeling of resignation, no one relished the idea of harming the Descendants who were enthralled by the Stone and bound to do whatever Elantra told them to do. Killing innocents was something the monsters did and they were all on the same side there, to protect humans from monsters.

"Ready your weapons," Ian called out and stepped through to the clearing with Sparah by his side.

Their army was a step behind. Ian and Sparah stopped walking when there was enough room for the entire group to be out in the clearing.

A cackle rose up around them and Elantra stepped through

the other side. She was dressed in a long black robe, her face streaked with blood, and she was vibrating with magic.

"Shit," Sorcha whispered, terrified at the sight.

"Sacrifices have already been made, sister. How many more will die before you step aside and give me what I want, what I deserve? My vengeance will be appeased!" Elantra shouted and raised her hand.

From behind her stepped the Descendants. They all carried weapons. A mindless army willing to be slaughtered. Sorcha's eyes sought out her sister and found Julie standing near Elantra, she was bleeding from a wound on her neck and that image burned through Sorcha, rage nearly overtook her. She stepped forward, ready to dole out punishment to the witch bitch.

Samson grabbed her arm and pulled her back to position forcefully. "Wait, Sorcha, think. We won't win this battle with rage; we have to use our heads."

"Fuck that, I'm pissed," she snarled but she didn't pull away, she knew he was right, she needed to keep her head or she would do more harm than good.

"As you should be, but don't let emotion rule you, Sorcha. Don't you see that's what Elantra did. Years and years of emotions have ruled in her, spoiled, and rotted inside her. There is nothing in her head aside from it and that is why she can be so cruel. You are not like that and whatever you do will live within you forever, be smart."

She took a breath and shrugged off his arm.

"Will you fight me one on one, sister?" Sparah asked.

"It isn't just your head I'm after. Death to all bloodsuckers and any who stand with them!" That was the battle cry.

Elantra's army rushed forward, and the werewolves swarmed forward around Sorcha, most still in human form but a few had shifted. They were the first line of defense. Their job was to detain and incapacitate as many Descendants as possible. Spilling as little blood as they could so as not to risk whipping the vampires into any type of frenzy.

Sorcha saw it go wrong immediately. A wicked laugh filled the clearing as the first yip and howl of pain erupted from a werewolf.

"Silver weapons," Ian hissed. "Vampires get between, we protect those who fight with us," Ian ordered, and the vampires rushed forward.

Sparah was lost in the frenzy now, too, and Ian joined his men.

Sorcha stood beside Beth, and Samson gave her a quick kiss before rushing in. Leaving her with a demand to not die. They'd said their tentative goodbyes just before sunset, not with words but with their bodies. Both desperate to make as many memories as possible in case it was their last chance. Now no words were needed, they loved each other and they wanted to see what they could make together when this was over.

First they had to make it through tonight.

"How do we help?" Beth asked, looking around at the clash of fangs, claws and weapons.

Magic prickled across Sorcha's skin as something exploded on the other side of the clearing. Sorcha couldn't see what it was, but she had a feeling Elantra was protecting herself with the deadly weapons.

"Follow me," Sorcha said.

Beth didn't question it, just ran after her as Sorcha slipped back into the trees and made her way around the clearing, trying to stick to shadows.

"Bitch." The word was sneered out of the mouth of Chase, a Descendant who lived to lick Julie's boots and really got on Sorcha's nerves.

"Move, Chase. I will not hesitate to bring you down."

"You chose the enemy, which makes you one of them," he sneered.

"Fuck you," Sorcha said and stepped forward, blade in hand.

Chase laughed and drew his own blade. He swiped it at her,

and she blocked it easily. He'd never been better than her in a fight, but the dead look in his eyes frightened her. He would be putting everything he had into this and she wondered if one of them wouldn't make it out alive.

"I don't relish the idea of killing you, Chase. Stand down, snap out of this," Sorcha begged.

"You were always trouble, Sorcha. Your sister had to save you from yourself, and you still chose the monsters over your own kind. Betrayer, whore and—"

His words were cut off by Sorcha's blade swiping him across the arm that held his own knife. It wouldn't kill him, but it did shut him up for a second and make him use his non-dominant hand. She was buying time, hoping the whole ordeal might end before she was forced to do something she couldn't take back.

"Bitch," he screamed and jumped forward. Knife out, he nearly hit her she was so surprised by the vehemence and the non-reaction to the hit he'd just taken. As if his pain sensors had been shut off.

Her mind floated to the blood on her sister and the way she'd stood as if she were fine. "Shit, Elantra has told them not to feel pain," Sorcha said as she dodged his second thrust.

"Fuck, that's not good," Beth said.

The third time Chase came for her she had no choice but to react, she swiped to block, and he feinted the other way. His calculations were a mistake though, leaving him open to her thrusting blade and she ran him through the belly because anything other than a death blow was not going to stop him and she couldn't waste any more time fighting with him. She had to save her sister. She had to stop Elantra before all of the Descendants were killed.

He gurgled and scowled, then slumped as she drew the blade back and his blood poured out.

"Shit, sorry, but that was mostly your fault," Sorcha said, then hurried away as he grunted and tried to stand.

Beth was still following and Sorcha wondered if the woman despised her now for killing Chase. Sorcha wondered if she despised herself.

She had to push those thoughts away. This was about saving the masses; Chase had been an unfortunate bystander. Hopefully he'd be the only one to fall tonight, aside from Elantra.

A howl of despair ripped across the night, and she knew that was already not true. No doubt that was the pain of loss the pack felt when one of their own fell. Some brave werewolf had given his life for this fight and that knowledge spurred her on. This was about so much more than the individual and sacrifices came with a fight between right and wrong.

She wouldn't call it good and evil, no one was all one or the other, but there was right and wrong in every choice, every decision.

She hurried her steps, making it around the rest of the way without incident. Now she stood on the other side of the battle. She crept forward, Beth right behind and they peeked out into the clearing.

Elantra's back was to them. Her hands were moving in quick motions, no doubt she was spelling. Beyond her the fight raged with a fury that was shocking. The clearing would run red by morning and that knowledge hurt. Sorcha saw more than one werewolf in wolf form with a Descendant pinned beneath their paws thrashing around but alive. But that took the werewolf out of the battle and made them vulnerable to attack because they couldn't kill the Descendant and they couldn't let it go.

Would it all come down to numbers, who had more people?

Sorcha wasn't sure who would win that, looking around it felt evenly matched.

Sorcha watched Sparah step through the battle, pushing a Descendant aside who was locked in the arms of a vampire who was just trying to hold on and not let the poor woman go. It was a relief to see that everyone was trying to use non-lethal techniques here, but she knew it couldn't last forever. More than one body was lifeless on the ground, and she shuddered, trying not to look and wonder who had fallen and why.

"Stop this," Sparah demanded of her sister.

"Not until I have their heads, and yours, betrayer," Elantra said.

The words hit Sorcha, the same ones Chase had spoken. Was this the fate that awaited her and Julie? Opposite sides of a battlefield because one of them had chosen love and the other had chosen an antiquated duty that led to misplaced vengeance.

Elantra lifted a hand to throw a spell. Sparah raised both hands and glowing magic bounced off harmlessly to the trees.

"You hate me because I am stronger," Sparah spat. "You hate me because I am the daughter of two great powerful species, and you are the daughter of only one. You hate me because mother married my father and they raised me with love, your father was a side piece, a thrown away night. You hate me because I was strong enough to choose the greater good over my own suffering and you ran scared from the best thing you could have ever had."

"Ha!" Elantra sneered. "Best thing? He was a beast, a monster and he used me, took from me. My body, my blood, my children. None of it belonged to me anymore. You are a monster, your father was a monster, a murderer just like them."

The two sisters stepped closer and the air crackled. Both lifting their hands to throw spells that would likely kill.

Sorcha was so entranced by the exchange she was caught off guard when the prick of pain lit through her side. Beth was paying more attention thankfully and she swept her own sword in front of Sorcha and caught Julie's blade before it could do more than scratch Sorcha's skin.

"Sister," Julie said with no emotion as she was pushed back from the force of Beth's blade. "You have to die. You betrayed us all."

"Julie, no. Don't make me do this," Sorcha said, one hand

pressing on the bleeding scratch. It stung but it wasn't deep. "I don't want to hurt you, and you don't really want to hurt me."

"You left us. You chose them. You fucked a fucking vampire. How could you let a monster between your thighs like a whore?"

Sorcha tried not to be hurt by her sister's words. She knew they weren't really Julie's, and yet she also knew that her sister probably really would think that exact thing. She'd just never say it. She'd only look at Sorcha with disappointment and shake her head.

"They aren't what you think they are," Sorcha pleaded.

"She is not going to listen to reason," Beth reminded. "We have to detain her."

"You won't harm her," Sorcha hissed.

"I also won't let her hurt us," Beth snapped.

Dallas appeared then, his shirt was torn, his hair was a mess, and he had a grin on his face when he looked at Beth. "Hey, lost you for a minute back there," he said, a little breathless.

"Can you hold her?" Sorcha asked, motioning to Julie.

"I can certainly try," Dallas said with uncharacteristic seriousness.

"Julie," Sorcha snapped and brandished her sword, hoping to distract her sister.

It worked, Julie held up her own weapon and they thrust at each other, blocking and attacking. They were a good match for a fight, always had been. But Sorcha wasn't really trying to win, just distract, so she let Julie push her back, stepping closer and closer to the clearing as Dallas circled.

Julie was completely focused on killing Sorcha and she tried not to let that hurt. She stepped back again and was fully in the clearing now, the sounds of battle roared behind her. Dallas wrapped his muscular arms around Julie, squeezing until she dropped her weapon then he winked at Sorcha.

"I can hold her all day, no big deal," he said with confidence.

"Sorcha!" Beth screamed then.

But it was too late, she felt a hand grip her hair and pull her around. She was suddenly pressed against Elantra's body and facing Sparah, Ian, and Samson, who looked ready to kill. Sparah was sweating and breathing heavy; Ian and Samson both looked like they were barely winded but they both showed scratches, proof that the battle hadn't been easy. Sorcha didn't want to know if they'd been killing the Descendants.

It wasn't their fault; wasn't her fault she'd had to take Chase's life.

This was all *her* fault, Elantra's. Sorcha kicked back at the witch. She screamed in frustration and fought against the witch, but Elantra's grip only tightened and if Sorcha continued to move she'd rip her own hair right out.

"What now?" Elantra said sweetly. "Going to rip through this innocent as well? This one seems happy to bed down with vampires, so you might want to be careful. Not that you care much about willing, do you?" Elantra sneered.

* * *

Samson was going to lose his mind. When he'd left her at the beginning of the battle, he'd assumed she'd stay back, safe with Beth, guarding each other. Now she was here in front of him wrapped up in the arms of Elantra and she was bleeding.

Who had hurt her?

He wanted to rage and kill everyone around him.

"Steady," Ian whispered just loud enough for him to catch the word.

It did settle him enough to think, but barely.

His gaze assessed Sorcha, she was okay, she was breathing a little heavily, but she wasn't gasping, the blood was not continuing to run which meant it was a minor scratch, not a grave injury. Her face was twisted in pain from the hair hold and she was pissed. Pissed was good, it meant she wasn't afraid.

"You can't win this," Ian said. "Sparah is too powerful."

"If she was so powerful, I'd be dead already. I think it is *you* who can't win," Elantra said with an evil grin. She lifted a hand and blackness pooled there. "Funny thing, power, it can come from all over. Sparah draws from Maeve, the first mother. Did you ever wonder if Maeve was alone? Just some light floating alone in the ether and then poof, started creating shit to keep herself busy?"

"What the hell are you talking about?" Sparah snapped.

"If Maeve is so great then why did she hide from you that she wasn't alone, that when she was creating this life all around there was another, a darker half, balance. Balance is always found in the universe, and I found her," Elantra laughed. "The dark to Maeve's light, the hate to her love. I was embraced by Byleria and I know her pain, the despised sister, the forgotten and alone. We know each other's pain and she feeds me her dark power. So much power!"

Thunder hit at her last word making the entire clearing stand still for a second before the roar of battle continued.

"I know of the sister. I know of the evil that Byleria houses," Sparah admitted. "Maeve told me of her sister's hatred and how she tried to protect the earth from it. She is mother to the monsters we contain in Atlantis."

"It didn't work, good never wins."

Sparah smiled. "That's where you're wrong, Byleria may have slithered in after Maeve gave herself to the spell, but she doesn't own this land, she only owns you. You are a tool, a weapon she wields and this is the last time she'll touch what belongs to us." Sparah's voice had taken on a new tone, something deep and sure and Samson wondered if it was Maeve herself speaking through the witch.

Elantra cried out in frustration and the black power in her hand grew. Samson didn't know what it was, but he was certain it would kill Sorcha if it touched her and all thought to anything else fled his mind.

He leaped across the space to sink his teeth into the offending arm.

Elantra was too fast, the black ball rushed toward him and the look of fear in Sorcha's face had him making a midair turn to fall and roll safely away. Missing Elantra, but also the black spell disappeared harmlessly into the night.

"Stupid vampire, ruled by emotion for this bit of willing flesh," Elantra sneered. She gathered another ball of black in her hand as Samson crouched on the ground debating his next move.

Elantra was facing him now and her grip had loosened in Sorcha's hair. She took the opportunity to drop her body then push back, knocking Elantra off kilter for a moment. Thorn grabbed Elantra from behind, a strong arm going around her neck and the witch smashed the black ball of magic she'd been holding into his face.

Thorn screamed as his face melted. Samson couldn't look, couldn't think about how that had almost been him, could have been Sorcha. He jumped forward, embracing Sorcha in his body and rolling them away from Elantra.

He jumped up and threw Sorcha behind him just in time to see two Descendants flank Elantra with swords drawn.

"Outmatched," Elantra laughed.

Ian and Sparah still stood in front of her, seemingly unfazed by all that had gone on.

"Stop her," Sorcha hissed behind him.

"I can take out one of the guards," Samson whispered back, expecting her to say *hell no* to the suggestion of harming a Descendant.

"Do it, stop this madness," she said.

Samson met the gaze of a werewolf on the other side of Elantra and with an understanding nod they attacked at once, each taking out one of the Descendants there, leaving Elantra open.

"No!" Elantra screamed in annoyance.

The distraction gave Sparah the opening she needed.

Sparah's head had fully transformed into a wolf head, pure white and missing one ear. She moved with lightning speed, her jaws wrapped around Elantra's neck and ravaged the skin. Elantra created another ball of death magic in her hand and slammed it against Sparah but it only sparked and dissipated as Sparah clamped her jaws until there was nothing to hold Elantra's head there.

A scream, an unreal, inhuman scream emerged from the bleeding neck hole and a darkness lifted from it and darted into the sky.

The world stood silent.

Sparah shook her head and it returned to its human form.

"Fuck that was hot," Brighton said with a growl, breaking the silence, his eyes ravishing Sparah.

Samson stood back from the dead Descendant and looked at Sorcha expecting to see rejection and anger, regret... horror and blame, he expected her to hate him.

She rushed to him and threw her body against his, embracing him and kissing him. His heart exploded and he wrapped his arms around her and squeezed as tight as he dared.

"My sister," she said and pushed him away. "Julie?"

"I'm here," Julie said with a snarl, pulling out of Dallas' grip. "What the fuck!" she screamed at no one in particular. "How did that bitch get the Stone?"

Sorcha looked like she was about to cry. "I gave it to her, traded her for a spell to block all memories of Samson. I thought she'd keep it away from the vampires, I didn't know she'd use it against us. I didn't know she was fucking insane or possessed."

"Sister," Julie said quietly and embraced Sorcha. "Why the hell would you risk something like that?"

Sorcha pulled back and looked at Samson. Samson could see the turmoil that burned in her eyes. "He betrayed me," she answered honestly.

Julie gave Samson a death glare.

"But I loved him, which made it hurt all the more," Sorcha admitted.

"Well fuck him," Julie said pulling her in close again as if she were going to shield Sorcha from Samson. "You don't need him."

"It's okay, we worked things out," Sorcha said and pulled herself out of Julie's grip, moving to Samson's side. She took his hand and raised it to her mouth, kissing his fingers. "We are good now and I have my memories back, too."

"We'll talk about it later," Julie said firmly as Descendants started to gather around her. She was quickly taking back her position as leader, checking on her clan and reassuring them, counting up the dead and injured while glaring at any vampire or werewolf that came near.

All around him the world buzzed as vampires and werewolves were checking on their own people as well. It wasn't all good news. Everyone had lost someone in the battle, and it wasn't long before the vampires and werewolves were snarling at the Descendants even though they'd only been mindless pawns and the Descendants were grieving losses as well and glaring at the vicious beasts who'd killed to protect themselves.

Someone dragged a body of a male Descendant to Julie who looked down with disappointment.

Sorcha turned from it and buried her face in Samson's chest. "I had to," she whispered, and his heart ached for her, having had to kill one of her own to save the rest. It was a decision no one should be forced to make. He stroked her back.

"Let me take you back to the bunker where you can rest," he whispered against her hair.

She pulled back and looked up at him with regret on her face.

"I have to help them. There's so much that will need to be done now." She pulled away and looked at her sister, multiple bodies now at her feet as the clan cried and mourned after the battle. "So much needs to be healed."

He wanted to argue, to tell her no, to force her to go back with him, but he knew she was right. She had to help her people and if he tried to stop her it would only drive a wedge between them. So he nodded and said nothing.

A flash of hurt passed over her face before she turned and approached her sister, who was giving orders. They would take the bodies back to the compound for proper and honorable burial.

"We can help carry," Dallas said, volunteering the werewolves.

Julie opened her mouth, an angry set to her face. No doubt about to deny the help, but Sorcha spoke up first. "That would be great, thank you, Dallas."

Beth stepped up too and smiled at Dallas. "You are very kind to offer," she said.

Beth and Sorcha shared a look of understanding. They'd been of their own mind during the fight, had fought against their own clan and it would forever bond them in that trauma.

"Fine," Julie said, "I assume there are vehicles somewhere?"

The rest of the arranging was lost to Samson as Sparah approached Ian who stood beside him looking down at a slim phone. He would have already told Felix and Katherine what had happened.

"The city is flipped, police and military are approaching Atlantis. We need to get back before our guards are forced to engage," Ian said. "I have the Stone; I am taking it back to Atlantis where it will be safe."

"Fuck that," Julie said, suddenly paying attention to them. "We will not have that thing in the hands of vampires again."

"After this massacre you really think the vampires are the danger?" Ian scoffed.

"I lost more people here than anyone," Julie said with a hiccup of emotion.

"We all lost, and any is too much. This was the work of a psychotic witch, not a vampire I remind you, and it is because you "kept it safe" that it occurred," Ian reminded.

"It won't happen again," Julie gritted.

"You're right, it won't," Sparah said. "I am not allowing anyone else to take it and I will fight you on that," Sparah said, glaring at Julie, then Ian. "Not a vampire. Me."

Sorcha put a hand on Julie's shoulder. "Let Sparah have it, sister, she only wants to protect everyone. I promise."

"Fine. Let's get out of here," Julie snapped and turned away, ordering her remaining clan to pick up the bodies and head to where the werewolves would meet them with cars.

Ian shouted for the vampires to get back to Atlantis and they moved.

Samson stood locked in place staring at Sorcha who stood stiff, staring at him. Only a couple feet lay between them but it felt like an impossible distance.

"I have to go," she said.

"I know."

She opened her mouth to say something more but shut it again and turned, hurrying to her sister's side.

A hand landed on Samson's shoulder and he turned to see Laric there. "You're just going to let her go?"

"What choice do I have?"

"We always have choices, Samson. Fate brought you two together more than once, that can't be a mistake."

He shook off Laric's hand and turned to follow the retreating vampires. His whole existence was a mistake.

Twenty-Four

KATHERINE RAN into Ian's arms as soon as he stepped onto the beach, finally taking a breath of relief. He was safe. She'd stayed far away from the battle, and she was in his arms again.

"You have no idea how worried I was," he whispered against her hair.

"For me?" she laughed. "I was stuck in a room with Felix complaining about missing all the action, you were the one in danger!" She kissed him, holding his face between her hands and looking into his eyes. "Did everything turn out okay?" She knew it wasn't good, no way death could ever be good, but she needed to know things hadn't turned for the worst.

"Well enough. We lost two good men, sacrificed to the protection of all," he said sadly. "We haven't had to deal with a death of one of our own in a long time, not since my father," he said with a shudder.

"And your brother," she pointed out.

"That was different," he said with a frown. "Jovi had left us a long time ago."

Katherine held him tighter, wishing she could take the pain

away. She kissed him again, deep and needy. She knew how to distract his mind.

"We need to wrap up this spectacle," Saul said beside them, making her break the kiss and her cheeks redden a bit. She'd almost forgotten they weren't alone.

Ian grunted and lifted his head. They were currently standing on Atlantis soil, a line of vampires assembled at the border and on the other side was a growing crowd of humans being pushed back by people in uniforms with weapons.

"This is going to be all over the news worldwide," Katherine said. "What's the plan there? Ignore and hope it becomes an unsolved mystery? I think I have been photographed too. That's going to raise some questions about my supposed death."

"Ignoring sounds good," Ian said.

"Katherine!" A scream came through the crowd and Katherine knew it immediately.

"Jenny!" Katherine called back and tried to step forward but Ian grabbed her arm, holding her back.

"What the hell do you think you're doing?" Ian snarled.

"It's my friend, Jenny. I worked with her at the museum. She must have seen me on the news. I told you I was photographed. She thought I was killed that night by Norgis."

"And you think talking to her now is a good idea?" Ian asked with a shake of his head.

"It's too late to deny I'm alive," she said back and they both turned to see Jenny yelling at a couple of vampire guards blocking her path.

The vampires turned and looked pleadingly at Ian, unsure how to handle the human's aggression.

"She's tenacious. She's not going to just go away, Ian."

"Let her by," Ian ordered the vampires and they moved so she could rush across the sand. Ian let go of Katherine's arm and she met her friend halfway and they embraced.

"You have so much to explain," Jenny said with a laugh and tears running down her face. "It's really you? You aren't dead?"

"It's really me, alive and well," Katherine said. "I don't think I can explain though."

"It's you, isn't it? You're the anonymous person whose been sending us those artifacts in such amazing condition?"

Katherine nodded.

"You're okay? We had a funeral for you even though there wasn't a body. Last month we finally said goodbye with no leads."

"I'm sorry it had to be like that, Jenny."

Jenny's eyes looked over Katherine's shoulder and she knew Ian was standing there.

"I am so happy now, Jenny. This is Ian. I was hurt that night but thanks to him, I survived."

"And he stole you away somewhere," Jenny accused.

"No, I assure you I was willing and I'm happy."

"I would never harm or let harm befall Katherine," Ian assured Jenny.

Jenny leaned close and stared into Katherine's eyes. "Blink twice if you're being held against you will."

Katherine just laughed and Jenny eyed Ian some more.

"Well, you certainly found yourself a sexy savior," Jenny said. "I bet you stopped missing that dusty old fiancé, huh?"

"Definitely," Katherine agreed.

The two women chatted for a while, Jenny wanting to know everything and Katherine being purposefully vague but promising to continue sending things in if Jenny promised not to tell anyone it was coming from Katherine.

"The military are too close," Ian said, stopping their gossip about the other people at work.

"Go on home, Jenny. I'll be in touch somehow."

"I am so glad to see you happy," Jenny said a little tearful as she embraced Katherine one last time then ran off, passing through the vampire guard line without hesitation.

"Sparah, take us down," Ian said.

"Can't until the sun rises. It's far too dangerous for me to take my moon magic before then. The werewolves would shift into wolf form suddenly wherever they are with no preparation for anyone's safety," Sparah explained.

Ian frowned at her, then back at the crowd. "Then can you at least do something about all this?" He waved a hand at the people.

Sparah looked thoughtful, then her eyes widened and she smiled. "I don't think I need to," she said, and from somewhere behind the crowd a hum started up. It rose and rose until it was ear piercing and laced with so much magic it made Ian cringe.

Katherine shivered, not particularly sensitive to magic, but it was affecting even her.

Soon the crowd started to disperse in a confused, wandering sort of way. The human citizens, the military, and the police. News crews and even the helicopters circling above left. Until only a group of witches stood, casting the magic.

One witch stepped forward, not crossing the line to Atlantis but close enough to talk. "We don't want this out any more than you do. That spell is one to fog and forget, they'll have vague memories but nothing solid enough and with a few well-placed suggestions, the videos and pictures will be erased as well. We can't stop what already went out, but it can probably be brushed off as some kind of publicity stunt by a movie studio."

"That's a relief," Katherine said but hoped Jenny would be immune, she wanted her friend to know she was alive and happy.

"Thank you," Ian said, a little wary.

"We picked the wrong side, and we want to make up for it," she said with a shrug and then met Sparah's gaze. "We will properly dispose of your sister's body; she will know rest."

"Thank you," Sparah said.

"We found the stones holding souls of witches." She held one out to Sparah. "And this."

Sparah took it with a gasp, tears sliding down her cheeks.

"Thank you," she said and pocketed the stone before anyone else could get a close look.

"A few of us will stay here until the sinking, vigilant for anyone wandering in," the witch explained.

"We appreciate the help," Ian said.

"And we appreciate not having monsters roaming about," the witch said with a laugh and then turned to walk away, calling out orders to her coven.

Katherine touched Ian's arm, gaining his attention. He smiled down at her then picked her up, making her squeal as he flung her into his arms.

"My men can take care of things for the next couple of hours, I want to celebrate success with my wife under me," he growled.

"My insatiable beast," she whispered and kissed his neck making him groan.

Hours later Katherine was on the beach with Sparah. The vampires were all hiding out in case something didn't go quite right, but Katherine wanted to watch the sinking. There were a couple witches still on the beach as promised and no sign of any humans about.

Sparah was mumbling, her arms spread wide and her head thrown back. One hand held the black stone that the witch had given her and as she mumbled it started to glow, then a white light shot out of it and disappeared into the sky.

Katherine felt a shudder under her feet like a small earthquake as the horizon began to brighten. Then they began to sink. Inexplicably they moved down, and the water moved up around them, flowing against an invisible barrier. Down and down they went until the water was completely enveloping them and then still further down. It became dark as they sank further from the surface and Katherine had one moment of claustrophobia before Sparah stopped her mumbling, flicked her wrist in an intricate motion and the fake sky lit up as if it were the dawning morning.

"Wow," Katherine said when Sparah finally slumped.

"Yeah, it's quite the spell."

"You're amazing, Sparah."

"I'm something," she said with a half-smile and started to slowly walk away as vampires emerged to celebrate the success.

Ian found Katherine quickly, embracing her and smiling. But Katherine couldn't stop watching Sparah who walked alone and slowly back to the pyramid. She was likely mourning the loss of her sister and the other vampires. Maybe she was exhausted from the spelling, but it was something else too, something that tugged at Katherine's heart.

"Do you think we could find Sparah a boyfriend?" she asked Ian.

He laughed. "Sparah hasn't been interested in anyone since my father died."

"Exactly, she has to be lonely."

He looked thoughtful and kissed the top of her head. "You want to be a matchmaker now?"

"I just want to thank her for all she's sacrificed. She deserves happiness too."

"She does," he agreed. "But sometimes you love so deeply that there is no room for anything else once they're gone. If I lost you, I would never take another lover," Ian said, and Katherine melted against him.

He always knew exactly what to say to make her heart burst. She wrapped her arms around his neck and pulled him down for a deep kiss. She would never get tired of this vampire. She couldn't believe how happy she'd been since accepting him and this life. A romance novel come true.

* * *

Sorcha sat in the back of a car and stared out the window. She was in shock, she decided. She'd murdered a clanmate, basically ordered Samson to murder another. Then she'd left Samson standing in the middle of a clearing without any promises of ever seeing him again.

What the hell was wrong with her? Why hadn't she told him she'd be back? Why hadn't she told him to come for her? Why hadn't she promised to never forget him?

Her eyes drifted to the front seat where Julie sat, tears silently streaming down her face still.

That was why. She'd done that to her sister, and she needed to fix it. She didn't deserve the love and comfort of Samson. It was her selfish irresponsibility that had allowed this horror to happen.

They returned to the Florida compound with the morning sun brightening the sky. It was destroyed, way more than just from what had gone down with Jovi. This was intentional destruction that Elantra had dealt out to make sure they couldn't use the place.

Julie burst into a new round of tears at the sight.

"She ordered us to break and burn so many things," Julie said quietly. "And we just did it."

"It wasn't you," Sorcha reminded.

"She came to the house and I was happy to meet her. I thought she was going to help fix the wards even though the witch coven we'd contacted had told us no. I invited her in, and she looked around then, all my will left me," Julie said with a shiver.

"I am so sorry for giving her the Stone."

Julie looked at her with a sad expression. "I don't blame you. A love like that vampire has for you would be impossible to forget. We are supposed to trust that the witches want the same thing as us. Betrayal by one never would have crossed my mind either."

Julie walked into the house, leaving Sorcha stunned by her words. She'd seen the love in Samson's eyes, and she hadn't called him a dirty blood sucker?

A spark of hope, of maybe someday, ran through Sorcha as she followed her sister into the house. Before she could think about that, she needed to fix this, her people needed her and she'd be here for them.

Would Samson be waiting for her when she was done?

Twenty-Five

THREE MONTHS LATER, Sorcha stood in her sister's office waiting to be yelled at. She'd confessed everything to her about the night of the battle months ago but Julie hadn't reacted at all at the time. Sorcha had been waiting for the anger and hurt to come. Blood was on her hands, she knew it. She deserved punishment.

They'd all been working hard at rebuilding and the witches had shown up to offer a new protection spell even. Surprisingly, Julie had turned them down, saying that she no longer thought it necessary, partially because every vampire in the area apparently knew where to find them anyway.

That was something else Sorcha felt responsible for.

"You're not happy," Julie said from behind her desk. More like accused, really. Her eyes were narrowed, and her lips were pursed.

"What the hell do I have to be happy about?" Sorcha demanded.

"You are alive. I am alive."

"Not everyone is," Sorcha whispered and looked away from her sister.

"No, not everyone is. But you are and I want you to be happy about it."

Sorcha scoffed.

"Sorcha, I want you to leave."

"What?" Sorcha gasped and snapped her gaze back to Julie. "Are you kicking me out?" Not that it would surprise her, she didn't deserve to be here among them, gaining any kind of comfort from the familiarity of their presence.

"Yes."

Sorcha nodded. "I'll pack my things and be gone today."

Julie shook her head. "I am not kicking you out because I don't want you here, Sorcha. I am kicking you out because your fucking moping is driving me nuts. Pining after that damn vampire."

Sorcha's cheeks flamed, it was true, she dreamed of him nightly. Woke up craving him and thought about him at least once every fifteen minutes throughout the day. She'd been distracted but had hoped no one else was noticing.

"I'm sorry I—"

Julie held up a hand cutting her off. "I don't get it. I won't pretend to. He's a vampire." Julie shivered. "But you love him."

Sorcha lowered her eyes and bit her lip.

"He saved your life more than once. You have saved his. Despite my best intentions, I can't keep believing he's a no good, soulless monster."

Sorcha looked up hesitantly. Julie was looking out the window now.

"I don't know, maybe monsters aren't connected to appetite, maybe they're made that way from shitty lives." She turned back to Sorcha. "I want you to go find him and figure it out. If you can have a happy life with him, then that's what I want for you, Sorcha. You're my sister and I never wanted to make you suffer. I just wanted to keep you safe."

Tears burned Sorcha's eyes.

"Julie, I don't want to leave you. There's still so much to do to rebuild here."

Julie waved a hand, her own eyes glistening with unshed tears. "We can do this without you. But if you decide you want to come back, if he ever hurts you or you just don't want him anymore. You come back or call me and I will come get you. No vampire will keep me from my sister in need," Julie said with so much emotion Sorcha could no longer hold back the tears.

Julie stood up and Sorcha rushed around the desk to embrace her. They'd never been close. Julie so focused on her role as leader and Sorcha always a bit of a rebel. Knowing that her sister valued her happiness over her own prejudice, knowing that her sister really did forgive her. It was overwhelming.

Julie pulled back and wiped the tears from Sorcha's cheeks. "Go, I have a feeling he's close."

Sorcha nodded. She could feel it too. Samson had been just outside the compound walls since she'd arrived here. Never approaching, never seeking her out, but there all the same, like a promise of salvation in the depression that she'd embraced.

She didn't wait any longer. She ran to her room and packed a small bag then rushed from the compound. It was still daylight so she would have to go to him.

He would know she was coming, and it sent a little thrill through her.

She rushed into an empty house. It wasn't old and abandoned, likely someone's vacation home sitting unused.

"Samson," she called as she searched for the basement door.

"Sorcha," he roared back, and she found the door at the end of a hallway. She rushed through it and down into his arms.

No more words were necessary. She wrapped her legs around him and kissed him deeply, moving her tongue into his mouth and swallowing his groans.

His hands gripped her ass and pressed her firmly against his hardening erection.

She ripped desperately at his clothes and moved her mouth to his neck where she bit down with her blunt teeth until she tasted the trickle of blood and felt him shudder with pleasure. She licked the blood and pulled back enough to offer her own neck to him.

He whispered *fuck* before dipping his head and slipping his fangs into her skin. It was her turn to shudder with the pleasure as he drew softly on the wound, always so careful with her.

He pulled back and their mouths clashed again, sharing the taste of each other in a delicious and heady mix. He turned and laid her on the bed, breaking the kiss long enough to shed his clothing. She wiggled out of her own and then he was there, on top of her and trailing kisses down her body. He licked and nipped at her breasts and traveled back up to bite her earlobe gently.

"I can't wait," he apologized, then he was moving her legs, spreading them wide and shoving in with a forceful stroke.

She arched her back and cried out as her body accepted him, more than ready for him.

Their lovemaking was fast and fierce. Sweat dripped from them both as they moved together to a release that came with a force that left them both panting and shivering with aftershocks.

When they had settled, Sorcha ran a hand over his cheek and smiled into his eyes. "I love you, Samson, and I don't know what kind of life we can have together or for how long. But I want it all for as long as I can."

"I don't deserve you," he whispered and kissed the tip of her nose. "But I can't let you go. Let me take you to Atlantis, let me give you an eternity of showing you how much I love you."

She nodded because she had no words to describe the joy that his words brought her.

"You hate Atlantis," she whispered.

"I would hate anywhere that didn't have you in it."

• • •

Samson wasn't sure what to expect when they arrived in Atlantis. After the initial decision it had taken a week of preparation for Sorcha to feel ready. She'd gone back and told her sister what she was doing and promised to stay in touch. Then she'd figured out how to pack and waterproof a few essentials that ended up being four large bags.

He told Beltar and his coven, all of whom were happy for him and excited to see how long he could stand to be locked on an island.

He had no fears over it, he'd live in a jail cell if it was with Sorcha. She was all he needed. The months he'd spent stalking her outside the compound had been hell. He refused to pressure her, but he couldn't make himself leave. So he'd sat outside the walls and watched, hoping to catch a glimpse of her, which he had a few times.

He had seen Julie often and she had almost approached him once, stared at him from a close distance and frowned.

Sorcha told him that Julie had accepted their relationship. But he doubted it was without reservations. He didn't care, he would prove to everyone that he deserved Sorcha, it was his life's mission and it had started with figuring out how to take blood from a less than willing victim without killing or fucking. He'd hated it, but he'd had to eat while he waited for her and each time he did it now he didn't hate himself. Because of her he knew he wasn't a monster for needing to eat and he didn't harm them in any way, aside from a little loss of blood which he told them to forget about.

He confessed it all to Sorcha and she'd just smiled at him and assured him that she understood. But that he was to never do that again if she was anywhere within a night's traveling distance or she would punch out one of his fangs.

The violence with which she loved him was astounding and he hoped it never ended.

When he dragged Sorcha and her many things up onto the

beach of Atlantis ready to start their lives together, Sparah was there waiting to greet them.

"You saw us coming?" he asked.

"No," she said with a frown and walked away.

"That was weird, she looked expectant," Sorcha pointed out.

"Maybe she's expecting someone else," he whispered.

They were only halfway up the path when Katherine came running out with a squeal and embraced Sorcha.

"Oh my god! I am so happy you're here. I am so excited to not be the only Descendant down here anymore." She leaned in and whispered conspiratorially. "Sparah's been depressed ever since we sank back down so she's been no female company worth having."

"Samson," Ian's voice boomed behind Katherine.

Samson looked up and met the vampire king's eyes. He wasn't sure how welcome he'd be down here, but he hadn't told Sorcha that.

"Ian, my wife and I wish to join the Atlantean colony."

Ian looked thoughtful for a moment, his eyes sweeping down to the bags Samson carried and Sorcha who was giggling with Katherine, then back up to Samson.

"Welcome brother," Ian said and embraced him.

They were given a room in the Pyramid where Katherine and Sorcha could always be close, and Sorcha would feel safe. She was still a little wary of being one of the only two humans there. No matter how many times Samson assured her she was safe, and Katherine agreed that she'd never felt uncomfortable with anyone in Atlantis.

They settled into a routine and Samson enjoyed training with Sorcha. She was strong and skilled and he was filled with pride at his wife's abilities. Reassured over and over again that she was not a weak brittle thing that he was taking advantage of.

She attacked him nightly with as much ferocity as he felt towards her and every time her blunt teeth broke his skin his love and possessiveness flared and built. He knew that all the hell he'd endured was the necessary path to her and he let go of some of his pain because he knew he'd do it a hundred times over to feel her pressed willingly against him, moaning in pleasure as she pierced his skin and lapped up his blood.

Charlotte's voice faded away and eventually never came back to prickle his worry. He couldn't forgive her for what she'd done to him and his mother, but he could let it go. She couldn't touch him now, and that was all that mattered.

Twenty-Six

SPARAH WALKED to the beach daily. She was waiting for him. She'd seen it and although she knew that it wasn't necessarily the future she'd get, it was the one she desperately wanted.

But each day that passed and no one arrived, she was taken deeper and deeper into a dark place she hadn't felt since the day she'd realized that the vampire king would never love her the way she loved him. Not that it had stopped her from trying, from giving him every part of herself for as long as she could.

She'd never been anyone's everything though and that was what she wanted, what she saw on a thin strip of possible future.

Everyone had settled nicely into Atlantis. Sorcha and Katherine were happy to have each other to spend time with when the men were busy with other duties. Sorcha didn't resent their happiness, but it did make her lonely life all the more evident. Before Katherine arrived, no one on the island had a mate and it was just the way of it. Now two very happy couples were among them, and it made more than just herself antsy for something more. The vampires were beginning to ask for leave days and going above under the watchful guidance of Beltar and Laric, to interact and explore.

Sparah predicted many more couples coming to live in Atlantis over time. Perhaps they'd be a bustling city once again rather than a paradise shielded prison.

Today she had dressed in a light blue sarong style dress and left her feet bare so she could dig her toes into the sand. She twirled a finger over the soft pale grains and conjured a few shells with a simple whispered spell.

She stared at their pearly white surface and thought about turning them into necklaces, a gift for the new brides of Atlantis.

The water rustled and she froze, standing up with tense shoulders. Was this it, would it be him?

A blond mohawk appeared first. Beltar dragging a wet dog. Next came a vampire with long brown hair. Prat also dragging a dog. She frowned. It was Lilly and Tray, she recognized them immediately.

Gasping and growling the two werewolves struggled up onto the sand and shook out their fur then transformed into humans and embraced with giggles.

"Wow, that was something else," Lilly said excitedly, and Tray just stared at her, investigating every inch to make sure she was okay.

Beltar and Prat stared at the water.

"Are more coming?" Sparah asked, trying not to sound hopeful but knowing she hadn't hit it when Prat gave her a wink.

"One more, my brother isn't as strong a swimmer."

Just then the water rippled again and a short brown-haired vampire, Trenton popped up dragging a werewolf with deep red fur that was sprinkled through with black, making him look dangerous. His eyes were a bright blue and they looked frightened as he scrambled up the shore. He too, shook off the water then shifted into the most beautiful man she'd ever seen. His human hair was pure black, his eyes so dark brown they could be called black and his skin the color of dark chocolate. Brighton.

"You came," she whispered, then bit her lip, knowing that just because he was here didn't mean her vision of the future was about to come true.

He grinned wide, showing all his teeth and stepped forward, unashamed of his naked body. Not that he had anything to be ashamed of.

"I had to get a second look at the pretty girl who ripped apart a witch in front of me with her bare teeth."

Sparah felt herself blush like a schoolgirl as he approached her and took her hand, lifted it to his lips and kissed her knuckles lightly.

"You came to see me?"

"I couldn't keep you out of my dreams, so I figured it was as close to fate as I was ever going to find."

Sparah had dreamt of him too. The way he'd looked at her like she was pretty while asking about her missing ear. How his eyes had showed pure desire after she'd decapitated her sister. She hadn't been able to get him out of her head even before she'd seen the vision of their future.

He grinned. "And you owe me a story," he reminded as he lightly ran a finger over her scars.

"I saw you too, I had a vision of our future together," she said in a rush. "You will stay here with me, and we will be together in eternal bliss."

She wanted to slap her forehead for the insane admission, he was as likely to run screaming from such a declaration as anything else.

To her surprise and whoops of approval from the others, he pulled her to him and kissed her. His lips were hungry on hers, tasting and nipping, and his tongue demanded entrance. She opened for him and groaned as her lower body pressed against him.

"You two need a room?" Ian's voice brought her out of the kiss, and she pulled back smiling up at the man.

"Yes," she said without looking at Ian.

Brighton growled agreement.

"I insist on knowing who's in my city," Ian said with a half smile. "And why the hell would werewolves make that swim?"

"We wanted to speak with Sparah about breeding," Tray said happily. "Lilly and I want to give it a try. We have the Blood Moonstone so we can prevent her shifting and losing the pregnancy but we're more concerned about what to expect it to be when it comes out."

Sparah had expected that question, but she'd been too distracted by visions of Brighton to think too much on it.

"I'll be happy to take a peek into the future for that," Sparah said, and Lilly smiled brightly at her.

"And you?" Ian asked with a cough to cover his laugh. "What are your intentions here?" he asked Brighton.

Sparah rolled her eyes, he was acting like a father who was interrogating his daughter's prom date.

"I couldn't stop thinking about her so when I knew they were making the trip I had to tag along."

Ian looked at Sparah and raised an eyebrow. "She's capable of kicking you out if she wants to, I suppose. Good luck," he added. "Welcome to Atlantis."

"You'll need to cover your shit," Samson hissed, having followed Ian down to the beach. He'd become quite the right hand man to Ian, replacing Thorn who'd been lost in battle. "There are women here," Samson grunted.

"And men," Tray agreed, looking at Lilly.

They made their way up the trail and Brighton stayed so close to Sparah, she could feel the heat coming off of him.

"I want to touch every part of your body," he whispered as they walked. "I want to run my tongue over the most delicious parts of you and savor every delicate bit."

Her steps faltered as her body trembled with the desire his words built. It had been so long since she'd felt anything even close. Had she ever felt anything even close?

Brighton easily caught her elbow and helped her find her footing. His grin was full of self-satisfaction and his nostrils were flaring.

"You smell like my mate. My wolf has claimed you."

Sparah didn't try to contain the smile of satisfaction on her own face. Something wild and feral inside of her was howling with delight at his words. *Mine.* It growled as she breathed deep the scent of him.

Vampires came forward to greet them and Katherine and Sorcha hurried to embrace and welcome Lilly.

They were taken to the pyramid and given clothes before she welcomed them to her room for a look at the future. As much as Sparah wanted to lock herself in her rooms with Brighton and have no need for clothes for at least a month, she needed to answer Tray and Lilly's question first. So she sat them on her couch and kicked everyone else out.

Brighton growled. "I'll be right outside the door."

She patted his chest and kissed his lips sweetly. "You do that big boy; I'll be with you next."

It seemed to satisfy him, and he leaned against the wall opposite her door. When she shut it, she was sure she heard him whine.

"Okay, so you haven't gotten yourself knocked up yet?" she asked, not wanting to waste any time.

"No," Lilly said. She was gripping Tray's hand and had a worried look on her face. "We just need to know what it will be if we do." She looked at Tray who gave her a reassuring smile. "We will love it no matter what, but we need to be prepared in case it's going to come out furry," she said with a strained laugh.

Sparah nodded. It was a legitimate worry.

"I was born from a witch and the first werewolf."

"But were you furry from birth, sharp teeth and claws? What did you eat?" Lilly insisted.

"I was born a normal small girl child. Much to the

disappointment of my father." As Sparah spoke she began gathering materials. She pulled out her bowl of summoning and filled it from a pitcher. She sprinkled in herbs she'd grown and dried herself and lastly she carefully dripped three drops of her own blood in. She stared down into it and waited for what the fates might allow her to see. Sometimes she did this just to see whatever random thing they might like to share. Other times like this, she concentrated on her question and hoped they would provide some answers.

Sparah's eyes drifted closed, the world around her dropped away and she floated to another time, another possible place.

She floated into the vision. A beach, Atlantis. She saw herself there, happily splashing at the water's edge.

She was about to pull herself out, this was not what she'd been asking for, she wanted Tray and Lilly's future, their children.

Brighton stepped into view then and she froze. She wanted to see this. Wanted more of what might be for them. He pulled her close and kissed her deeply, as full of passion as today and this felt years in the future. That meant there was a good possibility that their passion for each other wouldn't change or fade.

A small child appeared, running up to them. Sparah was shocked at first, then wondered if it was Tray and Lilly's child, but her skin was dark, like mocha, and her hair black as night. She looked up and squealed in delight.

"Ew, daddy and mommy, kissing is gross," she made a face up at them. Brighton laughed and picked her up swinging her around.

"Kissing is what people in love do," Brighton said.

"Is that why Auntie Lilly and Uncle Tray kiss so much? Are they in love too, are they going to have another baby?"

"I bet they will," Sparah said, stroking her daughter's hair and tucking it behind an ear. "You'll have a whole litter of cousins to play with if Uncle Tray has anything to say about it."

"And will I have a little brother soon?" the girl asked.

Sparah touched her stomach and sighed. "It feels like a boy this time," she said, and Brighton kissed her again.

Sparah was ripped out of the vision. Tears streaming down her face. She was looking at Brighton who was growling at Tray and Lilly to get help. Ian rushed in with sword drawn.

He of course only saw Brighton as a danger in that second, Sparah in tears unable to speak, and Tray and Lilly freaking out.

Ian grabbed Brighton and threw him away. Brighton shifted to wolf and growled and Sparah shouted.

"Stop!"

The room froze. Ian had his sword raised, Brighton had his teeth bared and Tray had Lilly shoved between him and a wall.

"Stop," Sparah repeated.

"Who harmed you?" Ian demanded. "I will kill this beast."

Brighton growled.

"No one harmed me, Ian."

Ian looked at her unsure. When she nodded reassuringly, he dropped the sword. Brighton shifted back to human and pushed past Ian to embrace Sparah.

"Why the hell were you crying? I heard your tears and you wouldn't wake up. Tray and Lilly were sitting there like idiots doing nothing," Brighton accused.

"Hey, we weren't sure if it was part of the fucking process," Tray defended.

Sparah shook her head. "I never know how a vision will affect me," she admitted.

"It was horrible, wasn't it," Lilly said quietly. Silent tears slipped down her face. "We will have a monster. We shouldn't ever. I can't give you a child, Tray," she said, her heart breaking.

Lilly collapsed as Tray embraced her and tried to soothe her with a hand stroking down her back and whispered words.

"I don't need a child, I only need you," he reassured her.

"No, it wasn't like that at all," Sparah said. She looked guiltily at Brighton, unsure how much to reveal.

"What was it? I have to know," Lilly said.

"You will have children and they will be wonderful. But you should do it here."

"In Atlantis?" Tray asked doubtfully.

"Yes. Here in Atlantis. You should stay here and create your family. It will be safest."

Tray and Lilly shared a look of hope and love that made Sparah's heart fill. Atlantis was going to become a place of love and family.

"Well shit," Ian said. "Is anyone going to ask if I want werewolves running around my city?"

"No," Sparah said with a wink.

Brighton leaned down and kissed her shoulder, her neck and then nipped her earlobe. "Can we be alone now?"

"Everyone out," Sparah demanded and shooed Ian, Tray, and Lilly out the door then shut and locked it.

She stared across the room at Brighton, once again naked and beautiful. She desperately wanted the life she'd seen and judging by the look in his eyes, he was ready to give her anything she asked for.

This was the balance, the good she'd suffered so long for.

"Welcome to Atlantis," she said as he pulled her into his arms.

Please Rate and Review

We hope you enjoyed
Descendants of Atlantis, book three in the Atlantis series, by
Courtney Davis.
If you did, we would ask that you please rate and review this title.
Every review helps our authors.

Rate and Review: Descendants of Atlantis

Meet The Author

Courtney Davis is an award-winning author of urban fantasy, urban fantasy mystery and space fantasy with a little romance and humor thrown in. She loves creating worlds and exploring human and inhuman interactions with fast-paced, action-packed stories. She resides in North Idaho with her husband and children–teaching, reading, writing and soaking up sunshine. She hopes you find joy and an escape in her writing.

Other Titles from 5 Prince Publishing

www.5princebooks.com

Secret Admirer Pact *Bernadette Marie*
A Trace of Romance *Ann Swann*
Descendants of Atlantis *Courtney Davis*
Holiday Rebound *Emily Bybee*
Rewriting Christmas *S.E. Reichert & Kerrie Flanagan*
Aristotle's Wolves *Courtney Davis*
Christmas Cove *Sarah Dressler*
A Twist of Hate *T.E. Lorenzo*
Composing Laney *S.E. Reichert*
Firewall *Jessica Mehring*
Vampires of Atlantis *Courtney Davis*
A Rocky Mountain Romance *Jessica Mehring*
A Copper Penny Christmas *Ann Swann*
Merry Mix-ups *Emily Bybee*
The Mrs Clause *S.J. Reisner*
Mistletoe Memories *Bernadette Marie*
Falling For Christmas *Amy L. Gale*
Liz's Road Trip *Bernadette Marie*
Back to the 80s *S.E. Reichert & Kerrie Flanagan*

www.ingramcontent.com/pod-product-compliance
Lightning Source LLC
Chambersburg PA
CBHW032212030726
47494CB00020B/993